Praise for Jody Weiner's
PRISONERS OF TRUTH

"Prisoners of Truth is an ambitious first novel, hilarious when you least expect it, laying out enticing clues to the central mystery while layering past over present and allowing the novel that Ollie is writing to intersect with the unfolding events of his life."

Donna Gillespie; author of
The Lightbearer

"Jody Weiner is a master of authenticity, putting his story down in all its hues with the deftness of a great realist painter. His characters vividly come to life in this funny and classy legal-flavored pot-boiler/morality play. I could feel Ollie Katz's breath on my neck."

Romy Ashby, editor
Goodie Magazine

"A very nice mystery . . . the characters are well defined and interesting . . . it makes you laugh enough to make the people around you stare. I'm not sure if this is Weiner's first book, but it deserves to be a success and to be the start of a series."

John Matlock
Amazon Top 1000 Reviewer

2005 National Semi-Finalist (IPPY)
Independent Book Publishers Award in Mystery/Suspense category

PRISONERS OF TRUTH

PRISONERS OF TRUTH

To Cathy:
My friend and compadre, thanks
for classing up the back cover.

Jody Weiner

Jody

S.F.

COUNCIL OAK BOOKS

Council Oak Books
San Francisco/Tulsa

COUNCIL OAK BOOKS TRADE PAPERBACK EDITION, MAY 2006
PRISONERS OF TRUTH
copyright © 2004 by Jody Weiner

Library of Congress Cataloging-in-Publication Data
Weiner, Jody
Prisoners of Truth/by Jody Weiner
First Edition/First Printing
Printed in Canada

ISBN 1-57178-197-8

Original artwork/book design by Nancy Calef
author photograph by David Paul Morris

Acknowledgements

Barth, John. <u>The Floating Opera</u>, New York; Knopf/Anchor Books, 1956. "Myriad Minds" excerpt from Dutta, Krishna and Andrew Robinson, <u>Rabindranath Tagore: The Myriad-Minded Man</u>, New York; St. Martin's Press, 1995. "Myriad Minds," appeared in the <u>San Francisco Examiner Magazine</u>, 26 November 1995.

This is dedicated to my parents, Leo and Sarah Weiner. He was a brave, honest man and she was the hardest-working woman not in show business.

Thanks to Paulette Millichap, Maurice Kanbar, and for edits from John Loughlin, Laura Wood and Nikki Lastreto. This book found its way through the trust and devotion of my wife and best friend, Nancy Calef.

The Human experiment is over. We have failed as a species. Nevertheless, you can always hire a lawyer to argue the other side.

-Kurt Vonnegut

Jody Weiner

PRISONERS OF TRUTH

Jody Weiner has been a practicing attorney for more than thirty years. He lives in San Francisco with his wife, Nancy Calef, an oil and mixed media painter.

This is his first novel. He is a contributor to *Kinship with Animals,* an anthology of personal stories describing interspecies encounters that changed how the authors view the world.

PART I

Two years ago, when the course of my life seemed inexorable, I ran into Lucien Echo inside the renovated criminal court building on Chicago's West Side. We'd first met in college and hooked up again in the early 80's. Our lives followed separate paths until coincidence brought me to the courtroom in which Lucien was performing that afternoon. Part of me had to admire his commitment to upholding the constitutional rights of unrepentant criminals, but I remember thinking that we were strangers cut from separate cloth. Now I've come to feel that we've known each other all our lives.

Oliver Wendell Katz is my full name. Call me Ollie. Following Jewish tradition my father chose Oliver because it began with the same letter as his recently deceased older brother, Oscar. Just before I was born my uncle Oscar fell from a stock ladder in his fancy department store and banged his head on the metal corner of the fluoroscope machine. Customers were supposed to operate this ancient foot-measuring contraption—a freestanding platform about four feet high—

by sliding their feet inside the hollowed-out base. X-rays' harmful effects were not yet known so shoppers peered down through a binocular viewing screen at the luminescent outline of their newly irradiated tootsies.

My father has never been devout. He defied orthodox teaching early on by marrying my mother, a fiery Roman Catholic, may she rest in peace. Despite their differences, my parents met and fell in love while they also toiled in Uncle Oscar's grand emporium. Then the War broke out in Europe and their honeymoon was postponed until my father came home from Anzio, which he doesn't talk about, and he borrowed enough money from Uncle Oscar to open his dry goods store in a working class neighborhood on the Northwest Side. There my dad has remained for over forty years, a stubbornly uncomplicated shmatta salesman whose lifelong motto is, "slow and steady wins the race." Since my mother died in `83, Dad's health has deteriorated in proportion to his increased alcohol consumption. Now in his late seventies, my father grows crankier by the minute sounding more and more like Diogenes whenever he goes off about "this world full of liars."

You might say that the same search for truth in my bones brings us back to the courtroom where I happened upon Lucien Echo defending Louise "Mama" Raspberry. I had no idea then how infamous the proceeding would prove. I remember thinking that Lucien's argument persuaded The Honorable August Rotini to dismiss the charges against Mama Raspberry without a trial. It had seemed routine except that Lucien had appeared in such a mundane matter rather than sending a flunky associate. I complimented him in the hallway afterward and we had no more communication until a year ago. That was shortly after the federal grand jury accused Echo of bribing Judge Rotini to throw out Mama Raspberry's case.

It's no surprise that I was obsessed with the sensational story following Lucien's fall from grace. Here was the most prominent citizen I knew charged with violating his sacred professional trust. What's worse, he'd allegedly done it right under my nose. Who was better equipped to examine the explanation Lucien might offer?

I'll resist drawing parallels between Lucien Echo and Jay Gatsby, or my other favorite fictional hero: *Mr. Littlejohn*, Martin Flavin's disillusioned scion of a Century of Progress. Not only do I lack requisite skill to create characters of their ilk, I don't want to be diverted from the tale that I'm determined to keep straight.

Lucien Echo is not his real name, a precautionary measure I've taken to forestall lawsuits. Without revealing his identity, I can tell you that Lucien is regarded passionately. Some have declared him a political scapegoat for threatening the status quo. Lucien was at the pinnacle of his career when the manure hit the spreader. I was shocked, to be sure. Not so much over whether the accusations were true, but because the case I was covering turned out to be the stage upon which the fix was allegedly played out.

I was attending the same courtroom to report on a front-page murder trial. Out of curiosity I hung around during a recess to watch Lucien in action. We hadn't seen each other in more than fifteen years, but I'd often read about him in newspaper accounts of other trials or in Kup's Column. I was freelancing for the Lerner chain, thinking I could sell a feature story about the "viaduct killer."

The viaduct killer's victims were a suburban family of four driving through the city on their way home to Evanston. Caught in a violent rainstorm on this muggy summer night, they detoured off the Dan Ryan Expressway smack into the remains of Robert Taylor Homes, world's largest high-rise ghetto project. The downpour had also flooded the L train underpasses in the neighborhood, further diverting vehicles into a creeping procession along dark, dangerous side streets. Near the 55th Street viaduct several punks in the milling crowd wielded bricks and a metal pipe upon terrified motorists stalled in the deepening pool of water. While threatening to smash windshields and/or heads, they were extorting cash in exchange for safely pushing cars through the swamped underpass.

By all accounts the viaduct killer approached the front passenger window of the Evanston family's trapped vehicle, pulled from his waistband a .45 automatic pistol and calmly splattered the wife's brains across her husband sitting behind the wheel. Upon hearing their two young girls screaming in the backseat the assailant turned and fired again into the darkness. The father survived if you call that living. I watched him testify with the same bullet that had killed his wife lodged in his spine.

When reliving the horror had sent the wheelchair-bound witness into convulsions, Judge Rotini let the jury go home early. Senses were dulled in the courtroom by the time he ordered Mama Raspberry's case to proceed. After waiting most of the day, Lucien Echo presented a motion to quash the search warrant executed at Mama Raspberry's residence.

The police had seized from Mama a cache of weapons, a roomful of designer clothes, sporting retail tags, and an array of natural and pharmaceutical substances. I should tell you that Mama was a fat and sassy middle-aged woman dressed to the nines. She resembled a rich family's nanny, a streetwise grandmother who served the North Shore liberals by imbuing their children with decent values.

I also remember that the prosecutor had been surprised by Lucien's cross-examination of Tommy Goyle, the arresting officer. Using photographs of the exterior hallway to Mama's apartment, Lucien coaxed Detective Goyle to admit that he and his partner initially went next door by mistake. Judge Rotini suppressed the evidence of Raspberry's drugstore and fencing operation and his ruling seemed perfectly acceptable to the few remaining spectators.

When I read almost a year later that Lucien and Rotini had been indicted for conspiring to dump the case, I thought that the government might be overreacting. The notorious Operation Greylord prosecutions and their progeny had been winding down for over a decade. These undercover federal investigations of the Cook County courts exposed some of the most sordid revelations of official misconduct in a city famous for political shenanigans. During its heyday, Greylord snared in its net several hundred lawyers, judges, court personnel, and law enforcement officers. The probe's effects persist to this day. Every so often a new undercover corruption investigation, much like the matter of Rotini and Echo, appears in yet another county department.

To me, however, realizing the depth of corruption was like a cold shower. I suppose it's evident that I've thought about becoming an attorney. I dropped out of law school after the first year when I realized that I didn't have the stomach for perpetual confrontation. Although I was naive I must've sensed that I couldn't spend my life getting paid to defend principles I didn't believe in.

Anyway, I'd never been good at sticking with things. More afraid of endings than beginnings, I guess, I was engaged once. Lately I was going out with Sally, and had been on and off for several years. I'm constrained to report that Sally recently retrieved the personal stuff she'd kept in my apartment.

My writing—something that I'd decided was an honorable alternative to law—was either "awkward" or "uneven" depending upon which rejection letter you read. Almost ten years ago, I submitted to New York publishers the draft of my first novel: *Stuff the Lady,* a black comedy about a professional basketball player busted on game day in a raid at his cocaine dealer's crib. After one cop is accidentally killed by his partner's errant bullet the player panics and runs away from the scene. He is charged with felony murder, fired from the team, forced into rehab and . . . yadda, yadda, yadda. . . . You get the idea. None of the publishers who bothered to respond were interested.

My baby sister, Annie, who fled Chicago after high school, thinks *Stuff the Lady* would make a good movie if I get around to writing the screenplay. As a matter of fact, I was working on another novel when Lucien Echo reappeared in my life. I also sent those early chapters to Annie, my most respected critic. She said they were "interesting." The worst comment possible. Like one of those disturbing dreams from which you wake up the moment before you're going to die. As if that isn't enough, Annie insists that I'm most readable when I'm funny.

Once in a while I sold stories to the weeklies: fanciful pieces and fluff, mostly. I sometimes wrote about heinous crimes, sending accounts like the viaduct killer to a local magazine. My story on the continuous line of gawkers at John Wayne Gacy's house was featured in the *Reader*. I also drove a cab and did a stint as the night deskman at a seedy residential hotel. Performing these subsistence gigs allowed me to carry around some high-minded literary aspirations of redemption, while in fact I probably resembled more a blind man selling pencils on the cold concrete sidewalks of La Salle Street.

When the criminal court corruption scandal first erupted I remember thinking that those bastard lawyers, caught with their hands in somebody else's pockets, deserved a public flogging. I was repulsed by the accusations of organized extortion among judges who split their weekly take from courtroom hustlers paying for verdicts like hockey tickets. Jesus, this sounds like some self-righteous diatribe motivated by my inability to make it through law school. The truth is that I had never before challenged my own faith, such as it was, in anything greater than Me, Me, Me!

Enter Lucien Echo who'd been a larger than life hero to me. He stood accused, belatedly, by Mama Raspberry herself, of rigging the very proceeding at which I'd observed him admiringly. I recall that Mama had appeared to me then as another opportunistic criminal. It was commonplace for former clients to make deals by blaming their lawyers, and I thought that she could easily have lied about Lucien to save herself. It wasn't hard to believe that the government wanted to bring Lucien down. He was too controversial; his causes were too unorthodox; and his fast-lane lifestyle slapped the establishment in its collective prune face.

On the other hand, despite her appearance and demeanor, Mama Raspberry was a neighborhood legend. Her open and notorious operation meant that she had local connections. When Mama was caught by the DEA in a large cocaine transaction, she had bargained for her freedom by thrusting a dagger of bribery and drug abuse into Lucien Echo's back. According to the sorry saga Mama recounted, Lucien had schooled her how to stay one step ahead of the cops for years while remaining her best customer. And Raspberry's long history of arrests for narcotics, weapons, and stolen property offenses was a matter of public record.

The press accounts of Lucien's indictment begrudgingly noted August Rotini's distinguished career, partly because he'd sentenced the viaduct killer to death. Unfortunately for His Honor, though, Rotini had already been named in connection with two earlier cases growing out of the same sting operation that allegedly netted Lucien. A court-ordered wiretap, approved by the Attorney General of the United States, no less, had been secreted in the judge's private chambers adjacent to the courtroom over which he presided for more than a decade. Of course, Auggie Rotini grew despondent from the massive media assault, including references to him whenever a sleazy new accusation emerged.

Lucien was crucified, his guilt all but assumed over his association with the tarnished jurist. I too may have fallen prey to the prevailing climate of mistrust. Or perhaps it was the coincidence of my shattered faith. Despite my usually aimless life, I found myself propelled into the breech. I wrote a nasty piece about sensational journalism destroying the presumption of innocence. Then, as if to further demonstrate this fit of self-importance, I sent it off to the *Tribune* in Lucien Echo's defense.

After every local paper declined to print my story, I mailed it to Lucien's office out of frustration. Nearly a month passed without a response, something I wasn't expecting, anyway. Then I received a telephone call from Alex Carlton, the woman with whom Lucien had been cohabitating for several years. Alex was a star in her own right. I'd read in the society columns that she originally hailed from a proper east coast family. Her reputation was forged in Chicago after she got together with Lucien and opened Rococo, a trendy restaurant in the artsy River North District. Alex's culturally inclined fund-raising and politically correct photo-ops, combined with Lucien's deep local roots, made them *the* exciting couple, the darlings of the social set.

Alex identified herself over the phone and went on to say that she was calling because Lucien had spoken highly of me. Out of the blue, Alex announced that Lucien wanted to see me. I found her desperate tone weirdly exhilarating and gladly jumped at the chance for an audience with Lucien Echo. Maybe then I was innocently compelled to uncover the truth about what I'd witnessed in the courtroom. But now I've come to believe that the truth often straddles a fine line between good and evil. For reasons that we'll endeavor to glean together, I'm no longer convinced that I can tell the difference between the heroes and the villains.

The first time I stepped off the elevator to Lucien Echo's penthouse, Alex Carlton was waiting for me in the carpeted hallway next to double oak doors. Alex's large brown eyes were bloodshot and puffy behind a pair of retro rhinestone eyeglasses. She wore a turquoise Lycra jumpsuit, cut out above the waist, with suspender straps pushing her round breasts through a skimpy T-shirt that advertised the sunny beaches of Aruba.

"Please come in," Alex said, giving me the once-over in an effortless, self-effacing manner. She appeared sophisticated, making me feel like the most important person in the world despite that she couldn't have cared a whit for me.

The spandex strained against her supple frame and disappeared underneath tie-dyed sweat socks as she padded across a black and white tiled foyer, leading me into a cavernous living room arranged into three groupings of overstuffed couches and chairs. At the far end, opposite a stocked bar with mirrored shelves and leather stools, was a grand piano, a snazzy drum kit and Big Band Era music stands. My footsteps resounded against the hardwood floor until we retreated through another hallway and arrived in an office library appointed with oak furniture and oriental rugs.

"I wanted you to see this," Alex said, matter-of-factly. She bounced over to Lucien's desk and, gingerly, she picked up the commentary I'd sent to his downtown address. "Lucien was touched," she added.

"Like I said over the phone," I began, using an officious, phony-sounding tone, "The newspaper won't print it. They will publish an interview. Isn't he here?"

"That's just it," Alex sighed. Then she plopped down onto one corner of the long desk and took off her glasses in resignation. She was living with a litigation pro and master prevaricator. Yet, I was about to learn that Alex was incapable of lying. First impressions may not be the most important, but they're everlasting. For I also recall her slumping eyes; her entire posture evinced the fear and despair she'd obviously been suffering since Lucien's public humiliation.

"It's eating him up," Alex went on, getting off the desktop. She stood very close to me and looked directly into my eyes. Her fragrance was definite: wild strawberries and a hint of fresh-baked bread. No doubt she'd been exercising when I arrived as long wisps of hair were still matted around her face where the sweat had dried.

"So . . . I thought . . . I made up that story about interviewing him to get you here," Alex confessed. "Lucien was moved by your article. I thought he might trust you. He has to trust someone," she added, while another misty cloud formed in her eyes. Alex shifted her feet, her frustration cutting through the sadness and anger. Then she turned away.

"If Lucien's guilty," I said, after she'd wiped her eyes on her sleeve and replaced her goofy glasses, "Maybe he doesn't want to defend himself."

"Lucien's gone off on a holiday. He packed a bag, left his office and jumped into his car like some damned kid."

"Well, I don't see . . ."

"If you really knew him you'd understand."

Alex must've thought she'd made a point about Lucien's character that she expected I would know. I was digesting the wild goose she wanted me to chase. I searched the room for an easy way to let her down, focusing instead on one particular black and white photograph within a cluster of framed snapshots mounted on the paneled wall. Five men resembling a pack of wild jackals in business suits had been arranged for posterity around a restaurant table. Lethal eyes collectively peered through an eerie shroud of cigar smoke lingering above the white linen tablecloth. First I recognized J. Arthur Penny, well-known civil rights lawyer. Seated next to him was a boyishly handsome and defiant Lucien Echo with wavy hair and scraggly beard. Lucien was the youngest in the group, the three other men unknown to me. Upon closer inspection I made out an inscription near the bottom of the photo: "Ed O'Ryan special prosecution team," and I realized that they were a formidable bunch.

Fresh out of law school, where Lucien had barely survived, he began his professional career working as a junior prosecutor in States Attorney Edward O'Ryan's office. Having known by then that he wanted to be a trial lawyer, Lucien managed to land this appropriate position despite his politics.

The marriage didn't last. After O'Ryan had accompanied a late night police raid on the Black Panthers' alleged local headquarters, in search of "automatic weapons and other tools of the revolution," Lucien abruptly quit the states attorney's office. The official bullet count revealed that a police invasion had taken place in the tenement where two Panther leaders were killed in their beds. Citywide outrage caused the appointment of J. Arthur Penny, an African American special prosecutor, and the special grand jury promptly indicted the ambushing police officers, along with Ed O'Ryan, for conspiracy to commit murder. Lucien Echo begged for a chance to work on the prosecution team. Although O'Ryan was eventually acquitted, his career was basically over, while Lucien Echo found himself advancing by bucking the system.

"Where did Lucien go?" I finally asked her.

"To Madison; to his friend's condo on the lake. Jake's an old hippie in the political science department at Wisconsin. Maybe you know him?"

"I think . . . I kinda remember one of Lucien's friends with that name."

As I moved about the office inspecting other mementos of Lucien's exploits, college memories began to distract me. Alex watched me finger a shiny harmonica resting on his credenza.

"Billy Joel gave that to him," she said. "I think Lucien helped Billy negotiate one of his recording contracts."

"You and Billy hang out much?"

Alex ignored the question and started toward me. She stopped in midstride, as if changing her mind. "I have something in the kitchen. Please think about speaking to Lucien." Then she turned and left me pondering their twenty-ninth floor perch above the Gold Coast.

Spread out before me were the city's bright summer-time colors of trimmed greenery, billowing white sails and rich aquamarine water. Shiny architectural steel contrasting dusty concrete framed this postcard panorama of Lake Shore Drive winding around Oak Street beach. Purchased for a sweet song during the conversion boom of the 80's, Lucien's apartment covered nearly half the top floor. The price per square foot increased with the altitude and the upholstered settees in the mirrored elevators were safe from vandalism. It occurred to me that despite the computerized intercom system the occupants could lead separate lives in this urban maze.

I grew up in a suburban tract home where my older brother Michael and I were forced to share a bedroom smaller than Alex's walk-in closets. We all seemed to live together in the family room. A revolving crowd of aunts and uncles minded my business, while my baby sister Annie's nasty little friends often paraded around, half-dressed, changing the radio station on the only stereo system in our house. Of course, when Michael couldn't hack City College he tried to escape by joining the Air Force. In spite of the escalating Vietnam War, I thought it wasn't such a bad idea. Never mind that I'd be getting my own room. Besides model airplanes and fixing cars my big brother's only other interests were roller derby and "Vargas girls."

Michael wound up flunking the induction physical owing to fallen arches. He moved into a greystone in New Town and, for a while, if you can believe it, became an auto mechanic. Yet, my graduation to solo living quarters was short-lived. Annie soon picked up the slack, requiring frequent escort through her high school freshman perils and spending too much biology problem solving time in my new private room. None of which personally involved me, I'm relieved to mention. And all of which serves to explain why I found myself coveting the vast stillness high up in Lucien Echo's world.

Until the calm grew uncomfortable. I was intimidated by the view, by the celebrity photo gallery staring back at me, and by the mountain of books lining the rooms and hallways throughout the house. I imagined Lucien sitting in his overstuffed chair near the window reading Anwar Sadat's memoir *In Search of Identity*, or maybe the signed copy of Saul Bellow's *Humboldt's Gift*, which I examined, stacked among many other first editions within his collection.

Some titles recalled my sophomoric days in Madison when Lucien had mentored me. He was in law school but took a liking to me after I'd sucked up to him because he was cool. That I was in *his den* posing as a writer left me feeling weak and unaccomplished. I moved back to Lucien's desk and instinctively picked up an autographed baseball from a polished wood stand. I began hyperventilating; I was going to run away. The importance of this mission had given way to my churning stomach and the soothing likelihood that I was just another loser with a bullshit dream. Then I read the handwritten scrawl: "To my adviser" signed "Dick Allen." I reeled. Richie Allen was my all-time hero on the White Sox. Baseball's bad boy, his MVP season in `72 had single-handedly catapulted the team back from oblivion.

I couldn't help wondering what Lucien must've done for *him*?

I replaced the spherical icon and hurried from Lucien's office in search of the exit. Forgotten was Alex Carlton's plea for help. I decided not to approach this man. But as I passed through the sprawling living room, the silken fabric of a winged couch invited me to catch my breath. "What's the rush?" it seemed to whisper. "Relax; enjoy the opulence."

"Are you all right in there?" Alex's soothing voice came over the intercom clear enough for me to hear through my fog. "I'm almost done," she added. "Make yourself a drink if you like and bring it to the kitchen."

I automatically walked over to the brass and mirrored bar with four soft leather stools lined up neatly alongside. Everything bearing Lucien Echo's friggin' stamp was organized, refined, and smooth like a gracious, slick machine. That's the way he'd appeared to me in court; his lifestyle was annoyingly corroborative, and I was cracking from the strain of comparison.

Not wanting to disturb the elaborate display of etched glasses and fine spirits, I poured what turned out to be a stiff drink of scotch from a crystal decanter on the shiny counter. It burned going down and I coughed in distress. Despite working as a bartender over the years, I could never stomach hard liquor. The irritant calmed my nerves. Then I headed in the direction of the warm, sweet aroma I'd inhaled when Alex stood near me. Thick carpet runners led me down several hallways past closed doors until I found the formal dining room. Beyond the open doorway at the other end of the room, Alex stood beside a butcher-block table in the center of a dream kitchen.

"Cinnamon loaf," she said, as I crossed the room and stopped to watch her transfer the contents of a molded baking pan into a glass tray. "Come and try some. It's way too fattening to eat," she added. "More like therapy, anyway. I end up throwing away most of it."

Alex had put on a pair of faded jeans, ripped at the knees and thigh, so her turquoise tights shone through the frayed denim holes. A men's tattersall dress shirt hung from her shoulders like a lab coat, as she cut through the warm, sticky bread.

"You're a writer," she said after I'd approached and taken a slice. "How does one decide to do that for a living?"

"Good question."

The doughy candy melted in my mouth before I chewed it.

"As a matter of fact," I added, once I'd swallowed the treat, "I can't help Lucien. You need a respectable reporter or a biographer. Someone whose opinion matters."

Alex looked at me strangely, as though I'd suggested that she might want a circus. "I like you," she said. "You have soft eyes and an honest mouth." Then she placed her knife in the sink and turned toward me again. "Lucien has to face the truth no matter what."

"If someone's searching for truth, pride is a dead battery in their flashlight."

Usually, I'm someone who thinks of the perfect thing to say immediately after I've uttered exactly the opposite. But this time, I remember, Alex regarded me seriously. I could feel her studying my face, as I was uncomfortable being exposed. Whatever she was up to, the notion also dawned on me that here was a ripe opportunity. How could I possibly run away? In order to discover anything about Lucien I would have to overcome my own pride and jealousy about his wealthy lifestyle. I'd somehow managed to hit upon a well-proportioned plan. "What if we drive up to Madison and I suggest an interview with him?"

"Lucien asked me to come up this weekend," Alex replied, somewhat hopefully. "Would you do this? I mean, there's no guarantee he'll agree, or even see you. Y'understand?"

"I guess we'll find out how much my story moved Lucien."

"What does that mean?"

"Nothing," I replied, innocently.

What a crock! You bet I was thinking about getting to know Alex. I recall the way her soft pale skin glowed with fresh cool excitement despite the withering summer heat. I also admit that I'd fooled myself into thinking Alex wanted to learn more about me. Although I knew she wanted my help exonerating Lucien, I had this eerie feeling that I was being born anew out of his dishonor . . . Well, that's about as deep as it gets lest I further expose myself. For I am rather handsomely superficial, I hesitate to add, but with no bankable profession and bad teeth. Suffice it to say, I was being asked to participate in Lucien Echo's odyssey, maybe influence the outcome, and it was the best damned thing I had going by a mile.

"So I left him in a bakery on Koh Pha Ngan," my sister Annie said to me.

We were sitting at the round oak breakfast table nestled in the front room of my one-bedroom apartment. Annie had shown up a few hours earlier, unannounced, straight from the airport following another one of her Asian adventures.

"I finished my breakfast," Annie went on, in her way of slowly drawing the picture, "and I caught the first boat back to Samui. That's Thailand, Ollie. If the tropics are right you can stay six months and never think about moving. When stuff happens it's like milk going sour. Get out as fast as possible. Anyway, Oskar was a cheap con-artist."

"Your ex-husband, Ray, was a cheap con-artist," I replied.

Whenever Annie's relationships failed my sister acknowledged the break-up or, in Ray's case, the divorce by branding her latest ex with the term describing his most glar-

21

ing fault. Annie's catalog of "irregulars," as she liked to call them, had grown steadily during the ten years since she'd walked out on Ray with their son, Jason, who was then two-and-a-half years old.

"Well, Oskar reminded me of Ray," Annie said, screwing up her sun-lined face; its youthful Mediterranean sheen remained despite the strain of bearing, rearing, and attempting to tether Jason.

"How is the mutant?" I asked, changing the subject.

"You know I don't like you calling him that. . . . Jason loves summer vacation with his Grandpa and his old playground buddies. Now they travel in packs. Bowling is the latest craze. I swear. It's the Midwest. In California, Jason doesn't hang out in bowling alleys."

"Is that where you live now? California?"

"What's the matter, Ollie? You've given me nothing but grief since I got here. Aren't you happy to see me? 'Cause I'm perfectly willing to go to Dad's tonight. I should see my son, anyway."

"That's right. You should see your son," I repeated. "It's been nearly three months," I added, as if she didn't know. "That's the thing, Annie. Whenever the mood hits, you run off to some damned island leaving your life to chance. Then you stroll back in here telling war stories about getting beaten up by some guy you fell in love with during an all night wavehouse, whatever the hell that is. For God's sake, you're my sister!"

"It's a *rave*, you dolt. They play *house* music on the beach. I'm touched, Ollie. But Oskar just slapped me once. He didn't hurt me. Six days together in a bamboo hut, without electricity after the sun goes down, and a person's true nature comes through. It's intense and personal and some people can't handle it. . . . Christ, he was only thirty."

"He only slapped you once? Your life is a 'B' movie."

"He was a hunk from Munich who stroked my ego. . . . Cocky and serious with loads of money off the currency market float, or something. Well, I guess I provoked him. I was talking about some silly thing Jason did when he was a baby and Oskar went on about the brilliant, handsome son we'd have together because we had the right genes. I mean we're talking breeding and Nietzsche. So I called him a Nazi and he lost it. . . . His face got fiery red, veins were popping out, and his body started to shake. He was weepy afterwards, begging me to forgive him. He kept apologizing and trying to hold my hand until, finally, I felt sorry for him. Just like Ray."

"Ray hit you too?" I asked, feeling guilty about those rare times during our childhood when Annie was my punching bag. The delight of having a younger sibling, whose care was often placed in your hands, depended upon the amount of torture you were able to inflict upon the kid for good measure. Moreover, the family chain of command required a fall guy. When Dad gave it to Michael, Michael gave it to me, if not for the same reasons that he got it from Dad, for something previously unresolved between us. In turn, I gave it to Annie. Sometimes I even had a reason. Oh, what have I done to her? I wondered.

"Ray never laid a hand on me," Annie responded. "He was such a bad liar. When Ray screwed up he'd make himself so nervous trying to keep it from me that he'd break down and confess five minutes after he walked in the door.

Ray ingratiated himself with gifts and subservient charm. It worked for ten years, the cheap con artist!"

Annie was my anchor. Although I don't remember the day she arrived, one of my earliest childhood recollections involves my father cradling Annie in his lap at the dinner table, singing "Pop Goes the Weasel" and trying to feed her with a soup spoon as large as her tiny head. Annie has always been our father's favorite child. She brought out his pride, something that rarely showed when Michael or I came home with a remarkable report card or some other important accomplishment. And while my old man was usually weakest around our mother—who tried to rule evenly all three of her children—only Annie could inspire my father to stand up to Mom when a family discussion deteriorated into a case of them versus us.

That's why our dad was so deeply offended when Annie, barely eighteen, ran off with Ray. Annie sent word via Western Union that they'd married in Las Vegas and were searching the West Coast for suitable surroundings in which to permanently settle. I figured Mom was relieved that her rivalry with Annie for Dad's attention was finally over. . . . That's exactly what it was. But as soon as Annie heard that Mom was dying, she came home and stayed with her to the end. And after Jason was born Annie insisted upon schlepping her new family back to Dad's for a visit, despite having recently returned to her job at Walt Disney Studios, no less. When Annie's marriage ended my father wanted her home again, where he doted over Jason while Annie worked odd jobs in order to put the pieces back together.

Annie prevailed, of course. She's the one who sings like a bird, dances the tango, doesn't need subtitles for most foreign films, and has the amazing ability to multiply numbers in her head faster than you can punch them into a calculator. At four years old Annie memorized all the state flowers and the Gettysburg Address. In high school she was captain of the swim team and collected scholarships instead of stamps. My sister taught deaf kids in India, managed a resort hotel on Bali and, I must confess, in addition to being my most insightful writing critic, Annie is a fan. Over the years, Annie's not only read whatever I've sent to her, she's also a crackerjack writer who hates to do it. Instead she calls frequently with encouragement and bits of likely information. Annie gave me *Mr. Littlejohn* to read in the first place.

Too bad my old man still resents Annie for leaving home all those years ago. I suspect, though, if Annie were a man, Dad would champion her lifestyle the way he once rooted for her from the poolside risers during her high school swimming meets. Things are tough on him now. His grown sons are hanging around while one of the two women in his heart left forever and the other returns to use the place as a way station or a day care center. There's something else about Annie that our father probably won't ever understand. He's from the Depression generation; Dad measures success by the territory one acquires, by the cost of their American car, and by the number of vacations they take each year.

The key word here is vacation. The way our father sees it, a person who travels out of the country for an extended period of time is a kook or a bum, or worse: a Bohemian who, like the French, doesn't wash. So it's no surprise that Dad doesn't recognize Annie's genius. Annie never looks back. She's the only one of us who has the ability to throw it all away in order to appreciate the experience. Yet, our father can't appreciate that his lifelong struggle to survive enabled Annie to demand so much more from life than mere survival.

"I'm going up to Madison tomorrow," I finally said. "You're welcome to stay the weekend if you and Jason need to escape from Dad's."

"You've always refused to go back there," Annie replied. "Does this mean that a woman's involved?"

"Yeah, right."

Annie silently savored her croissant while her eyes searched over me and out the window toward Lincoln Park. She's such a good detective, I thought, she might've noticed that since her last visit I'd replaced the dead Wandering Jew with the Boston fern hanging over her head.

In truth, my routine hasn't changed much during the decade since my last move from a studio apartment about a mile south on Clark Street. Turn on the "Today Show" at seven a.m., grind the coffee beans, go downstairs, and walk around the corner to the newsstand for a *Tribune*. I cancelled my subscription years ago because the punk on the first floor worked nights and managed to come home right after the delivery boy. He'd either steal the paper or read it and return it covered with food stains and creases. Although the creep eventually moved away, I continue to purchase the newspaper, a la carte, as it forces me to go out into the world each morning. Of course, there's also my toasted bagel, usually sesame, with butter and cream cheese. On rare occasions I'll have an English muffin. The fact is that most things go better for me when I'm regular.

I'm no Einstein, though, whose wardrobe reportedly consisted of seven identical sets of one complete outfit, including pants, shirt, jacket, shoes and socks. I guess Albert didn't waste time in front of the mirror wondering whether his outfit matched. Whereas, some of my clothes, my furniture, and most of my odd collection of stuff have been around too long already, from time to time, I've managed to acquire some interesting art and other curios. My teeth have definitely grown old before their time. Spurred on by periodontal disease causing bone loss, I recall that my bridge on the upper right-hand side had loosened severely a few days before Annie showed up. I must say, now I understand why novelists are always advising young readers to take good care of their teeth.

Anyway, Annie might've detected the self-conscious shift in my smile. Instead she was gazing out the window toward the tree-lined sidewalk below. Shafts of sunlight streaked between the high-rises, two blocks over, and reflected off the row of tightly parked cars across the street.

"Annie? Can you hear me? . . . Hello?"

"I'm sorry. I was out there for a second. I was thinking, I miss Chicago this time of year. Maybe I'll come back for a while."

"It would be great for Jason," I said, excited by the prospect. "He'll find his cojones here."

"The mutant's already thinking about prep school," Annie blurted out. "I swear, I had nothing to do with it." she added.

We laughed for the first time since Annie arrived, and she promptly fell asleep on my bed. Bangkok to Chicago, via Hong Kong and Los Angeles, was a long flight home.

The next morning I called for Alex in my car and we headed up the Kennedy Expressway. You'd think rush hour would've ended by ten forty-five a.m., yet we inched along out of the city. A limp July breeze pushed factory soot and exhaust fumes through the open cabin of my ancient convertible. When the sun beat this muggy mess into our faces I offered to pull over and put up the top. Alex said that she enjoyed the heat, as it was a fine day.

The voyage acted like a tonic, making it easier to carry out our surprise attack on Lucien. I glanced at my companion leaning back and studying the gridlock. Alex saw me looking at her and smiled without turning around. She reached into her purse and pulled out, of all things, a leather tobacco pouch. Then she extracted a pack of Zig Zag papers and a plastic baggy, and she expertly fashioned a joint.

"D'ya mind?" Alex asked. "I'll understand. I just like rolling 'em. . . . I'm so addicted," she added. "But don't worry. I have a California prescription."

I pushed in the cigarette lighter.

Alex proposed to tell me her real name if I promised not to tease her. When I was sworn to secrecy she confessed that it was Dorcas Marie Carlton, which, she said, explained much about her parents. I laughed, anyway.

She offered me a toke and I declined. Not because I'm averse to smoking marijuana. Like with booze, I've always been a lightweight when it comes to mind-altering substances of any kind. After a double shot of Nyquil I won't get behind the wheel for at least twenty-four hours.

Traffic thinned once we passed the airport cutoff and we sailed along at a good clip. The hot wind tossed Alex's sun bleached hair while she raised herself above the windshield in an effort to cool off. A diesel horn blast announced the approach of an eighteen-wheeler and I caught an approving twinkle in the eyes of a leather-faced shit-kicker as he roared by. For I must say, Dorcas Carlton, by her own admission, possessed a communistic mind trapped in a capitalistic body. Moreover, she was a triple Scorpio raised in New England when Camelot reigned.

"I know I'm a little nuts," Alex said, curling her long legs up under her on the worn-out leatherette seat."

"Is that the clinical diagnosis?"

"My mother's fault, mostly. She's had a screw loose for as long as I can remember. It's good I'm an only child. . . . She's the lone female of five siblings," Alex went on. "In her conniving mind she's always believed that men won't take her seriously unless she outdoes them."

"Oh, c'mon."

"Basically, my mother rejects authority. She makes up crackpot remedies and scams insurance companies with phony lawsuits. *'Learn it from your mother rather than the gutter,'* she loves to say. In the best restaurants she'll stuff her purse with everything on the table that fits inside. When I was a kid we weren't allowed within fifty feet of any buffet in town."

"Is your father still around?"

"Since my dad was forced to retire last year, she controls him full time now."

Alex looked over at me, hesitatingly, deciding perhaps whether to divulge more personal history. "My father worked for the space program when I was growing up," she said, rather proudly. "A genuine rocket scientist. But he ended up with a mega healthcare corporation instead."

"You mean talcum powder and q-tips?"

"Dad developed the suture that dissolves in the body after surgery. As a reward, they promoted him out of the lab to the board of directors. Of course, they kept the patent."

"Too bad he couldn't invent a kleptomania machine."

"I'm glad he went into medical research," Alex replied. "'Cause I was a sickly child. . . . My mother's had her way with him for over forty years now."

"They must've been married a long time before they had you."

"She made her beauty work for her, all right." Alex replied, slyly busting me for my comment. "My mother snagged him with it, and my father swears he'd marry her again despite the humiliation she's caused. I wish I had better things to say about her."

"Oh, I dunno. It sounds kinda romantic."

"I feel sorry for my father. Now that my mother's looks are fading and her health is failing all she has left are neurotic obsessions. It can't be much fun for him anymore, married to an aging pain in the ass with a face that's been pulled and tucked so many times it's beginning to resemble a large-mouth bass."

We rolled through the hilly farms of northern Illinois and I watched the steamy blacktop stretch on, unchanging. Livestock stood still in the dry, yellowing fields. Occasionally a windsock wriggled or a weather vane slowly twirled atop the sloping red roofs of corrugated aluminum barns.

"In this novel I've been working on," I said, trying to impress her, "the main character is a successful obstetrician who finds out that he's dying. . . . Y'see, despite his formal scientific training, Dr. Rob—that's what I've decided to call him—was brought up believing that human experience is individually determined by the moral choices we make along the way. Respecting a system that may reward obligatory good deeds or punish errors and omissions at any time—by practicing his own version of karma, if you will—Rob has been served well in his medical practice and his personal life."

"I'm listening," Alex said, after I'd looked over to see if she was paying attention. "I know what karma is. Go on, Ollie."

"People come to see Rob because he's a healer. They know they can trust his advice on any subject. And he's been so responsive to the ailments of others that he hasn't had time to enjoy his own life. When Rob is diagnosed with an incurable, degenerative disease he can't understand why it's happening to him. . . . He's barely middle-aged, he has a lovely wife, two grown kids, and he's brought a thousand healthy babies into the world not to mention all the additional lives that he's saved. There must be some mistake, Rob decides. He can't think of a single act he could've committed that requires this ultimate punishment.

"Meanwhile, acute episodes of intense pain ultimately land Rob in the hospital. At night he tries to relieve his suffering despite the painkillers by forcing himself to drift back over the significant events of his life. During the day he stares out a window near the bed in his private room, growing obsessive about incorporating past transgressions into his attempts to stay alive. Rob finally decides to flush out his most egregious wrongs, desperately believing that this self-discovery will at least allow him to die in peace."

"How horrible," Alex interjected. "Not the story. Everybody's worst nightmare is facing death honestly."

"Unfortunately for our hero," I replied, delighted that Alex was still with me, "since the disease and the medication have affected Rob's brain, his recollections grow quite precise. It's no surprise that he has memory hallucinations, thinking that he's being transported back into his past. But then he realizes he can undo the evil things he's done in his life if he's able to recognize the precise moment when each one is about to reoccur. Rob figures that if he acts appropriately this time around he'll alter the path of his existence, his life's purpose will be found and this death sentence will no longer be required. He'll be cured."

"The will to survive is born of the innocence of imagination."

"That's beautiful," I replied.

"Steven Spielberg," Alex said. "It's from that movie *Empire of the Sun*."

Then Alex looked over and put her hand on my arm when she realized that I might be brooding about her interruption of my story. "I like it," she said, reassuringly. "Now I gotta pee."

We pulled into a Shell station near Beloit, where the absence of bulletproof glass at the cashier window served notice that we'd entered Wisconsin. Alex hurried off for the key while I pondered an issue I'd been struggling with since I began the friggin' novel: Can we ever correct our mistakes? . . . Suppose we did have the power to return to the past, after all. Maybe in a time machine, or through hallucinations. How would we recognize the precise moment of our error if we didn't think we'd done something wrong in the first place?

People can and do change, I thought. Forgiveness and rehabilitation are uniquely human ideas, the essence of religion. An atheist would have to admit that the *concept* of God remains the most significant life-altering force humanity has had in common throughout civilization. If God has been inside each of us for eternity, I wondered, why couldn't we be transported back in time with our more evolved sensibilities intact? Wouldn't we be better equipped to recognize the difference between right and wrong when we're given a second chance to choose? . . . God must guide us when that precise moment arrives, I concluded.

"Want some?" Alex asked, suddenly returning with a box of Raisinettes that she thrust into the driver's side window. "I thought they only sold 'em in movie theaters," she added, pouring me a handful.

The sun, directly overhead now, baked her muscular legs as I watched her stride around the hood of my car. Her baggy khaki shorts, tank top, and baseball cap were fresh and seductive to me.

"Y'know, Ollie," Alex said, after she returned to the passenger seat, "the character in your book reminds me of Lucien."

I didn't respond as we drove off. Alex settled back for a few minutes and then began fiddling with the radio stations. After hearing all of them we wound up driving in silence. Soon I recognized the capitol dome in downtown Madison rising on the horizon. When we exited the Interstate a freshwater breeze off Lake Mendota cleared out the remnants of humidity clinging to the upholstery. I hadn't come back to the university since I'd left with a useless liberal arts degree and no connections. In those days I had big plans. That they hadn't amounted to much was not attributable to my tenure at this noble institution, I assure you.

"Where're we going?" I asked after we'd reached the town square and were circling on the wide, one-way drive.

"Jake's condo is a broken-up old fraternity house at the end of Langdon Street," Alex went on. "Lucien and I have stayed there while Jake is off on summer holiday."

"I lived in a fraternity house at the end of Langdon Street. It's not the Phi Pho House?"

"How would I know? It's an old brick place with a rolling lawn down to the lake."

"You're kidding? How much has Lucien told you about the time we spent here?"

"He said you were friends who had a fight and didn't keep in touch over the years. Your editorial surprised Lucien. . . . Not a whole lot of support's been coming in lately."

"He said we were friends?"

"Is there something else?"

"It's been a long time, that's all."

"You're going to find out," Alex suddenly offered, "those accusations about Lucien's past drug use are true. I went to Mama Raspberry's with him a few times."

"D'ya think he'd appreciate your telling me this?"

Alex leaned forward and tugged on her baseball cap in what seemed to be a show of determination. "You promised to help," she said.

I drove instinctively toward my old fraternity house along Langdon Street, a winding tree-lined row steeped in campus traditions: goldfish swallowed in stuffed telephone booths, sorority house lawns littered with filched panties and empty beer kegs, and bricks and chairs hurled through tear gas clouds at National Guardsmen passing by.

"Here's the place," Alex said when we approached the cul-de-sac at the end of the same narrow brick road on which I'd regularly walked years ago. Standing before me was *my* three-story Tudor mansion fronting a broad lawn sloping down to the lake. With green painted shutters and a clay-shingled roof, the retrofitted structure had retained its ivy-covered walls and the small portico extending over the main entranceway. A hand-carved wooden door stood open underneath. Only the cluster of shiny mailboxes and doorbells on the archway indicated that the Phi Pho house was gone.

"There's Lucien's car," Alex said, and I parked next to it.

We followed the footpath down the long bank beside the house. Through some trees ahead of us I could see a newly painted wooden dock bobbing above the lake. The tide beat against the stanchions caressing the shoreline. A figure was lying face down on the pier asleep in the hot sun. I pointed in that direction and the shirtless body stirred although we were fifty yards away. Alex waved when she recognized Lucien smiling up at us, and she hurried down the stone path to the pier. They embraced as I came along at a normal pace. When I stepped onto the dock they were exchanging pleasantries. I heard Lucien say, "I've been expecting you." He was looking at Alex. His voice was loud. I swear he was talking to me.

"It's nice to see you again," I said after I'd stopped a few feet away and he came over to shake my hand.

"I wasn't sure you'd feel this way," Lucien replied.

Something about our meeting there, of all places, compelled my warmest emotions toward Lucien. My nostalgia notwithstanding I had reason to dislike him. Lucien was the personification of everything I hated and wanted to become. The contradiction ran deep into my soul, reminding me of my own inadequacies when I came upon a person of influence and achievement. As I sized him up on the wobbly pier, Lucien's gaze was fierce as ever. Yet his handsome, angular face composed a compassionate visage, and I concluded that he was not a person easily impressed anymore. Lucien had probably seen and done it all.

Alex approached us and slipped her arm into his. Lucien smiled at me while he kissed Alex's cheek, and I wondered what the hell I was doing there.

Then I experienced the most amazing sensation. Words do not adequately describe what transpired, but a force surged through me that catapulted my puny level of understanding beyond the wildest expectations. I saw behind Lucien Echo's eyes a dark rattle of terror and shame. So gripped was I by this powerful swell of confidence that I knew I had stumbled upon the precise moment in time when I could alter the course of my life. Convinced that we'd been transported back in time, standing on my fraternity house dock, if this was my second chance I wasn't going to muck it up.

An ominous cloud appeared overhead. It hovered above the lake, abruptly covering the sun's blazing heat with a chilly gray blanket. Alex must've sensed that something had passed between Lucien and me because she slipped away from him and regarded me strangely. Lucien's body relaxed and the horror disappeared from behind his eyes. He mumbled something to Alex. It sounded like, "Don't bother about dinner." When Alex said that she hadn't heard him, Lucien apologized instead for his inattention, and he asked her if she wouldn't like to freshen up as he had something that he wanted to talk over with me. Alex took the cue and smiled at me gratefully. I gave her the car keys so she could collect her bag from the trunk. She kissed him and left us alone on the dock.

"Heroes are only lucky fools," Lucien said right off. "Are you trying to be a hero, Ollie?"

"I don't understand," I barely uttered, having remained quite confused over what time and space we were really experiencing at the moment.

"Alex thinks people should mate for life, like wolves," Lucien explained. "Don't bother getting a woody over her."

I tried to change the subject, feeling embarrassed that he sensed exactly how attracted to her I was. "Some people think you're a hero," I said. "Does that bother you?"

"There's always an instant of decision when the outcome is spontaneous," Lucien responded evenly. "An opportunity presents itself and you take the risk or you don't. Anybody who follows that plan for life is a fool. . . . That's why I'm surprised at you, Ollie," Lucien went on, startling me as he said, "Didn't you take a risk coming here? . . . Or are you following the path of some deep truth like that doctor in your novel?"

"How did you? . . ."

"Never mind." Lucien interrupted me with a wave of his hand while a drizzle began to fall. "You're here. That's what matters. Now listen to me."

I was too shocked to listen. The lake was alive with tiny circles made by the lightly falling rain. Off in the distance I saw an approaching shape that appeared to be a small boat. I felt naked and afraid without the slightest clue how Lucien could know anything about my writing. Then the anger began to bubble inside. "Alex must have . . ."

"Alex has nothing to do with this. Take a chill pill," he added, turning on the charm. "I'm trying to help you finish your book. But you gotta stop floundering over this ridiculous notion of some universal truth that transcends time."

"I still don't understand how you . . ."

"All right with the naive bit," Lucien interrupted me again, this time growing agitated as he went on to make my skin crawl. "No crutches, like your believing in some metaphysical God . . . Ollie, if there is a purpose to our existence, as you say, then the cure for your Doctor Goody Wimpass must come when he's forced to choose between saving himself at someone else's expense or adopting your What Would Jesus Do plan. If I'm any judge of human nature, he won't change anything."

"People don't change? . . . That's it?"

"Who wouldn't want to go back and correct some mistake they've made? Time travel and God? That's cornball slop for children's stories. You want to talk about evolution, how people have adjusted themselves right to the brink over millenniums of civilization, now there's a fine topic. But you can't reduce such heady things to the singular hallucination of a dying man and declare the cure for all humanity. Now can you?"

I assumed that Lucien was pulling some cruel mind control trick on me. I've yet to figure out how, especially since I don't believe Lucien was expecting me to show up. Alex could have phoned him on her cell but she denied having anything to do with it. Notwithstanding the source of his fakery, I was drawn in by Lucien's intellectual challenge to my novel's premise. Maybe I couldn't resist the jumpstart to my ego. No matter how I looked at it, Lucien's point *was* aptly put.

People do evolve very slowly, at separate rates. Ever since we crawled up from the ocean slime, aggression has been essential to the food chain. As Lucien just decried, shall humans continue to kill each other in greater numbers than any natural occurrence until we destroy every living thing on the planet? Or does the fact that we have selfishly evolved into the lone species with the capacity to survive against the dictates of nature mean that we possess inherent life-preserving qualities too? How can we know? Those things we now believe to be life preserving might be the implements of our extinction one day, as harnessing nuclear energy begot the atomic bomb and space travel may yet beget alien aggression.

"If the truth remains constant," I heard myself wondering aloud, "How can anyone change? Especially if we believe that we exist right now. You and I, distinct beings, individual particles massed together in separate casings. . . . It's impossible."

The rain was coming down harder and my panic grew. I heard a voice on the lake and realized that the distant vessel was the crew team's racing shell gliding on the water. I couldn't make out the face of the lone person in the long boat, but I heard a faint cry: "Stroke . . . stroke."

"When the time comes in the novel for Rob to choose," I said, offering the one solution I could think of. "He'll do the right thing so long as he recognizes the truth about himself."

"Not bad," Lucien replied. "The cure must come from within. Not bad at all," he repeated, patting me on the shoulder and flashing his annoying grin again as he walked to the edge of the pier. "Assuming the noblest of purposes," Lucien went on, "should humanity's survival depend on good versus evil? When it comes down to reason versus instinct, or turn the other cheek, who knows what's right? Isn't that the question no matter how well you know yourself?"

"If we rationally control our instincts," I said, "We *can* change the course of events."

The heavens opened in a downpour that rattled the deck. Lucien looked at me smugly, putting his hand out as if he had invoked the storm to drench my enlightenment.

"The truth is something we can't control," he declared. "By your standards nature is corrupt despite our belief in God. The duality of man may have been forever cast when Adam ate from the tree of knowledge, but a volcano, a hurricane, or a man-eating tiger doesn't consider good or evil before striking."

When I turned to run for cover from the rain, the racing shell passed near us and I heard the coxswain bark, "Ollie . . . Ollie."

I looked over and saw a middle-aged man dressed in a silk surgeon's gown sitting up on the narrow bow. Alone in the rapidly moving shell he cupped a tiny megaphone in his hand. Surrealistically, as he went by, I noticed eight oars moving in unison although nobody was attending to them. Then the little man looked back at me and smiled through the drenching rain. I recalled that moment when I'd looked behind the blackened eyes of Lucien Echo.

"You're guilty, aren't you?" I declared.

"Relax Ollie," Lucien responded good-naturedly. "Don't take this good and evil thing personally. If you get maudlin people won't buy the story."

Then he wrapped his hairy arm around my shoulder and led us toward the house. "C'mon," he said. "We'll find out together."

AUTUMN 1967

In Burgerville's game room Ollie Katz and three of his Phi Pho brothers are crowded around Lucien Echo, who's been known to work the Cowpoke pinball machine for an entire afternoon on a single dime.

"I've always wanted things that aren't mine," Lucien declares, injecting himself into their discussion about an absent fraternity brother.

"That's no explanation," Ollie replies, figuring Lucien must be into some Zen thing. What other reason would make him bare his soul? The discussion doesn't concern Lucien.

"Admit it," Lucien taunts. "You've all pilfered stuff from time to time—things you can never use. We take them because we're not supposed to.

"You're full of shit!"

John Trundle's reply takes everyone by surprise. Usually silent and obsequious, "Creach"—short for "the Creature"—Trundle has apparently had a bellyful of Lucien's dime store philosophizing.

"He's a thief," Creach adds. "It's easy for you to defend him, Lucien. Your stuff isn't missing. Why do you care anyway?"

"Excuse me!" Echo answers. "Getting together behind some guy's back to blackball him is cool. Especially since you think he's stealing your dope." Lucien looks at the others. "That's one of the reasons I never joined a fraternity."

Lucien saunters off leaving them to finish his pinball game. Thinking that Creach won't escalate the dispute, Ollie grabs the flippers when Chicken Man and Davis hesitate for an instant. Most of Ollie's buddies are afraid of Lucien. Lucien isn't a bully or a karate freak; he carries himself in a cool and indifferent way. A loner and street kid from Chicago, Lucien seems to be biding his time in Madison waiting for the place to catch up with him. And he's the best damned pinball player Ollie ever saw.

Ollie probably should've accomplished more last year than pledging the house, playing pinball, and pulling his penis. But he was away from home for the first time and that's what they did—well, most of his pledge brothers, anyway. Creach and Ollie were dormitory roommates. Now they're sophomores, numbering twenty, living in the Phi Pho house with thirty older actives. Their world consists of Burgerville, Bascom Hill, and the Risk game board, from which they occasionally retreat to swill another beer out of the tap on their wood-paneled bar in the basement. Ollie's association with Creach played a part in his acceptance into the house. Creach had been an all-state catcher in high school, coveted during rush week by every fraternity, and Ollie benefited from being a package deal. Ollie coined Creach's nickname after he confessed to taking a foul tip under his cupless jock that left him with one testicle.

Ollie keeps a journal for days like today. When raging hormones and rampant curiosity bring him to the brink he tolerates his present crisis by reviewing past whinings. He also thinks that maybe he'll be a writer someday and lately his anxiety seems to be running deeper than usual. Halloween is around the corner and the green lingers on Bascom Hill beneath a cover of fallen oak leaves. The red and white image of Bucky Badger is prominently displayed over campus. But something's been plaguing Ollie since he arrived for the fall semester. His classes seem stilted and angry. Confrontations have replaced discussion and more students are milling around daily. People are choosing sides and Ollie's not prepared.

To make matters worse his chemistry mid-term was returned with a large red question mark where his grade should've been. In the past, Ollie managed school and exams effortlessly. Organic chemistry has been his carbon-based Waterloo since the first class. Here's proof, he thinks, medicine may not be in the genes. Things have been complicated because Ollie spends the lectures mooning over some brown-eyed girl who doesn't know he exists. She's a vision of grace whose soft-eyed gaze Ollie avoids from two rows back and one row over in the amphitheater.

An hour ago, Ollie endured his last emotional straw. When he left the Memorial Union on his way to Burgerville he ran into a raucous protest against ROTC recruitment on campus. Paralyzed with conflict Ollie watched the loudest demonstrators lob trash and rocks at student cadets marching in the parking lot.

"Fergeddabout those geeks," Davis said, after Ollie recounted what he'd witnessed. "Were any chicks there?"

"C'mon, Ollie," Creech broke in, realizing that Ollie was shaken. "Why do you care if they kill each other?"

"The problem is," Ollie said, "you guys only think there's a problem when no ballgame is on the tube or you run out of beer."

That's when Ollie decided to talk to Lucien Echo. Lucien is a law student via some advanced academic program and Ollie believes that Lucien has special wisdom. Rumor has it Lucien belongs to the Weathermen. Jerry Rubin supposedly spent two nights on Lucien's dining room floor. Ollie overheard this discussion in the produce section of the Mifflin Street Co-op, where militant neighbors have risen up to compete against the imperial Kroger grocery chain by opening the first organic market in Wisconsin.

Ollie used to think it was more important to belong. He no longer understands what the fight is all about. If he flunks out he'll be forced to choose between going to Vietnam and running off to Canada. The choice could be infected by cowardice since Ollie has never before questioned whether we're the good guys.

Growing up in Morton Grove, Illinois was akin to living in John Wayne territory. Ollie's knowledge of wars is limited to the Veterans' Day parade, Audie Murphy, and *Run Silent, Run Deep*. In high school Ollie learned about the Domino Principle and the Marshall Plan. Occasionally he'd hear that one of the greasers or the shop jocks had been shipped over there. But Ollie was editing *The Buffalo* and planning on a college deferment. The Gulf of Tonkin Resolution didn't seem like such a bad idea at the time.

Now it's impossible to ignore the Big Lie. Southeast Asia is crawling with American soldiers who possess no jungle warfare skills. The government doesn't bother to deny America's commitment to war, while its reasons for having hidden our involvement seem murky to Ollie. His professors are telling him that unification of Vietnam will be communist by majority will. Everybody knows, they say, we're trying to defeat an army that isn't threatening us.

What Ollie hears sounds villainous, as if we are the bullies. He wonders whether it's wrong to save a country that doesn't want us there. What's worse, the times are calling upon Ollie to put his adolescent distractions in the back seat and rise up outraged over the suspect morality of our government.

Lucien and Ollie end up together in the back game room. The speckled Formica countertop stretches around the narrow alcove all the way to the back. A late afternoon chill creeps in as "96 Tears" comes over the jukebox. The pinball machines lined up against the wall are silent and the calm is reassuring to Ollie. At Echo's nonchalant insistence a lone silver metal ball bounces between two rubber-rimmed bumpers. The rapid-fire clanking competes with the music.

"Do you think we'll lose the war?"

"Why not?" Lucien replies, tapping the right flipper like an electric typewriter. "We lost Korea didn't we?"

"We did?"

"Yeah, right."

"We're having a Hawaiian party at the house next week," Ollie says. "It was pretty wild last year and I thought . . ."

"Keith told me about it," Lucien cuts him off. "Fraternity parties? Never mind," Echo adds, dismissing it with a wave. "Here take a ball."

"The faculty is voting on ROTC recruitment tomorrow," Ollie says. "If they kick `em off campus people will be forced to notice."

"The institution is finished, including the faculty bullshit about peaceful change. We have to tear it down and start over again. Shut down the schools, the courts, the jails, the big corporations and turn off the goddamned televisions!"

"But if we stop the war we'll do something no other generation's accomplished."

"The war is a symptom, man. This is a decolonization."

"I don't understand. Isn't the point of protesting to get attention?"

"Who said anything about protesting? Anonymity is key. With any luck, Ollie, people won't notice until it's too late to stop the *big* change."

On the Monday evening in October after the clocks fall back, people scurry along surprised by the early darkness. Ollie dawdles up State Street wondering why he's unconvinced about the proliferation of protesting. The navy-blue, plaid-lined jacket he's been guarding for weeks in the men's store window distracts him. As the flower shop next door is about to close, Ollie worms his way in with a story about his girlfriend's forgotten birthday and purchases one red rose to spring on his brown-eyed chemistry classmate.

She must have transferred here, he thinks, pondering how to present this declaration of affection. Ollie would've noticed if she were around last year. Her long curly hair, the color of bleached almonds, and those big round eyes were carved into Ollie's feeble brain when first he'd spied her entering the lecture hall. Ollie followed her home from class pretending on the way to take photographs of people on the street with his empty camera. Waiting for the appropriate moment his fear grew with each passing day. After struggling with dioxide ring formulas for a month and a half, the meaning of life was slipping away and all he could do was stare at her with a goofy, lapdog grin.

Deliver it anonymously, Ollie decides, remembering what Lucien said. He stashes the rose beneath his flannel shirt and takes a shortcut through the parking lot behind the Beta house. When he approaches Langdon Street he turns homeward, not willing to risk discovery by his mystery woman, and he walks away from her apartment building located a few blocks up the street.

The cul de sac is jammed all the way down to the house. Gleaming new sports cars line the cobblestone alleyway. In the moonlight owners pretend not to watch the football being tossed around their polished chrome status symbols. As Ollie approaches the front door he avoids an errant spiral that skips across the windshield of Pushead's MG and lands in the bushes next to him. After hurrying into the house, Ollie ducks past the living room full of brothers hanging out. Clutching the rose to his chest he climbs the brick staircase to his room on the second floor. The door is stuck. Ollie notices *his* towel wedged underneath and realizes that Bork is getting high again. He calls out to his roommate while struggling against the blocked door.

"Why do you insist on getting me in trouble?" Ollie asks as he finally brushes past him into the room.

"I keep tellin' ya to try some," Bork says with his dumb grin. "You wouldn't be so uptight all the time."

What is *that* supposed to mean? Ollie wonders, as Bork hands him the joint and walks to the doorway.

"I'm going to dinner," Bork adds, disappearing into the hall without asking Ollie to come along.

Ollie carries the roach over to Bork's desk and places it in the folds of his psychology textbook. He's tempted to retrieve and light it but continues out onto the small terrace at the end of their room.

The night breeze is chilly. Rustling leaves have replaced the laughing, familial sound of the Greek pre-dinner ritual in the street below. Although Ollie lived for this time all summer, the thought of joining his brethren en masse for their nightly dose of starch and snappy comebacks knots his stomach. Suffocating under his shirt nearby is a thorny reminder of his inability to do what his gut tells him.

After retreating inside the narrow room, Ollie leaves the French doors open. He places the rose on the bunk bed and retrieves his spiral notebook from within a stack on the desk in his portion of the quarters. The wind comes in off the lake through the terrace. Ollie begins to scribble in his journal as he hears a boat banging against the pier down at the end of the path.

SHORT STORY IDEA: A lonely hero with the courage to be unpopular. Someone who understands a person's true value despite the social baggage hanging in the balance. Recognizing value in another often requires us to admit we're wrong about ourselves and to appreciate our intuition particularly when it is not self-aggrandizing. If this helps us honestly reflect our inner-selves, does the strength to act follow from this knowledge?

When Ollie hears the dump truck grinding up the hill alongside their house he figures that conditions are safe to venture downstairs. Springing from his bunk, Ollie leaves Harlowe's monkeys for another session. It's Saturday and Bork is off somewhere. By now he's probably in The Pub, drunk. Since the hapless Badgers took it on the chin again this afternoon, no post-game celebration will occur in the streets. Tonight promises a different bacchanal amidst the half-ton of sand just dumped on the dining room floor.

Chicken Man, a.k.a. Keith Strobar, peeks his pointy head into Ollie's open doorway. "Can I borrow your shampoo?" he asks.

"In Bork's bookcase," Ollie replies after slipping on his jeans and a wool pullover sweater. "You have a date tonight?"

"Nah," Keith says. "Last year, I puked my guts out at nine-thirty and passed out. I woke up with some chick gobbling my knob."

"Yeah, right."

"I swear to God! I'm swirling in a pool of ectoplasm, a bell is ringing in my ears, and my pants are down around my ankles while this townie's sucking on my pole like a clarinet. So I've decided. This year no punch, no date and I'll have the pick of the litter."

Ollie's heard enough to beg off quietly and head downstairs. Colorful paper and straw palm trees mark the entrance to the cavernous stone living room. The clubby furniture has been removed and the tweed rug is rolled up against the wall. Tropical flowers hang from the brass and wood wagon wheel chandeliers, their electric candles dimmed past the point of suggestion. Only the television set remains lighting up its usual spot in the corner, while the Rockola blasts out J.J. Jackson's "But It's All Right." Ollie winds halfway down the main staircase before he sees Ring behind the wood paneled bar at the bottom.

"Waxing Wally again?" Ring asks him.

"How do you polish a Q tip?" Davis cuts in.

"Wanna beer?" Ring offers.

"No thaa . . . why not?" Ollie changes his mind upon reaching the landing, stopping next to Davis who's leaning up against the bar. "So the band is Fever Tree?" Ollie asks him. "Psychedelic music seems stupid for a Hawaiian party."

"Rocky's an acidhead," Ring replies in a gossipy tone. "Nobody else wants to book the bands. I heard some big name soul group is still in the running."

"Who cares?" Davis says. "By eleven o'clock it won't matter if the Beatles are here."

"Fuck the Beatles!" Ring snorts. "Mick is the main man."

"Morrison is *the main man*," Davis retorts.

"Jim or Van?"

"Piss on those Limey bastards!" declares Davis, the true American. "There's one Lizard King."

Ollie peers around the corner into the dining room. The long dining tables have been folded and stacked outside on the patio leaving the open space resembling a sandbox with fake palm trees and beach umbrellas. A large rubber garbage pail next to the remaining table in the room will soon contain fresh fruit and hard liquor punch. Plastic sheets cover the framed color portraits of past fraternity classes hanging in rows along the walls and adding the padded-room touch.

Ernie, the Phi Pho cook, is in the adjacent kitchen pantry preparing to go home. A squat, graying black man, Ernie has been standing over the pots and pans absent-mindedly dropping Lucky Strike ashes into his institutional concoctions for the likes of them since Korea. On Sunday mornings, when breakfast is a free-for-all and Ernie takes special orders for the few who wander in before ten o'clock, conversation is the main ingredient. Now his manner seems indifferent as Ollie watches him grab his checkered apple-cap from the hook behind the door and make for the back stairway exit. Ollie peppers him with small talk, following Ernie into the late afternoon chill and all the way up the street toward the Student Union.

Once he's inside the main hallway of the building, Ollie falls in line with the crowd of students and townies making their way. A slideshow of ancient temples in India is letting out and there are drunken stragglers drowning their sorrows after the football game. Ollie passes under the

Rathskeller's gothic archway searching for familiar faces to avoid. His timing couldn't be worse. On the far side of the room Lucien Echo and Ollie's brown-eyed girl sit together at a small table. Lucien is speaking, punctuating the air with a hand he has just removed from the young woman's delicate wrist. Ollie's mind retreats into the hallway while his feet carry him in their direction.

"Hey Ollie," Lucien says. "Doin' some research? C'mon over."

Lucien rises and makes the introduction that Ollie's been craving for weeks.

"Elise Franklin meet Ollie Katz."

"I'm . . . gratified to meet you," Ollie says, drawing a blank on the speech he's meticulously prepared for this moment. He reaches over for Elise's outstretched hand hearing a single drop of his sweat plop loudly onto the plastic tabletop between them.

"I've seen you in chem class," Elise replies, seemingly unaffected by his bumbling. "You in pre-med?"

"Ollie is the latest Kerouac," Lucien responds.

"I decided on med school because my father wants me to be a lawyer," Ollie says without looking at her. "I'm not sure I'll make it through."

"I'm sure you'll do whatever you set your mind to," Elise says.

Their eyes meet and Ollie's heart races. Lucien doesn't seem to notice. He gets up, asks whether they want anything, and goes off toward the cafeteria line.

Following a silent moment, Elise smiles at Ollie, and he wonders if she's as uncomfortable as he is.

"How do you know Lucien?" Elise asks.

"He's teaching me the finer points of pinball."

"Lucien's a master of games."

"He takes the war seriously."

"Lucien likes danger associated with tearing down the system," she adds. "I don't understand how anyone thinks that peace over there will come from violence at home."

"I never considered that," Ollie says, thinking of ways to ask for her help with his chemistry equations.

Lucien returns with a bottle of Special Export and Ollie notices that around Lucien's neck is a porcelain pendant on a gold chain.

"How's your new story coming?" Lucien asks.

"It's not. What's that necklace you're wearing?"

"The Yin Yang," Lucien replies. "A Chinese symbol for balance between aggressive male energy, Yang, and Yin, the maternal nurturing side of us. When the Yin and Yang are balanced a person is supposed to be in perfect harmony."

Before Ollie can remark how he's a big hairy dude without a lone spark of female energy in his body, Lucien takes off the pendant and hands it to him.

"Here," Lucien says. "Try it. If your voice doesn't change you can give it back."

"Thanks," Ollie musters.

"Don't sweat it," Lucien says. Then he suggests that they head off. Elise nods affirmatively, and when they stroll away she slips her arm into Lucien's.

Ollie isn't surprised that they're together. Yet, he feels guilty plotting to steal Elise away when Lucien was expressing his friendship. "Screw the excuses," Ollie declares. She's the cutest girl he's ever met and the way she said, "tear" and "war" with her New England accent excited him. How can

Ollie compete with Lucien for her attention? Ollie wouldn't know what to do if she begged for it.

Ignoring the cold night air, Ollie walks over to the East Side wearing a flimsy windbreaker. A small crowd is forming inside the Nitty Gritty. He ducks in hoping to find an empty pinball game and a view from the bar to watch the girls do their Saturday night mating dance. Within the long row of machines, Hearts and Spades has fewer than five dimes lined up on the glass cabinet top. A burly guy with thick, red beard and a lumberjack shirt grunts at Ollie, takes the first dime off the glass top, and fumbles for the front slot on the machine. Not a long wait, Ollie concludes, making his way over to the horseshoe bar with racks of glasses, like stalactites, hanging down around it.

The bartender happens to be standing near the open spot into which Ollie drifts. Without bothering to check his ID the young man gestures for Ollie to order something. Ollie glances over at two glasses of draft beer next to him, and he realizes that the brews are attached to two young ladies with loads of perfume and matching paisley dresses. He decides to chance it. "Tequila Sunrise," Ollie says, a tad softly.

"Whadjusay?" the bartender asks.

"Tequila Sunrise please!" Ollie shouts as the Box Tops' finish, "My baby done wrote me a let-terrr!" and the room grows silent. Sensing that the girls are watching him, Ollie catches another whiff of their cheap scent. Incredibly, though, the bartender says, "That'll be a dollar-fifty, Bud," and he goes off to mix Ollie's drink.

"Hi there," Ollie says to both of them, feeling full of himself.

"You twenty-one?" the suspicious cutie on the right asks.

Ollie realizes that the only way he can tell the young ladies apart is by the half-pound of additional make-up on the face of the one on the left. He figures them to be high school seniors from somewhere in town. "Don't I look twenty-one?," he says to the one on the right.

"Don't worry," she replies. "We won't turn you in. My name's Jen, in case you're interested. This is my sister, Renita."

"It's Rennie. Thank you very much," she jumps in. "Jen knows how I hate that name. She's showing off."

"Stop it, Rennie," Jen says back to her. "We're twins in case you haven't guessed," she continues with Ollie. "I'm older."

The bartender sets his drink on the bar. While Ollie removes his wallet the girls grab for their beers. After placing two dollars on the counter, Ollie watches them drain their glasses without taking a breath. He extracts a five and swaps it before the bartender's wet hand arrives. "Two more beers," Ollie says.

"Oh, thanks ever so much," Jen replies with a smile that seems encouraging to him. "You must be a Greek," she adds.

"You got me."

"What's with the 'ever so much' business?" Rennie asks her. "You auditioning?"

"Don't mind my sister," Jen says to Ollie. "She's upset because her boyfriend stood her up. Where you from?"

"'Burbs of Chicago."

"Dad was stationed there in the Navy," Rennie interjects. "Last summer, Jen and I took the train down to see Manfred Mann. Someplace on the North Side, I think. Near the lake, right Jen? Remember? `Cause those hoodlum boys gave us a ride to the train station after they tried to park with us at the beach.

"Can you believe it?" Rennie goes on. "We were practically kidnapped in this ugly guy's Cadillac convertible. He kept trying to kiss me with his greasy face and get me to play with his thing."

"Ren, cut it out . . . I told you . . . Why are you always such a p.t.?"

Ollie's not much of a drinker. Now his goes down like pink lemonade. The twins quickly respond in kind. Jen's face is smooth and a little flushed. Upon closer inspection Ollie notices that Rennie's eyes are darker and set a little deeper despite all the makeup. Their silky chestnut hair appears eerily identical, done up with Buster Brown cuts that shine crimson under the bar lights.

"D'you wanna go to a frat party?" Ollie asks directly.

They look at each other for a moment in conference.

"It's not going to be one of those sex orgies? Is it?" Rennie asks.

"No, it's a Hawaiian party. There will be a lot of leis."

"Whaa? . . . Oh. Heh, heh, heh," Jen giggles and her body vibrates on the barstool. Ollie notices her small breasts bobbing through the thin material of her dress. Rennie sees him staring at her sister and downs the remains of her beer.

"Okay," Rennie says. "I'll go. But we gotta be home early. Remember, Jen, tomorrow is Manchesters' anniversary sale. I have to work," Rennie adds for Ollie's benefit.

During the walk to their car Ollie learns from Jen that they attend Wilson High and turned eighteen on Wednesday. On account of school, Jen says, they waited till last night to begin celebrating. Rennie gets behind the wheel and checks out her makeup in the mirror as Jen and Ollie also squeeze into the front seat. Rennie takes off driving like a maniac, cutting around cars and screeching the tires when she turns the corners. Ollie feels Jen's hand on his leg, and she smiles at him to convey that she's steadying herself from the jostling about. Rennie seems too intent on breaking the sound barrier to notice.

They arrive unharmed at the cobblestone alleyway leading to the house. No parking spaces remain so Rennie backs up onto the lawn and shuts off the engine. Ollie exits the car and hears live music coming from inside. He sees people standing on *his* darkened balcony above the entranceway and prays that Bork hasn't leased their quarters for the evening again.

The living room is jam-packed with revelers in a semicircle, ten deep, surrounding five middle-aged crooners wearing gold lamé suits and wailing in choreographed harmony: "She's pretty as a daisy but look out man she's crazy." Behind them near the fireplace a much younger zebra band cranks out rock and roll rhythm to the sweaty, bouncing room. Ollie pulls the girls inside and soon they're able to penetrate the throng standing in the foyer. Women wearing grass skirts and couples dressed in Hawaiian prints dance together in the tiny space between the performers and the audience. "Late at night when you're sleepin' Poison Ivy comes a creepin' around—arounnnd . . . La di la di la da, la di la di la daa."

The clamorous show keeps everyone dancing and inspires encores. The group snake dances around the living room until the singers eventually head up the staircase out of sight. When Ollie spots Ring leaning against the stairwell, sporting a pork pie hat, he's staring off into space with a chemical grin on his face. Ollie starts toward Ring, doing a one-eighty as soon as he sees Chicken Man intercept the sisters. Having lingered at the edge of the foyer, they're still gaping at the unfolding scene.

"You came with Katz?" Chicken Man asks Rennie as Ollie hurries to rejoin them.

"They sounded just like the Coasters," Ollie replies first, ignoring Keith's not so subtle insult.

"It's them, Pinhead," Chicken Man says, casting lecherous eyes over the length of Rennie's body. "Rocky came through. Are you going to introduce me to this lovely creature? Or not?"

"Where's that punch you've been bragging about?" Jen asks Ollie, paying no attention to Keith. Much to Ollie's relief, she drags him off.

"My uncle owned a big house like this on the other side of the lake," Jen says as they wind through the crush of bodies buzzing about the living room. "The government took it away. Something to do with tax evasion or something like that. Nobody in the family talks about it but my mother told me it was because he was a communist."

"There are two floors upstairs," Ollie replies. "I promise no communists live here."

"Hey, Ollieee! Hubba hubba!"

"Hubba hubba?" Ollie repeats without turning around.

"What a skank," Bork whispers into Ollie's ear. Then he comes around to greet Jen. "Ollie's little chickadee," Bork says in his drunken W.C. Fields voice. "How thrilling to make your acquaintance, my dear."

Bork spends most of his life in front of the mirror practicing dialects and speeches. His impressions are occasionally funny. However, Bork believes that one day he'll be the Democratic US senator from Iowa. He wears black engineer boots and smokes those skinny European cigarettes. Right now, Ollie wishes that he'd do his imitation of the Invisible Man.

"This is my roommate," Ollie says to Jen. "Nothing you say will offend him or make him go away."

"Am I ever going to get any punch?"

Ollie thinks that Jen is exhibiting good sense by dusting off his friends. On the way downstairs to the dining room, however, Ollie realizes that she was staring at him with a "go fetch" look. Scantily clad females in tropical attire easily distract him in the stairwell, and he can hear loud groaning sounds coming from below. A bottleneck in the barroom blocks the entrance to the dining room, but Ollie sees Creach and some other guy rolling around on the floor in a sloppy mixture of sand, beer, punch, and food. As Ollie pushes his way into the room people are laughing and shouting encouragement, and he can't discern whether those two are really fighting.

The crowd erupts in a chorus of "Ugh, Oogh, Go! . . . Ugh, Oogh, Go! . . . Ugh, Oogh, Go!"

From outside the patio doors, Davis rushes in and dives headlong into the slippery mess on the floor. He skids on his belly down this makeshift runway, landing on top of

Creatch at the other end of the room. A pile of slithering bodies soon develops under the table nearby, threatening to overturn the remaining punch. Ollie rescues the stuff, retreats to the kitchen and secures an empty pitcher from the sink. The moment he manages to take a gulp Ring shows up from inside the pantry.

"Didjuseedem?" Ring asks.

"Yeah I saw them," Ollie says. "Where'd they go?"

"Didjuseedem?" Ring asks again. "For a moment time actually stopped. A window appeared and it opened into a sunlit passageway filled with musical notes riding by on the waves of a multi-colored scale. Like a cartoon or something."

"Are you OK?" Ollie asks, taking another swig of punch.

"The notes were from the song they were singing," Ring drones on. "I don't read music, but I swear I was able to sing along as the notes went by. . . . I know an epiphany when I see one."

Now Ollie's fingers are tingling and his head seems to be encased in warm dough as he wanders through the darkened living room searching for the twins. While some of the crowd has spilled outside, the place vibrates with music and laughter. After he interrupts some couples groping on the terrace, Ollie decides to head upstairs. It occurs to him that he's doomed to be alone tonight despite his firm conviction that he could finally go the distance.

When Ollie comes upon the door to Chicken Man's room, he hears muffled sounds coming from inside. It's locked. He hurries off down the hall and, feeling like a house detective, Ollie flings open the door to his own room. There sit Jen and Bork on Ollie's bunk. At least he thinks it's Jen. It's dark and the air is thick with marijuana smoke. In the hallway light, Ollie notices that the girl's hair is mussed and Bork is fidgeting with the buckle on his pants.

"Where've you been?" Bork asks, jumping up to greet him in the doorway. "We waited for you forever. C'mon," he goes on, pushing Ollie out into the hall, "Let's discuss this."

"What's to discuss?" Ollie says. "You're getting high in the room with my date."

"Your date? Don't pull that shit with me, Ollie. They're townies you picked up in a bar who can't wait to get porked. Right now Keith is warming up the other one. For once in your life can't you just let it all hang out?"

"Which one is she?"

That's all Ollie can think of to say. They re-enter the room and Bork locks the door behind him. Ollie brings the pitcher over to the desk next to the bunk bed, picks up a glass, and fills it without looking at her.

"I'm sorry," Jen says, patting the bed invitingly. "But I didn't think you'd mind if I smoked a little grass."

"Here's your punch," Ollie replies with a dry throat as he sits down on the edge of his own bunk. Jen skootches over until Ollie feels her leg again. She takes a big gulp from the glass, smiles at Ollie in a devilish way, and the blood in his body rushes to you know where. Bork comes over and settles in, sandwiching Jen between them. While Jen passes the glass to Ollie, Bork lets his free hand slip on top of her paisley dress just above the knee.

"This is cozy," Bork says, looking at Ollie.

Ollie is paralyzed with fear. He's also randy as a toad. Without Bork's interference, he thinks, who knows how this could end up? Jen seems unconcerned about Bork's hand, which has crept a little farther up her leg. Ollie places his own hand on Jen's other knee and stares straight at her. She closes her bloodshot eyes and her breathing immediately grows heavy. Ollie boldly rubs his hand under the thin dress and along her thigh. A cooing sound comes from Jen's throat and she opens her eyes in a struggle to focus on Ollie's face. She leans toward him and her hot breath on Ollie's mouth makes his neck hair stand up.

Without removing his hand from her thigh, Ollie kisses Jen's gaping mouth and, losing his balance, pushes the two of them backwards onto the narrow bed. Her tongue explores the caverns of Ollie's throat while his body rests half on top of hers and half scrunched up against the wall. She squirms under him when Ollie reaches for her breasts, and he senses that Bork has moved in again. Jen tosses Ollie aside with surprising ease and sits up. Ollie sees Bork on his knees next to the bed, stroking her bare thighs.

"Okay," Jen announces, "I'll do it. But he's first," she says to Bork. "You gotta leave us alone."

"You promise?" Bork implores.

"I promise," Ollie answers instead, as he gazes at her white cotton panties illuminated by the light streaking in through the balcony doors. "I promise," he repeats.

Jen laughs. She takes Bork's head in her hands and kisses him softly on the mouth. Bork gets up off his knees, grabs the joint from the ashtray on the desk, and climbs the ladder at the other end of the bunk bed. Jen pulls up her dress past her hips and over her head, exposing to Ollie her smallish breasts, accentuated at their point by big red nipples.

This is it, Ollie decides, sliding slowly toward her. As he brushes his palm across her nipple, Ollie's fingers are electrified, and he's driven to cup both taut bosoms in his sweaty hands. Jen tugs his shirt out, undoes his belt buckle, and opens his pants. The wind whistles out of him and Ollie's head starts to spin when she grasps his hardness through the straining flap of his boxer shorts.

"Feel me down there," Jen says, while she slings her hips, allowing him to slip her panties down below her knees. Her private scent is intoxicating as he feels his way over her soft peach fuzz and inserts a finger into her gooey crevice.

"Jeesus," Ollie says, as she falls back onto the bed and kicks off her panties. "I gotta stick it in."

"Get on top of me," she orders. "Take off your pants," she says when Ollie tries to mount her too quickly. Ollie hears snickering above them as he scrambles out of his clothes. He climbs up again by pressing his heaving chest onto hers. Jen spreads her legs beneath him and guides his hips toward her until her delicate warmth touches the edge of his stiffness. And just like that, *it's in*.

"Whooooh," Ollie blurts out, feeling her surround him. Jen draws him into her while she writhes under him, and his brain is overwhelmed by the sensation of gliding in and out of her wetness.

"Whoooah," he exclaims, as the message rushes back through his tingling body to the source and he explodes inside her before he's able to glide out again.

"Not yet," Jen says into Ollie's ear, while she moves a little faster under him. "Oh, ooh . . . oh? . . . Did you come?" she asks, when he starts to slip away.

Dizzy with experience and too much drink, Ollie rolls off Jen's body onto his side. And just like that, it's over.

"You pulled out in time?" she wants to know.

"Sure," he lies.

Jen runs her hand over his belly and feels around on the sheet between them. Then she wraps her arms around him while she snuggles her face up against his chest.

Ollie's confounded by this display of intimacy. He doesn't want to hurt her feelings, but he is awfully tired and the annoying scent of her perfume is everywhere. When Jen promptly releases him and sits up, looking into his eyes, Ollie thinks that she's about to whisper something tender.

"You're cute," she says. "But you're a bastard like the rest of your frat buddies."

Jen collects her things, rising to her feet, and Ollie considers taking her home. Then he sees her peeking over the top bunk, where Bork's apparently fallen asleep. Ollie's relief that she's leaving turns to jealousy when he watches her climb the ladder.

He turns onto his back and closes his eyes. Ollie's okay with being a bastard like the rest of his buddies, he thinks, as marijuana smoke wafts across his face. He conjures up Elise Franklin wearing only the pendant that Lucien gave him, and he feels Bork's bunk bed begin creaking above.

"We're in perfect harmony," Elise whispers, and Ollie drifts off in his rocking cradle.

Five minutes into his Sociology lecture Professor Zeitmar goes off about news reports of Vietnamese village babies burned with napalm. Ollie and the other students, more than a hundred of them, are dismissed as Zeitmar storms out of the amphitheater to participate in a planned demonstration against the university. The professor has vowed to boycott classes so long as Dow Chemical Company job recruiters remain in the lobby of the Commerce Building across the street. That's where those genius regents have invited the napalm makers to set up their enrollment table. Although Ollie's thrilled to find an excuse for missing classes, why must this confrontation envelope him?

He doesn't thrive on controversy, particularly when physical threats are involved. During high school Ollie never fought with anyone outside his family. Last year, on the dorm basketball courts, Ollie took his first swing at some guy who wouldn't stop elbowing him under the basket. It was more of a slap than a swing, which is all you need to know about Ollie's pugilistic talents.

Who knows why adolescent boys are compelled to engage in turf wars? Ollie's predisposition to explore and conquer probably goes back to those glorious summer days when his parents permitted him to ride his royal blue Schwinn Racer as far as he could go so long as he made it home by dinnertime. Ollie and friends, usually a group of four or five, would start out early in the morning, their baseball gloves hanging from the handlebars and a playing card stuck with a clothespin in the spokes of their rear tires. Ollie can't remember how many times he ended up in the doghouse after his parents' family club meeting sat down to play poker and discovered that the Ace of Spades was missing from a brand new deck of cards.

If Ollie brought a dollar and a quarter along on the voyage, he could purchase a hamburger, fries, a Coke, and a long strip of button candy. Enough change remained for a Kayo and a pack of baseball cards during the afternoon return trip. His crew never rode all the way to the Loop, frequently making it as far as the city limits. There the traffic would multiply, the faces of their contemporaries would grow dark and menacing, and they'd invariably turn back.

Mostly they roamed the north suburbs searching for new schoolyards and playgrounds in which to challenge the locals to a ballgame, or maybe negotiate a major baseball card trade. Nothing satisfied Ollie more than buying a pack of bubble gum trading cards at some foreign neighborhood candy store and finding inside the card of a star player missing from his own collection. If bicycles were the ships bringing these modern day explorers to a new world, baseball cards were the currency they used to communicate with the natives who inhabited it.

Ollie's rather tame childhood memories contrasted sharply with the turf gang stories of Lucien's childhood. As it happens, Lucien recently told Ollie how he'd negotiated the Chicago public high school in his district, a concrete prison-like structure on the fringe of the inner city. There were upwards of two thousand students. Disappearing would seem easy, but Lucien maintained that everyone risked rough times unless they'd already joined some "social club" back on the street of their neighborhood.

Lucien guessed that he was recruited by the Top Hats one day when ten club members cornered him next to their lunchtime hangout and dragged him down into the basement gangway of a nearby building. They alternately kicked and punched him into the fetal position during this strange initiation ritual. Although Lucien briefly ran with the Top Hats, his association ended after their pyromania phase spun out of control. They used to scour the neighborhood filling stations, after closing, looking for gasoline residue trapped in the pump nozzles. By draining enough hoses they were able to collect a couple gallons of gasoline, which, for kicks, one night they poured along the concrete seam that runs down the center of the alley behind an entire city block of apartment buildings.

Moments after the match was thrown, the spreading line of fire caught a breeze and jumped through somebody's open garage door onto a pile of oil-soaked rags. By the time they reached the renegade flames, half a block down the alley, the blaze threatened to incinerate an old gray Packard parked in the cluttered garage. Lucien said that they'd panicked and fled, failing to smother the fire, when they heard an approaching siren. Lucien returned to the scene the next day finding the burnt out shell of the automobile. That's when he decided to join the football team. By wearing the colors of the toughest gang around—his varsity letter sweater, Lucien could safely cruise his high school corridors.

Ollie's present state of high anxiety has not been diminished at all by recalling those childhood adventures. Standing in the parking lot behind Bascom Hall, he's in the middle of an overflow crowd of angry protesters. There is much shouting. Ollie was just pushed backwards by some guy in a stadium coat, with strong B.O., who was shoved into Ollie by the person standing in front of him. Campus police have formed a barricade using their bodies and nightsticks to prevent this swelling mob from advancing further. The people behind him didn't get the message, so the cops were pushed. Now they're pushing back. There looks to be several thousand young people caught in this ping-pong match between the police blockade surrounding the parking lot and the adjacent Commerce Building.

Within the previous thirty minutes, near the carillon tower, speakers had formed a makeshift podium by passing around the bullhorn. While someone was condemning LBJ's decision to step up the B52 bombings, the commotion erupted. Four youths wearing black berets, blue shirts, and one black glove charged from the lobby and flung the corporate recruiting pamphlets into the horde of coeds who had either joined the demonstration or were caught traveling between classes. Nobody would've begrudged this civil disobedience had they not grabbed the megaphone and threatened to toss the Dow employees into the assembly. After a brief scuffle, however, the disrupters were drowned out by a chant from the vociferous crowd: "STOP THE WAR. STOP THE WAR. HELL NO WE WON'T GO!"

It sprang up around them, growing louder and louder as more people realized that student power was solidified behind the conscription issue.

"STOP THE WAR. HELL NO WE WON'T GO!"

Suddenly, there was Lucien Echo with the megaphone urging a mass march on the State Capitol. Authorized to speak about obtaining conscientious objector status, Lucien made one helluva speech announcing that he was going to burn his draft card on the Capitol steps. "Being a moral person requires doing what's morally right," he said. "If refusing induction is against the law then I choose to be an outlaw!" Lucien and the others stormed off the dais and led a procession through the center of the assembly. When news of this destination spread across the lips of the surging crowd, everybody in the parking lot was swept in the opposite direction, directly into the path of the campus police barrier.

Now the cops are badly outnumbered by the wave of demonstrators breaking through their ranks. Ollie must decide whether to defy the pigs or go back toward his next class. He's tempted to risk a clubbing for *the cause*, but it's freezing out here and he left his gloves in his room. Still, his adrenaline runs high from marching with this scraggly band of revolutionaries.

All winter long, Ollie's been desperate for something extreme to happen in his wretched life. Final exams ended with a cold, miserable break at home. Ollie's father seems to have lost interest in the clothing store. The commute from the suburbs is too much and his dad has started to drink. His mom's been trying to convince them to sell the place. But Ollie's trouble started when he found out that his father had cashed in his life insurance policy to send him to Madison.

Ollie came home complaining that fascists in league with the military-industrial complex were running the university. One evening, Michael reminded him that a lot more than draft dodger crap was expected, since Ollie was the privileged offspring to go to college. Then their dad got pissed off at Annie. Recently turned sixteen, Annie's been staying up all night dropping acid with her friends and she nodded out at the dinner table. "In no uncertain terms," their father insisted, Ollie was going to law school and it didn't matter how much *more* money he had to borrow.

Ollie can stall no longer. The campus police have apparently given up their resistance to the march, fanning out to direct the crowd in a manageable parade. Most of them retreat toward the service road that winds down behind Bascom Hall. Up ahead, Ollie sees the front line of demonstrators traversing the sloping, frozen lawn at the crest of the huge hill. He follows along in a column of people stretching across the wide parking lot. Icy patches on the sidewalk remain from a recent snowfall. Folks are slipping and sliding past the college buildings situated along the steep route, and Ollie realizes that the police must have diverted them this way to slow them down.

A loud cheer erupts from the pack of marchers in front of him. Then a wooden chair comes crashing through the second floor window of the Liberal Arts College. He sees shattered windows throughout the brick building and people leaning out in support of the demonstrators filing by. Ollie's frozen ears are stinging so he puts up the fur-trimmed hood of his Air Force explorer jacket. No sooner does he zip it up, surrounding his head in the warm rabbit hair, than he spots Elise Franklin walking away from the Law School Building.

"Hi," Ollie says, quickly removing the hood again. "Your hair looks different."

"I cut it back home."

"It looks nice."

"Thanks," Elise says, smiling. "How're you? I haven't seen you since our chem final."

"Is mine all messed up?" Ollie asks, running his hands over his head.

"Just a little. . . . Ollie, do I detect vanity?"

"It's this stupid hood. I forgot my gloves so my ears got too cold. Are you marching to the Capitol?"

"I was supposed to meet Lucien here, but that was almost an hour ago."

"He's down there somewhere," Ollie says, pointing towards the front of the crowd. "Lucien made a speech refusing the draft and the next thing you know everyone was following him. . . . I'm tellin' ya', it was inspired," he adds when she looks at him incredulously.

"The law school will expel him."

"Lucien thinks the war is illegal. He wants to void the draft because Congress hasn't authorized combat troops."

"I guess he doesn't care about his future."

"I know he cares about you," Ollie says for no apparent reason.

"YOU ARE ASSEMBLED ILLEGALLY! DISPERSE IMMEDIATELY OR YOU WILL BE ARRESTED FOR CREATING A BREACH OF THE PEACE!"

It came from a bullhorn in the street at the bottom of the hill. Another traffic jam on the path backs up toward them slowly. For a minute they stand around and leap up to see what's happening. Then a loud chorus of "Turn Around. Turn Around" spreads through them like a wave.

"Whaddiya think?"

"Go for it."

Ollie grabs her arm, pushing his way through the column of people in front of them. They're probably thirty yards from the two brick stairways on opposite sides of the wide lawn leading down to State Street. People are stacked up, stuck on the steep stairs. Some are spilling off the paths onto the center ramp of turf that resembles a frozen riverbank running all the way down the hill.

Mass confusion best describes the "T" intersection at the base of the incline. People are jammed in together, surrounded by a ring of uniformed city cops with police cars and wooden horses blocking the streets leading away. When the marchers surge across the intersection into the mouth of State Street, a phalanx of police closes ranks to deny them passage. Those in the rear are pushing in all directions, trying to find egress, but the only available avenue is back up the stairs through the rushing crowd. Some at the top are attempting to negotiate the slippery lawn in order to avoid the gridlocked sidewalk.

"Here goes nothing," Elise says to Ollie. She gingerly inches down the grass, crouching, and promptly slides on her butt when Ollie lets go of her hand. Ollie follows, sideways, keeping his balance with a Herculean effort.

"Thanks a lot," Elise tells him after he helps her up. Then she brushes the icy dirt off her thick, Navy pea-coat and retrieves her earmuffs from where they've fallen on the ground.

At least *she* has gloves, Ollie thinks, while they try again to descend this precipice. Every few steps one of them slips to the ground until they end up half-sliding and half-crawling down to the retaining wall above the street. With their hearts pounding and their backsides covered in cold, wet mud, they collapse in nervous laughter.

"YOU ARE IN VIOLATION OF LAW! DISPERSE AT ONCE OR YOU WILL BE ARRESTED!"

Although the retaining wall on their side is only a few feet tall, it's nearly a seven-foot drop to the pavement. Across the intersection Ollie sees fights breaking out between cops and demonstrators. Police clubs are swinging and people are shouting and running in all directions. Elise scales the wall and he shimmies down after her. Once they're in the street Ollie hears sounds resembling skyrockets firing and notices tiny clouds of smoke rising above the intersection. The panicked mob pushes through the barricades on Park Street, where the police are finally allowing people to depart. Ollie gestures in that direction, but Elise starts toward the intersection instead.

"That's teargas," Ollie says.

"I gotta find Lucien," Elise replies, and she disappears within the sea of flailing bodies.

All hope of being heard is shattered like the heads of those who refuse to surrender. Ollie is nonetheless compelled to follow her. His stinging eyes begin to water as he runs toward the line of police cars blocking off State Street. Any civilian venturing inside the forbidden space between the wooden horses and the uniforms gets cracked. Three at a time, the police drag people along the bloodstained pavement and stuff them into two large bread trucks with meshed wire on the back doors. Ollie sees the same look in every cop's eyes telling him he can have as much as he wants. He simply has to cross that line. It occurs to Ollie that maybe he's destined to be an observer; someone who marches to the edge of history and then stands around watching while others make it.

He thinks Lucien must've been hauled off by now. Ollie's shivering and his eyes are burning, when he finally spots Elise running up the sidewalk toward the Natural History Building. Giving chase, he stops to pick up her earmuffs, which she's left behind on the ground. "Elise, wait up!"

"Oh, Ollie," she says, tears streaking her reddened face. They're out of gas range and Elise blinks repeatedly, trying to see through her swollen, bloodshot slits. "Why do they have to beat on people?" She holds her frozen leather gloves up against her eyes for some relief from the burning chemicals.

"Rubbing them will make it worse. Here," Ollie says, handing her the earmuffs and trying to console her. His head is throbbing and he's no longer distracted from the cold. "C'mon," Ollie adds. "We have to get out of here."

They duck inside the hallway of Natural History and walk through the long corridor that dissects the main floor.

When they emerge on the quad it appears to be a typical gray afternoon on campus.

"I guess the revolution is only happening on the other side of the building," Ollie says.

"You look awfully pale," Elise replies. "Come home with me and get out of those clothes. I'll make some soup."

Believe it or not, initially it doesn't dawn on Ollie that he's experiencing one of his fantasies when they enter Elise's apartment. She tells him that her roommate, Eleanor, is home in Highland Park having her wisdom teeth pulled. Then she throws him a terry cloth bathrobe, which she claims is her own, and disappears through a doorway. Her parlor is warm and intimate with a vinyl beanbag chair, an overstuffed couch, and a weaver's loom resting off in one corner. Ollie removes his wet clothes, save his boxer shorts and socks. The powder blue gown smells like patchouli. It fits okay, so he sits on the couch, plucks a photograph album from the coffee table, and feels something in the pocket. Surprised, Ollie stares into Ulysses S. Grant's face and quickly replaces the bill.

Elise glides into the room wearing a flannel robe buttoned to the neck and a towel wrapped around her head. While her eyes appear red and swollen, she reveals no other scars from their experience. "That's my mom and dad," Elise says, after she sits next to him and points to a photograph in the album taken poolside at some mountain resort.

As Elise goes on about her parents, Ollie barely listens. Gripped with a twisted sense of deja vu, he perceives them in the future, when they're much older, maybe even married, discussing their own kid. Concluding that he's feverish, Ollie excuses himself in order to get cleaned up. In the cluttered bathroom he can't help thinking that he's seen his life pass before him and if he doesn't do something he'll regret forever the missed opportunity. When he returns Elise is in the kitchen pouring a pot of soup into two large mugs on the Formica counter. She carries them over as Ollie throws another log on the fire and stokes it. He wears a shit-eating grin, trying to hide his hard-on that keeps popping out the vent of his boxer shorts, threatening to escape through the folds of her robe.

Now the fire is roaring and they're sitting close together. Before he's able to talk himself out of it, he strikes with catlike precision, stealing a kiss on her satiny lips. They're pouty and soft, and she's responding for an instant that sends sparks flying up and down his spine. Then Elise puts her arms up to Ollie's chest and pushes him away.

"Why do guys only have one thing on their mind? Behave or I'm going to ask you to leave."

"I, uh, . . . I'm sorry. I don't know what came over me."

"You're forgiven," Elise answers, smiling easily again. She senses his panic and takes his hand in hers. "People aren't intimate overnight," she says, kissing his cheek the way Annie used to when Ollie helped her with her home-work.

"How long does it take?" Ollie replies, thinking about the poem in his wallet that he wrote about her but is too embarrassed to let her to read. "Is it romance you want?"

"It's not the right time. . . . That's the truth," she goes on when Ollie doesn't respond. "Something you can't control. Did it occur to you that we might be friends?"

"Friends? Hmm. Now there's a novel idea," Ollie considers it for the first time, really. Friends. Spiritual intimates who support each other with unwavering loyalty; allies with no sexual complications putting them on opposite sides of the struggle.

What's it called? Platonic. That's it. The mere sound of the word causes Ollie to recoil from the sissified notion that he could be identified with her on that basis. Frustrated, he finds himself scrunching up the forsaken greenback with his hand buried deep inside her bathrobe pocket. "Look," they'd say, "there goes Elise and Ollie. They're . . . Shhh! . . . *platonic* friends."

"Try Howie's canolies loose and our love beckons a funeral tire?" Ollie repeats the lyric out loud, while he's stretched out on Lucien's living room floor staring at the plaster speckles in the ceiling. Ollie figures that he's stoned on grass, but the sensation isn't at all what he expected. He continues to quiz Lucien after the record album ends: "What the hell does it mean?"

"Try now we can *only lose*," Lucien responds, "And our love becomes a funeral *pyre*."

"What the hell is a pyre?"

"You're a hopeless primate."

Ollie jumps into a gorilla-like crouch, grunting, and he bounds over, scratching himself. Then he leaps onto the easy chair next to the couch and sinks into the recliner feeling dizzy.

"Take another toke," Lucien says, grabbing one of the brass-tipped hoses that emanate like octopus tentacles from the ornate water pipe on the coffee table. "You're obviously not off yet."

Ollie doesn't know why he's having so much trouble with this new experience. What with Bork smoking all the time, and his other housemates experimenting with LSD and mescaline, it feels like he's living in a pharmaceutical shopping center. Things are way too extreme, so Ollie's decided to move out as soon as he finds someone to share a place with him. But there's more to it than the drugs. His romantic notion of brotherhood has not materialized. Beneath their facade of wisecracks and disdain, Ollie's friends are burying important realities. Their secret bonding rituals seem meaningless, and Ollie's tired of withholding opinions that aren't in keeping with the mob mentality. That's why he trusts Lucien more than the others.

""What's happening with your suspension?"

"They want to kick me out just for being arrested," Lucien replies. "The dean says my conduct was detrimental to the law school's image. But he also said that if I grovel, maybe I could return to classes. I guess their FBI spies didn't arrive soon enough to have any witnesses."

"Are you going to apologize?"

"Fuck'em!"

Ollie doesn't mean to seem ungrateful, but it wasn't Lucien's proselytizing that made him hitch a ride over here in the first place. When Ollie awoke this morning he was enraptured by the warm, early spring day. The scent of blooming lilacs drove him into the street, where sorority girls in halter-tops and cut-offs washed cars and chased frisbees. After Ollie wandered over to the terrace behind the Memorial Union, he watched the sailboats glide across a mirrored lake, decided that medical school would be a mistake, and then promptly fell asleep on the grass. It's funny how his mind works. Most of the time Ollie over analyzes a problem, obsessively, and can't make a decision. The moment he enjoys being alive, without a plan or needing to please anybody, solutions to the most troublesome issues pop right into his head.

Lucien convinced Ollie to celebrate his independence by getting stoned. They take another hit off the pipe and Ollie asks if Lucien wants to accompany him to a party at some farmhouse outside of town. Creach and Ring have promised to swing by and pick up Ollie in a few minutes. It turns out that Lucien's friends Jake and Nikki are the couple giving the party. It's sort of a commune, Lucien says, where they allow kids to squat in exchange for doing the farming and cooking chores. But when the doorbell rings, Lucien decides not to go along. He begs off with a look that says his mind is brooding over serious things.

Ollie rides shotgun in Creach's Malibu, which has the appearance of a gym locker wired for sound. Jock itch powder, damp sneakers, and a dirty t-shirt cover the floor. Above Ollie's knees, up under the dashboard, Creach installed an eight-track tape deck. "Take it, take another little piece of my heart" originates from a new FM stereo radio cartridge that plugs into the deck. As they head out past the Beltway, Ring keeps pestering Ollie to replace it with the tape of "Highway 61 Revisited."

Twenty-five minutes later they turn off the county road and cross a ploughed cornfield. Afternoon sun still warms Ollie's bare arm hanging outside the window. An old brick and wood house on a raised foundation is visible through the dust kicking up on the flat dirt path beneath them. Many cars are parked on the grass at the end of the road. Ollie notices a weather-beaten barn out behind the house and several ramshackle lean-tos inside a corral. People lounge under the shade of a sprawling oak tree and mill about on the sloping, grassy area between the house and barn.

"Hippie chicks," Creach says, while he parks next to the last car in line and shuts off the engine.

"I told ya'" Ring answers, "the guy who sells me acid lives out here."

"This is perfect," Ollie says after they walk around to the trunk and Creach retrieves two six packs. When he also removes a baseball bat, two gloves, and softball, Ollie adds, "You better wait until we're invited in."

"It's a picnic, Emily Post. We're playing baseball."

Ollie isn't good at crashing parties. He's afraid that he'll be publicly disgraced. Lately, though, Ollie wonders whether avoiding embarrassment is too high on his list of life lessons to remember. His friends don't seem to mind making fools of themselves whenever the opportunity arises.

Take Ring for example. He never goes to class, borrows Ollie's notes, cheats on exams, and he's barely passing his courses. Ring is thinking about attending the clown school up in Baraboo, after graduation, or pursuing a stand-up comedy career. For every ten jokes he tells, Ring considers himself lucky if two are funny. This seems to be his basic philosophy in life.

Townies and long hairs inhabit a ratty overstuffed couch on the wide wooden porch encircling the farmhouse. Others lounge on the floor, leaning up against the aluminum siding. Creatch walks around back toward the barn, while Ring and Ollie climb the two front steps in search of a refrigerator for the beer. They're met inside the hallway by a tall, dark-haired, twenty-something beauty with big blue eyes and a honey smile.

"I'm Nikki," she says. "There's a cooler out behind the kitchen and plenty of food. Try to stay on the first floor."

"My name's Ollie. He's Ring. I have regards from Lucien Echo. I don't think he's coming."

"Hmm," Nikki replies. Then she smiles warmly again. "Lucien and my old man, two jerks from the same soda fountain. I'll tell Jake you're here, after I take care of this," she adds, showing them some gauze and a tiny bottle of Mercurochrome in her hand. "One of the kids fell in the corral and skinned his knee."

"Was it his left knee or his right knee?" Ring asks.

"What difference does it make?" Nikki wonders aloud.

"Don't put it on his weenie," Ring replies.

Nikki looks at Ollie, as if for help, but there's nothing he can do to save Ring. Then she makes a "Hehh . . . hehh" sound, like she's clearing her throat, and pats Ring on the head. That's funny to Ollie, since Nikki is three inches taller than Ring.

"Cause you're Lucien's friends," Nikki adds with a conspiratorial look toward Ollie, "There's a bowl of purple haze on the top shelf, above the kitchen sink. I haven't tried it, but people say it's pretty mellow. Don't tell anyone else, and make sure you return the bowl so the kids can't get it."

"I'm in deep lust," Ring says after Nikki goes out through the parlor and they head down the hall toward the rear of the house. "Tall babes are my meat."

"You're a putz," Ollie replies, walking into the large kitchen. A round oak table in the center of the room overflows with platters of meat, side dishes, and desserts. Ollie continues out to the back porch and sees acres of gold and green fields rolling out to a line of trees on the horizon. Two bikini-topped ladies walk along the path through the field beyond the nearby corral, and Ollie figures that there must be a pond or a river on the far side of the trees.

Ollie shoves the six packs, minus two cans, into the cooler on the patio. When he returns to the kitchen, Ring has opted for the acid instead of vittles. "You gotta take this on an empty stomach," Ring says, popping the capsule into his mouth, grabbing a beer and washing it down in one swift motion. "Wait at least a half hour," he adds, handing Ollie another capsule.

"I don't know," Ollie says, slipping it into the pocket of his cut-offs. "Maybe later. I'm gonna check the place out," Ollie adds. "I think they have animals out in the corral. Maybe pot-belly pigs, `cause I don't get to see them up close."

"Why don't you pretend you're a scarecrow and shove a corn stalk up your ass," Ring snaps. "Hang out in the barnyard feeling right at home."

Ollie ignores him, heading back out onto the rear porch and down the steps.

Ring follows as they trudge along the grassy slope. "It's all right to call me a putz?"

"I'm tired of your cynical remarks," Ollie answers, stopping to face him before they approach a circle of people sitting on the rolling lawn under the big oak tree.

"Whaddiya gettin' all sensitive about? It was only a joke."

"Well, it wasn't funny. So shut the hell up already."

"What's your fucking problem, Ollie?"

Ring's voice is loud enough to cause two nearby kids, who are passing between them a joint as big as a cigar, to turn in their direction. Ollie restrains himself from slugging Ring, staring him down instead.

"You're a putz," Ollie says, softly now, and walks around the rim of the gathering toward an open space on the grass. Ollie sits next to a couple whose attention is focused on an exuberant, leather-skinned woman with silver-streaked hair. Out the corner of his eye, Ollie sees Ring stuck in the same spot, staring a hole through Ollie's back. Ring finally shuffles past the big tree down the slope toward the barn.

"Because the property has good feng shui," Ollie hears the attractive woman say to a man sporting trimmed red beard and tortoise-shell glasses, seated, cross-legged, next to Ollie. About twenty-five years old, he's beside his female companion, probably Ollie's age, who has the new greaser look like the Jefferson Airplane singer.

"For centuries," the streaky-haired lady goes on, "the Chinese have employed feng shui masters to inspect their property before they build on it or plant some crops. Judging the position and direction of the stars, and by measuring the cosmic energy about the place--the Ch'i, a master can divine the most propitious spot on which to put the house or dig the well."

"C'mon," the Beard says. "Evil spirits in real estate?"

"The Buddhists have spirit houses," she responds evenly. "They're lovely, particularly in Thailand. Intricate doll house altars in front of their homes, decorated with flowers and candles, and incense burned everyday in homage to sharing their Ch'i with these earthbound squatters. Buddhists believe that keeping the spirit house better maintained than their own humble dwelling promotes harmonious coexistence."

"We were *talking* about going back to the land as an alternative lifestyle," the Beard retorts snootily. "The reason this fucking war goes on is because it's the greatest boom to our economy we could ever devise. That's the serious issue. Without political organization there is no economic strength. Who in hell is going to listen to a bunch of hippie farmers preaching self-determination through higher consciousness?"

"Spoken like a poli-sci T.A., Eric," the streaked lady answers, smiling brightly. She shifts position on the grass briefly exposing her tanned legs underneath an otherwise frumpy cotton dress. "A collective's beauty is apolitical; the absence of rules or the imposition of will on individuals who share a simple, common goal of self-sufficiency."

"I wonder how long I could handle living without rules?" Airplane girl says. "Being raised a Catholic, I know I believe in certain things. Freedom is great and all that. Except, without guilt, or some higher judgment, the whole thing sounds godless."

"The feng shui isn't good for everyone, my dear," the woman responds before Eric interrupts. "But which culture is better suited for our little experiment? It seems to me, anyway, western religion and philosophy are based on the idea that God is the center of the universe. Although we aspire to know God during our lifetime, unless we live a Christian life and accept Him when we die we won't go to heaven. I know that's an oversimplification of the basic rules, but we must forever choose between good and evil . . . right and wrong.

"In my opinion," she continues, "most Eastern religions spring from the concept that *we* are at the center of the universe, along with God, in all earthly and eternal forms. We exist in one form now, as we've always existed in others, so we already know God inside us. Since we are free to experience the *now* without external prejudgments, rules naturally evolve from the universal spirit within all of us, not from conflict between us. It seems that this value system fits more comfortably with the self-governing concept."

"The only rule is the Golden Rule?" the Airplane chick asks in a way that causes Eric to regard her differently—almost with scorn. "I could live with that," she adds, not seeming to notice.

"Wonderfully put," the streaked lady says, punching the air in exclamation. She stands up without bothering to gather her frock around her and stretches her arms up above her head. She turns around and bends all the way over to stretch her back and legs without the least bit of concern that she's waving her ass in front of everybody's face.

"Shall we try some of Hakeem's shrimp salad?" she says to the smallish man with high cheekbones who's been sitting silently at her side, nodding, and smiling, since Ollie sat down. As they wander off, Ollie notices Hakeem's beaten-up leather vest and those psychedelic stringed pajama pants Ollie's been afraid to buy.

"Did you get that?" a soft female voice says into Ollie's ear. He turns toward the pretty young face, realizing at once that he's seen her before. Maybe on campus, Ollie thinks, wondering what she missed. "`Ere," she says, passing him the joint that he'd failed to notice in her hand.

She's a dropout from the Bronx, she says, hanging around off her monthly allowance check hoping her parents won't find out. Sometimes she crashes here. She keeps her stuff in the pantry of the Gilman Street apartment that she shares with three other friends, including Joel, who forced her out of her room after she'd taken *him* in as an act of mercy. Ollie forgets that she told him her name is Cathy. However, Cathy doesn't seem to mind, informing Ollie that she thinks he's cute, for a guy. When Ollie asks whether Joel is her old man, Cathy makes a face and says she doesn't get off on being a sex slave anymore. Ollie concentrates on not staring at her pendulous breasts—nipples and all—visible through her crocheted sweater.

They end up down in the corral, where the lean-tos are home to rabbits and a few sitters. With his chin on the fence post, Ollie watches a few innings of the seven-on-a-side softball game that's come together in the adjacent field. Cathy goes off about, "Margaret and her guru stooge's plan to maternalize the world. It'll never work," Cathy sneers. "People take care of their own. No way they'd throw out their small, prejudiced lives in favor of uncertainty."

It occurs to Ollie that Cathy's getting turned on having someone listen to her rap. He has no solutions to the world's problems, but they play kissey-face behind the last shed and Cathy finally allows him to touch her under her sweater. Then she runs off and, before long, Ollie lets her keep up with him in a race along the dirt path across the newly planted field. When Cathy stops, out of breath, Ollie jogs on through a thicket of trees and comes out onto a long stretch of tall grass sloping down to a man-made lagoon. Mostly nude bathers cavort in the shallow. Others lounge on the flats at the edge of the pond's muddy banks. The warm and windless sky is filled with the sound of a flock of migrating ducks that call down to a group of children, shrieking with delight as they dive off a large inner tube floating in the water.

They stand in the freezing water inspecting each other shamelessly. There's a smell in the air that Ollie knows will trigger a timeless memory when he writes a novel about this place. Cathy stops complaining. She's willing to accept that they're all in chains. She can't make up her mind whether she's destined to pull them through life or get dragged along. What seems cruel to Ollie is the sun threatening to set just when he's discovered the importance of an endless day.

Soon they lie in the tall grass at the top of the hill, drying off and swapping "knock-knock" jokes. They talk of a midnight movie at the Green Lantern and the upcoming Cream concert. However, their eternal connection may be severed after they return to the house for dinner and Cathy drifts off for another piece of pie. Not too much later, as Ollie watches from his solitary perch on the lawn, darkness falls with a thud. People have scattered into tiny groups, illuminating the hillside with campfires and filling the air with music. Creach and Ring decided to split, claiming they had dates. Ollie sent them off with a story about writing a farmhouse article for the *Daily Cardinal*.

Now the sound of a screen door, slamming repeatedly against the side of the barn, annoys him. Ollie ambles toward the lights shining through the loft windows and he's surprised to find a large propaganda factory inside complete with hand-operated printing press. There are anti-war posters, draft disobedience pamphlets, and newspapers denouncing American genocide. A couple of students tend a mimeograph machine resting on a long printer's table midway into the cavernous space. It's too late to split, so Ollie shuffles through the room like he's stumbled into a scene from a French Resistance movie.

Nobody seems to mind when he stops to read a flyer detailing Ho Chi Minh's apparent mandate to reunify the country. It's all news to Ollie, this stuff about puppet dictators and rigged elections. Ollie wishes he felt more like a committed protester and less like someone afraid of getting killed. At least these people are serious, he thinks, noticing two biker hippies sitting on a large area rug at the end of the long walkway through the barn. Next to them on a folding chair, some teenager in army fatigues is speaking to a genteel looking guy in his early twenties. He's sitting at a roll-top desk propped up against the back wall.

"You can stay here until you're confirmed with the people in Toronto," Ollie overhears the fellow at the desk say when he approaches the group. "You can always stick around and try the peanut butter trick," the guy adds, causing the two longhairs sitting on the rug next to him to crack up laughing.

"The peanut butter trick?" Ollie can't help asking the biker closest to him as he sits down.

"If you go to the draft board physical with a glob up your butt, the doctor's gonna wonder what the hell is up there. So you scoop out a finger-full, put it in your mouth, and say, 'Mmmm, tastes like peanut butter.' It works for a psychiatric with some doctors."

"Hey Jake," the bigger biker says. "You think maybe this one's a pig?"

"I don't think so," Jake answers with an easy laugh, while he looks Ollie over from his perch at the desk. "He's looks too straight to be a cop."

"I'm Katz," Ollie says. "The one thing I do know is I am most certainly not a pig. I repeat . . . not a pig. No siree, not me. Absolutely not a p-i-g."

"Well, I don't believe him," the bigger one responds sarcastically, and the other one rolls his eyes at Ollie in a signal to ignore him.

"Now, Ed," Jake says. "Let's be hospitable. You're Lucien's friend, right?" he goes on, recognizing Ollie. "Nikki said Cathy has the hots for you. See," he says to the others, showing his approval, "Cathy usually doesn't like anybody."

"This is some great place you have here," Ollie says, embarrassed to be labeled a lothario. "I was wondering, how much would it cost to stay here till the semester ends?"

Jake seems surprised by the question. He looks at the bikers, snickering at Ollie's bravado. Then Jake smiles at Ollie. "I don't know if you understand," he says. "Some of the things that go on around here aren't exactly legal."

"I keep pretty much to myself," Ollie replies, not at all certain what other things he means. He knows the government would love to seize this propaganda mill; and this kid in the army fatigues is obviously a passenger stopping at Jake's underground railroad station.

"There's going to be a lot of extra heat on us now," Jake says. He rises from the desk, motioning for the young deserter to follow him toward a door on the opposite side of the back wall. They stop, talk for a few seconds, and the kid goes outside. Ed and his buddy are silent, so Ollie gets up off the floor and plops into the folding chair. When Jake returns he looks at Ollie, shrugs at Ed, and pulls his desk chair over to the edge of the carpet. "Ed just came from town," Jake finally says. "Tonight somebody torched the Kroger on Mifflin Street."

"I gotta tell ya," Ed adds. "What a beautiful thing, watching those bloodsucking imperialists get a taste of their own medicine."

"It's a supermarket, fer Chrissakes," the smaller longhair replies. "They got insurance. In three weeks they'll reopen and jack up the prices again to pay for the damage."

"Gonna take longer than that," Ed says. "When I left the fire department wasn't finished yet. Seems to me, Katz, if that's your name, your friend Lucien Echo did a first class job."

"Hey, cool it, Ed," Jake implores him. "You don't know what happened."

"Yeah, right," Ed replies. "Don't worry, Jake. Nobody's gonna find out. Shit, man! The guy's a hero."

"Who am I to judge Lucien Echo?"

"You know something you're not telling me," Elise replies, pestering Ollie over the possibility that Lucien set the fire.

"All I said was, as your friend, I think he's too unstable for you. C'mon, we're supposed to be celebrating."

"I believe Lucien even if you think he's guilty . . ." Elise's voice trails off at the end. Still, she examines Ollie's eyes for a reaction. "I can't get over how much Dustin Hoffman reminds me of you," she adds, changing the subject.

"Don't ya' think the ending was kinda heavy-handed?" Ollie says. "Holding everybody off with the cross while they escaped into the sunset."

They're sitting at a small table in the noisy dining room of Smokey's steakhouse. The moment they arrived Elise made a face and exclaimed, "The specialty is red meat?"

Ollie invited Elise to celebrate her acceptance into the early graduate school program. But there simply aren't any fancy restaurants in Madison, a town acclaimed for haute fondue and smorgasbord. He'd planned on a romantic dinner in Chicago, at Café La Tour, atop a new high-rise overlooking the lakefront. Creach wouldn't lend him the car overnight and, ultimately, Ollie was spared the trauma of asking Elise to share a hotel room. Instead, she insisted that they see this Mike Nichols movie everyone's been talking about lately. After waiting in a long line, of course, they got stuck in those shitty front row seats.

"You obviously didn't get it," Elise says, reacting to Ollie's analysis. "When they rode away on the bus, after all the excitement was over and reality set in, I saw two frightened kids who didn't have a clue where they were going next, not to mention what they were going to do with their lives together. I give 'em two years, tops."

"Why do I think you're talking about us?"

"What about us?" Elise demands.

"I meant us, as in people. Look, Elise, don't you realize they're training you to keep moving at warp speed? Your future is already scripted. Go to graduate school, get a cushy job on Wall Street and meet some rich professional genius at a charity affair. You'll get married, redecorate your dream house in some gated community, have two-point-two kids, and become the high priestess of the local PTA. By the time you're forty you'll stop making love to your husband, who's cheating on you with his secretary or his nurse, and you'll wake up one morning in your four-poster bed wondering what the hell became of your life."

"It doesn't have to be that way."

"What's so great about growing up, anyway?" Ollie wonders aloud, avoiding the issue and, possibly, the opportunity to make peace. He's surprised to notice for the first time a tiny dark spot in one corner of Elise's left eye. Her hair is held up on top of her head by a wooden barrette resembling a coconut shell. With her graceful neck exposed, and wearing make-up and a sleek cotton dress, Elise is the picture of maturity.

"Sometimes I don't understand you, Ollie," Elise replies after wolfing down her creamed spinach.

"I'm just sad about the prospect that you won't be here next year to reject me."

"Please don't start that again. If it wasn't New York City I wouldn't be considering the program at all."

"Someday you're gonna take me seriously."

"You see," Elise responds emotionally now, putting down her fork in between bites. "You say these off-the-wall things just to get my reaction. You don't know what you want, so how can I believe you when you tell me you're serious?"

"I suppose Lucien has made clear his intentions?"

"His intentions?" Elise repeats it in disbelief. "You're not my father."

Then she smiles at him as if to acknowledge that she was making a little joke. Ollie smiles back while staring a hole through the point above the bridge of her nose where her soft eyebrows meet. After a moment of silent searching between them, her eyes fall like a car driving off the edge of a cliff with Ollie inside. He's sure that she's really saying, 'Ollie, you know how I feel about him.'

Elise fails to comprehend the irony. According to Ollie, anyway, Lucien doesn't care for her any more than she cares about Ollie. Moreover, if Ollie discloses that Lucien practically confessed to setting the supermarket fire, she'll probably never talk to Ollie again. On the other hand, if Ollie comes clean, maybe she'll dump Lucien. The fact is, Ollie can't avoid thinking that he should turn Lucien over to the cops.

In the days following the blaze, investigators found few clues to what they suspected was arson. The local newspapers and television stations played it up as the possible work of a radical student group unwilling to claim responsibility. Last Monday, the fire marshall issued his report that the point of origin was likely a trash bin left too close to an old wooden delivery door in the rear alley. The police had detained some vagrant hippie who'd been living off the discarded fruits and vegetables. Since the transient admitted that he might have fallen asleep in the dumpster, with a lit cigarette and a half-pint of ethanol, the press squelched any further notion of political motives associated with the event.

Ollie may have learned the truth yesterday. After cutting class, he wound up running into Lucien at Burgerville and jokingly remarked that Lucien was off the hook. Lucien didn't flinch, pretending instead to brag about having executed a commando raid.

"Got a plebe haircut," Lucien said, mockingly, in a clipped, military tone. "Put on a suit and kissed the law school dean's ass. That same night Special Forces climbed a drainpipe and got in and out of the market in ten minutes through a second floor window," he crowed.

"If you're serious," Ollie replied, "I think the whole idea was chicken shit."

"Your problem is, you're afraid to make a commitment to anything."

"So it's all right to watch some innocent derelict take the rap?"

"My wild days are over," Lucien announced. "I'll be a lot more effective screwing with the system as a lawyer."

"Doesn't it matter that somebody could've been killed?"

"What is it with you?" Lucien finally grew excited. "Things don't always come down to black or white. . . . I suppose you want me to give myself up?"

"It's the only way you'll be able to forgive yourself."

"Maybe, you'll be a good writer someday. Stick to fiction because you have no clue about reality."

"Are you planning to tell Elise the truth?"

"Don't preach to *me*, Ollie. I know you've been trying to put it to Elise for months, you little shit. Keep your mouth shut about this discussion!"

Ollie couldn't recall ever feeling more betrayed. A strange gurgling sound came from deep inside his throat and, overwhelmed with rage, Ollie shoved Lucien up against the jukebox. Embarrassed more than anything else, Lucien easily subdued him, grabbing his hand, judo style, and bending Ollie's fingers back, bringing Ollie to his knees. During the brief exchange, Ollie yelled obscenities and wished Lucien dead. Lucien silently backed off, allowing him to vent. Yet, Ollie got up and walked away feeling much better than he'd felt in a long time.

Now Ollie's having too much trouble convincing Elise that Lucien is not the man for her.

"I'm gonna let you drown," Ollie says to Elise when she lifts her eyes from the table to face him.

"What does that mean?"

"A relationship ought to be like banking. You put in your money and the bank takes care of it. I feel like I'm making all the deposits and not getting any interest."

"It's not a big deal, or anything," Elise says. "But did you happen to find fifty dollars in my roommate's robe a couple months ago? She's been harping on me over it."

"I can't believe you're accusing me of stealing."

"I am not. Don't get paranoid, Ollie. I believe you. Haven't I been your good friend?"

"Maybe that's not enough."

Their coffee arrives and he watches her fiddle with her silver-plated teaspoon, tapping it against the edge of the saucer. She is noticeably upset, while Ollie senses some weird power over the situation. He can almost read Elise's mind. Her eyes mist up and she puts on a pair of tinted wire-rimmed glasses to hide behind.

"I'm sorry you feel this way," Elise says softly. "I won't apologize for being your friend."

Ollie pays the check and they exit into the warm spring night. During their return drive to campus, Elise doesn't give up without a fight. By this time, Ollie is high on being noble, and they ride the rest of the way in awkward silence. When he pulls up in front of Elise's place, and she thanks him for the evening, they are nearing the point of no return.

"I guess I'll see you around," Ollie says in the phoniest voice he can muster.

Elise reaches for the door handle. Then, she turns around to face him. Finally, she darts from the car.

Ollie is so proud of himself that he isn't aware of what a terrible mistake he's made until he's alone in his room and the blessed silence drives him out onto the terrace. He breathes the warm night air, escaping in his thoughts to the unresolved ending of a short story that he's been massaging for a while. A voice suddenly comes from out on the lake past the pier. Although Ollie's never known the crew team to practice at night, it sounds like a coxswain shouting through a megaphone. Ollie hears the person calling *his* name.

He isn't given to the supernatural and, to the best of his knowledge, possesses no other deep spiritual belief. Nobody's really calling for him and Ollie's feeling alone in the world right now. Yet, he isn't lonely. Despite making a colossal fool of himself, twice, he's proceeding, undaunted, with his grand plan. For, as he tried to explain to Lucien, the truth demands responsibility. And just like that Ollie figures out the ending to his short story:

Robert J. Stephens, M.D., plopped onto the low wooden bench adjacent to his locker in the doctors' lounge. Rob's green surgical gown was drenched with sweat. Feeling dizzy and nauseous, he had fled the operating theater immediately after the obstetrician in charge, Dr. Patrick Crane, acknowledged that the young mother on the table was dead. Dr. Stephens normally wasn't bothered by trauma. In addition to his stint in the ER, Rob had spent seven months of residency in intensive care. However, this was the first time he'd lost an otherwise healthy person in surgery.

"She was only twenty, for Chrissakes!" Rob sat motionless, lamenting to himself. Only three hours ago she was a young woman undergoing a routine C-section. The woman had a name. She had a husband and a sister who happened to live on the property adjoining Rob's big new house in the woods. When the excruciating pain of her impending breech delivery left the woman screaming and delirious, Rob had reassured her. Then he clutched her sweaty white hand as they wheeled her down the corridor to her doom.

Not even Dr. Crane seemed to know exactly what went wrong. The woman's heart had stopped beating several minutes into the procedure. Crane worked decisively to get it started again, furiously pounding on her chest while the defibrillator was prepped. At the same time, he barked out separate instructions for enabling the baby to breathe independently from its mother.

"Thank God, Doctor Crane didn't request any assistance from me," Rob reflected. Rob had to admit that he was mesmerized as Crane repeatedly thrust the electrified paddles onto the woman's chest. Everyone stood clear while twice her heart began to beat again. Following the second time, Crane managed to get the baby out of there and onto the equipment. However, they couldn't keep the woman going, and the oxygen deprivation had lasted too long, leaving the newborn girl on a respirator in what would probably be an advanced vegetative state.

Patrick Crane, MD, came into the lounge. Rob was hunched over on the bench, with his head in his hands, apparently staring at the shiny Italian loafers on his own feet. Dr. Crane was a tall, elegant man of fifty. Penetrating eyes peered over custom-fitted bifocals attached to a gold chain hanging around his neck. He walked over to Rob's slumping figure and stood for a moment. Then he placed a steady hand on Rob's shoulder. When Rob did not look up, Crane simply muttered, "It happens," and moved over to his locker at the other end of the bench.

Rob was only twenty-six years old; the youngest resident Dr. Crane had permitted to associate with him during his tenure at Children's Hospital. "This is the finest teaching and adolescent care facility in the Midwest," Crane had said when he hand-picked Rob out of medical school and promised to make him the richest OB-GYN in town by the time he was thirty five. During Rob's initial months at Children's, Crane had come to believe that Rob's instincts were similar to his own when he was Rob's age. "He'll come around," Crane thought to himself, deciding it was an inappropriate time to talk this out.

Rob tried to focus on his brick, split-level home, fronting an acre of rolling lawn, which he and Beverly would own free and clear after only three hundred and fifty nine more payments. Rob desperately sought to visualize their son, Ricky, who yesterday had delighted them by climbing out of his crib and stringing together what sounded like two words: "fall down." Instead Rob's brain was overloaded with thoughts of flood and fire and pestilence. There was a smell of death in his hair and on his clothes. He couldn't shake the cold, clammy feeling at the base of his spine that radiated through him to the pit of his stomach.

Beverly waited for Rob in the driveway when he pulled up in his shiny new Sting Ray. She shepherded him through the lightly falling rain with a kiss on the neck and an arm around his waist. Marge, the dead woman's sister, had already been over with the tragic news. Bev refrained from the usual chatter concerning Ricky's progress and gossip about the neighbors. When Rob was in medical school, Bev used to come home late several nights a week from her cocktail waitress job. She'd find him wide-awake at their tiny kitchen table pumped up with coffee and cracking the books. During their five and a half years together, Rob had been dedicated and loyal, and Bev was content with her perceived role in the relationship. She was happier at home, not having returned to teaching since Ricky was born. And it was no secret that Bev knew how to get through to Rob.

At first, Rob didn't want to talk about it. He hardly touched his favorite dinner of Yankee pot roast and potatoes, prepared from his mother's special recipe. After their second batch of margaritas, which they'd begun to share again, Rob was finally able to describe the incident in detail. When Bev told him it sounded like somebody had screwed up badly, Rob insisted that Dr. Crane had done everything possible to save both mother and child. Nevertheless, Rob realized that people were going to investigate the incident.

Despite Beverly's comment, Rob could think of no reason to assume either legal or moral responsibility for the woman's death. Rob had merely observed the fatal procedure and he'd only seen Marge's younger sister twice during her entire pregnancy. She was the first of three patients who Bev had referred to his brand new association. Rob had dutifully introduced the woman to Dr. Crane, who became her primary obstetrician. Beverly certainly knew how to cut through the bullshit. This time Rob hoped Beverly's suspicions about Crane were wrong. She gave Rob too much grief already over his hero-worship of the man.

After Ricky was asleep in his room, Rob lay more comfortably before a warm fireplace. From within the deep cushions of their sectional couch, Rob loved to play with the new-fangled remote control on his Zenith color TV, trying to watch the programs on all three channels at once. The horror receded from his consciousness as he watched Bev pad across the carpeted rec room in her nylon shorty. Rob was compelled to absolve any doubt about his conduct in order to protect his family from the outside world.

Rob was not a ladies' man, having surprised his only friend in the med school dorm when he brought Beverly over one night. Sex hadn't been too important to him. Rob was drawn to Bev because she seemed interested in what he had to say. Of the few women he'd known, Beverly was the first who listened to him. They didn't manage to do it until after they'd been dating for months. She understood how critical it was for him that they trust each other, to be loyal friends and comrades above all else. Rob was amused that other people were knocked out by her looks. Everyone who knew Bev in high school thought she was so beautiful that she'd become a fashion model.

Beverly's ample breasts bounced as she walked over to the couch. Although her pantyless butt was exposed, Bev knew when it was time to close ranks. She was still young and firm, having gotten her figure back easily within a few months following Ricky's birth. Bev usually decided when they would make love, choosing those moments when Rob was at his weakest, when he was troubled and needed to remember he wasn't alone. "It's been almost a month," she whispered sweetly, while she touched him through the fly of his cotton pajama bottoms. Beverly appreciated manipulating him because he always responded. Tonight their love-making was purposeful and exhausting. She got off twice on the power, while Rob's mostly flagging faith in spiritual matters was temporarily rejuvenated.

During the next three weeks "Baby Girl" remained in her tiny incubator, sustained through tubes, with no hope for measurable brain activity in the future. Marge's daily vigil was soon the only outside connection this little being had. A week after her sister's funeral, Marge's parents and her brother-in-law stopped coming to the hospital. Marge confided to Beverly that her sister's husband wanted to pull the plug, while her parents were talking to lawyers about insurance policies, trust funds, and lawsuits.

Rob was buried in double shifts, lab work and teaching sessions. The surgeons kept the operating rooms busy nearly twenty-four hours a day. Whereas Rob and Dr. Crane had not yet discussed the incident, Rob managed to check on Baby Girl daily. He no longer felt guilt over the incident, for his mission was to bring healthy people into the world. And he no longer cared to know why the woman had died, that was better left to the hospital's board of inquiry.

At the end of this particularly long day, Dr. Crane noticed Rob in the hallway and motioned him into his office. Crane's facial expression was stern, as if he'd seen something under the microscope that he didn't like. With a grunt, Dr. Crane ordered Rob into one of the two chairs opposing his desk. Then Crane leaned back and stared at the ceiling until the quiet became unbearable. Finally, he looked at some papers in a folder on his desk and began to shuffle through them.

"I've been reviewing the dead woman's chart," Dr. Crane said matter-of-factly. "In anticipation of the board hearing on Monday. She was such a strong woman going in you'd never figure her pump would give out."

"I didn't know . . ."

"Don't say anything until I'm finished," Crane interrupted him, picking up a roll of lined graph paper from inside the folder. "In particular, I noticed the EKG ordered when the patient first came to see you. I'll bet you never bothered to read this. Well, read it now. You're such a good doctor tell me what condition the patient suffered at the time of her surgery."

"Oh my God!" Rob thought to himself, as he took the paper and began unrolling it across his lap. The short p to r intervals on the graph were obvious, and the prolonged qrs complex was unmistakable. Staring at these diagrammed peaks and valleys for the first time, Rob could feel his entire body trembling at the inevitable conclusion: Wolff-Parkinson-White Disease! A minor heart condition akin to an arrhythmia or irregular heartbeat, it should have no effect on the longevity or quality of the patient's life. Treatable with medication, it often went undetected because there are no symptoms. But the use of certain general anesthetics during surgery has been known to induce cardiac arrest in patients who have the disease.

Rob threw down the electrocardiogram as if he'd discovered that the paper was crawling with bugs. He reached for the woman's medical history report on the top inside flap of the folder. Rob's own signature was on the line at the bottom of the second page next to the date when he first saw the woman, exactly one week after he had started at Childrens. The same goddamn date that appeared on the automated printout at the beginning of the graph paper roll! It was true. He had authorized the test per the standing policy with all new pregnancy workups. The woman had failed to display any signs of a heart problem during his examination, so Rob hadn't pushed for the results.

"As you can see," Dr. Crane went on evenly, "I assumed you never read her EKG because there's nothing from the cardiologist in her chart, and there's no mention of this disease in the woman's history. I realize how busy we've been keeping you, and getting a report out of those primadonna cardiologists can be like . . . Well, let's just say, Dr. Mitchell was as surprised to see this as you are. But you ought to know we use Demerol in the operating room unless you tell somebody that it's going to kill the patient."

Rob's right knee began to shake at a rapid pace. He was forced to press his hand down on top of his thigh to stop it from banging into the front of Crane's desk. He opened his mouth as if to speak and began to suck great quantities of air into his lungs instead. There was nothing Rob could say in his own defense.

"You know I'm not one to pull any punches," Dr. Crane went on in an almost fatherly tone now that he had Rob's attention. "How did you expect the anesthesiologist to know Demerol was the wrong drug to give her? There wasn't a clue about that anywhere in the file."

Crane removed his bifocals, allowing them to dangle from his chest next to the monogrammed initials on the breast pocket of his silk shirt. "Apologies to that woman's family simply won't cut it," he said, anticipating what Rob must've been thinking. "It's ironic, but that baby's death would be the best circumstance for all concerned. Put the poor thing out of its misery and end the family's suffering. Frankly, any malpractice award would go way down, since the cost of maintaining her on machinery could run into millions."

"What's going to happen to . . . me?" Rob sputtered so softly Dr. Crane had to lean forward to hear him.

"We should throw you to the wolves," Crane replied matter-of-factly. "Except, it seems we've all made the mistake, and we'd be hypocrites to hold you responsible alone. I've tried to instill loyalty among associates. We're a team and that includes sharing the blame. If I didn't think you had what it takes I wouldn't be willing to give you another chance. Here's how Mitchell and I believe we should handle the situation."

Dr Patrick Crane sat back in his chair and fished a gold-plated cigar lighter out of his pants pocket. He held up the roll of graph paper in his other hand and flicked on the lighter. "Nobody finds out she had the condition," Crane said, looking at Rob as if he were simply waiting for a signal to ignite the paper. "I strongly suggest you tell no one about this."

Rob's mind raced off into a thousand directions, many involving places and methods of survival he'd never thought of before. He came to think about the morning of his medical boards, when he was in the bathroom throwing up for the first ten minutes after they passed out the examination booklets. Then Rob remembered the moment he knew he was in love with Beverly. She had stared deeply into his eyes without hint of suspicion or private agenda, her vulnerability a call to arms. It was the same way Beverly had looked at him the night he asked her to marry him. That same look she gave him at the cabin by the lake when Ricky was conceived. The same look when he told her about his appointment to the hospital staff under Dr. Crane. Rob finally focused on the flickering yellow and blue flame, while he visualized Beverly's all-consuming look, and he nodded his head up and down

By the time Rob pulled into his driveway he was momentarily giddy with relief. He felt a strange sense of confidence from his complicity. This wasn't about getting away with it; that was a cinch without any written follow-up from the cardiologist. And if anyone checked the patient's billing record, they would pass off the routine test—ordered but never done—as an administrative error. Rob felt instead he had somehow earned acceptance into an elite group possessing special responsibilities. Consequently, he was more resolved than ever to be a credit to his profession. "His profession." Rob turned the phrase over in his head, dubious again that the path was brightly lit for only so long as he could keep their secret.

Beverly was in the kitchen feeding Ricky. The dining room table was set for two. It was candle lit and covered with their finest tablecloth. As Rob approached her, the smell of roasted garlic wafted into his nostrils. When they kissed, Bev immediately detected something wrong. Since Rob was jabbering and pretending to be cheerful she sent her two men off to play horsie, although Ricky would probably puke up his mush. Beverly's news would wait.

"Do you think I'll ever be a good doctor?" Rob asked her later, after the dishes were cleared and they were sitting on the couch.

"Don't be silly," Bev replied. "You're the finest person I've ever met. I'll be proud to have you deliver all our babies."

"I have to tell you something," Rob blurted out, not paying attention to what she'd said.

"You didn't hear me, honey," Bev pressed him. "This was the most incredible day. I ran into Marge at the drugstore and she remarked that her family decided to pull the plug and get on with their lives. I know I said it was wrong before, but the strangest thing happened when she told me. I felt queasy right in the feminine hygiene section. So we picked up the Daisy test and guess what? Marge insists that it was divine providence. I believe her."

Rob fell back into the tangled folds of his sofa. He no longer needed to confess unless doing so led to something greater for their future.

"So, what did you want to tell me?" Beverly asked, looking at him differently than he'd remembered in Dr. Crane's office a few hours ago. It was a look that Rob had never seen before.

"If it's a girl," he replied. "Let's call her Marge."

PART II

I awoke in the guest room of Jake's condo somewhere on the first floor of my converted fraternity house. I could hear Lucien Echo bellowing instructions over the telephone to one of his young associates back in Chicago. During that strange weekend when Alex brought me to Madison, it was also business as usual. Lucien was the maestro of instant communication. Operating on Jake's dining room table, he revised letters and briefs via his laptop, dictated into his digital recorder, and made cellular calls around the world.

Success had transformed Lucien Echo. After our nasty confrontation in college, I hadn't encountered him again for over a decade. Then we briefly fell in together around Chicago's Division Street bar scene. In those days Ronald Reagan was beginning to trickle down and Disco was already dead—having been officially murdered out in center field of Comiskey Park one hot summer night a few years earlier. Lucien was still trading on his counter-culture style, defending drug smugglers and white-collar criminals out of a LaSalle Street office adjacent to City Hall. Of equal import, though, Lucien was cultivating his more respectable corporate client list.

By the time of our reunion weekend in Madison, Lucien had long shed the vestiges of his radical lawyer image and developed into the nerve center and titular head of a highly regarded downtown law firm. He was cajoling and consulting with people who laughed a lot, and sometimes he spoke to them in a foreign language. Lucien had come to favor polished board rooms with executives in silk suits who kept him hopping for four hundred dollars an hour and/or percentage points, on a case-by-case basis, only if it was ethical, of course.

I snooped around the condo, mulling over how he'd bushwhacked me on the rainy pier with apologies and some spooky hocus pocus concerning my stagnant novel. Although I remember retreating inside from the downpour, you know that I have never figured out Lucien's mind-boggling demonstration of omniscience. Something about my rekindled spiritual curiosity may have left me vulnerable to suggestion. For I confess that I was too easily tempted by Lucien's promise to transform me into the person I longed to be.

After Alex hunkered down in Jake's kitchen, she prepared one of her makeshift soufflés for dinner and I willingly fed the conversation among the three of us. When Lucien and I digressed, waxing nostalgic over our college days, Alex made certain that the conversation returned to the future.

Lucien didn't mind talking about anything. It was easy understanding how he persuaded judges to do his clients' bidding. He was a rapper, the sincere purveyor of phrases like *in good conscience* and *life is priceless*. I was engrossed in Lucien's stories and impressed by his candor. For a moment I even thought that Alex was miffed because we were getting along so well. At some point, however, it became clear that she was frustrated because Lucien seemed unaffected by the serious trouble he was in.

Lucien wouldn't admit that he bribed Judge Rotini. Whenever the discussion returned to his plan for defending himself, he assured us everything would work out fine. "It's Swiss cheese," he said of the government's case against him. "They won't take it to trial." Then Lucien also said that he was surprised at Alex for reacting so emotionally. "Search within yourself for any sign of deception between us," he told her. "I need to know that you're on my side."

It was the only instance that weekend in which Lucien's composure waned. Alex seemed satisfied with Lucien's appeal to her loyalty, for she finally brightened. Soon, though, she grew tired and excused herself. Lucien was just getting started. But I begged off, too, distracted by a ringing in my ears from the Armangac and the flood of memories that had surfaced.

The next day, Saturday, following breakfast involving eggs benedict, asparagus, and wild berries, Alex and I spent time sunbathing on the pier while Lucien conducted business. That night Lucien treated us to dinner in a revolving restaurant on the roof of a downtown hotel. I got a swelled head from the attention and fawning service and made a pass at Alex when Lucien went to the bathroom. My flirting had begun in the afternoon, on the dock, after I'd asked her whether Lucien had ever spoken of Elise Franklin.

"That was a different civilization," Alex said, lifting her head up from a rubber raft upon which she was stretched out in the sun. "Sorry. I don't mean that you're ancient. But aren't you and Lucien continually disheartened by the state of the world?"

"Where do *you* live? On Mars?"

"While I was growing up, activism was something you treated with Clearasil," she replied. "Self-examination, self-improvement, and self-promotion, that's what's happening today. Face it Ollie, you looked through a tiny window in history that won't be open again."

"You don't give us much of a future," I replied, unintentionally slipping in a double-entendre.

"I can't imagine my life if I reach forty," Alex said, not reacting to my comment. "The planet's out of control. My life's out of control, and I don't seem to do anything about it. Four, sometimes five nights a week, I'm not home from the restaurant till after midnight. In the morning there's the food buying and menu prep. Then there's promotion and bookkeeping. Between worrying about Lucien, if I squeeze in exercise and half an hour of piano practice . . . I don't know, Ollie, I admire your lifestyle."

"Art is more self-indulgent."

"Maybe. Once you finish a short story it's gone. A painter moves on to the next painting, an architect goes on to the next building, but their creations remain a tangible contribution. I have to pump the same dream every day otherwise it has no value. On top of that I have to make sure the dishwashers have green cards."

Alex sat up on the pier, leaning forward on her beach towel, and I caught a glimpse of one taut breast while she straightened the strap on her bikini top. She was blessed with an innocent look. While I'm sure she was aware of her sexuality, Alex didn't flaunt it or jiggle it in your face the way some other women did. "Mind you, I'm not complaining," she went on, "I'm drained and feeling guilty that I'm not doing enough for anyone other than me right now."

"Sounds like you need to hear more often just how beautiful you are."

She grew noticeably embarrassed and I sensed that this tension remained with her the rest of the day. I waited, like a snake, when Lucien went off to the toilet at the restaurant to tell her what a lovely afternoon it had been. But Alex failed to acknowledge what I'd regarded as a come on.

Lucien was like a sponge soaking up everything going on around him. In turn, his energy was commanding. He asserted himself when he could render others more comfortable or keep things moving. Effortlessly controlling it all, Lucien made people feel just important enough to do what he wanted. As I couldn't detect any sign of concern on Lucien's face, it was a gutsy performance from someone whose life might've been crumbling around him.

I was not immune to Lucien's charms inasmuch as he treated me like a long lost relative. When the time came to discuss my part in all of this, Lucien was offhanded. "I don't think there's much of a story here," he said, following dessert and espresso at the revolving restaurant. "Alex thinks I need a keeper," he added, paying the check from a wad of bills that he kept loose in the front pocket of his custom-tailored trousers. "There is something. Have you done investigative work?"

"No, not really," I answered. "I've covered a couple of fires, and I did a piece about the vicissitudes of traffic court."

"It's more like . . . I want you to deliver a message to Mama Raspberry. I can't go near her and I don't want to hire a detective to do it. It's a simple thing, really. You'd be doing me a favor. If she decides to talk to you, that's great. All I want you to tell her is, 'The truth is something you can't control.' Mama will understand."

"That's it?" Alex demanded. "That's what you want him to say to her? After all those times you bailed her out at three in the morning? If it wasn't for you she'd already be in prison."

"That's all I want you to say," Lucien responded.

They'd evidently been down that road before, as Alex raised her eyebrows to the heavens in a sign that Lucien was nuts. At the time it didn't occur to me that their exchange might have been staged for my benefit. I was caught up in the glamour of this so-called assignment, blinded by an opportunity for some validation of my existence.

I should tell you that for many years, while toiling in the obscurity of my prose, I sought that place in all of us where we choose to hide from the rest of the world. I took solace from the fact that my deepest fears and emotions were written down and locked away from public viewing. I was not one of the dedicated and committed professionals. We know who those esteemed folks are: the doctors, lawyers, developers, and other financial wizards who make judgments about people's lives and take control of their fortunes without the slightest hesitation. Movers and shakers who dispense their valuable expertise along with their prejudices and zealous devotion to whatever self-improvement scheme helped them attain their lofty perch in the first place. No, I've never been one of those arrogant hypocrites whose ration of daily bread is directly proportionate to the size of the screwing they're able to inflict upon others.

There was a time, right after college graduation, when I believed it was fashionable to forge a career. Having lucked out in the draft lottery I no longer needed an army deferment. Coursework and exams had been cancelled so often that pass-fail grading was adopted simply to get us out of there in time to make room for an incoming crop. I was totally unprepared to enter the work force. Since my father's dream had landed me there, I decided to enter law school.

By the end of my first year, worshipping the art of advocacy, I was becoming a competitive and contrary individual. Somehow I had tapped into the mindset, picked up the Latin lingo, and quickly mastered the Socratic method. I had scored well on my exams and, to my surprise, I was leaning toward a career in criminal law. I never told my father that I aspired to become an assistant United States attorney. I couldn't bear him bragging prematurely to my relatives. He is such a proud man. I guess I still don't want to disappoint him.

I suppose it will always be open to debate whether I just couldn't hack it, or whether it was my contraction of an inner ear infection during the summer that caused me to slip off to Europe with the student loan money for my second year's tuition. Perhaps my reaction to the immorality of justice unhinged my emotional balance as well. But eight months later I turned up on the Marrakesh Express heading to Casablanca with a story and pictures about disaffected draft dodgers living on hashish and Cadbury bars in the Djeema. I was on top of the world and the thought of earning my living by sending people to prison made me ill.

It was during those glorious days, when I disdained the drudgery of life's sad commitments and dreaded compromise, that I hatched this plot to save my soul with the swipe of a pen. Through honest reportage I was able to make use of my prodigious diary-keeping skills and, after too many years of fits and starts, I determined to finish my first novel. The words came in a mad rush sometimes hitting the paper faster than my ballpoint could record them. At night I often typed out my shorthand, coffee-stained scribblings from the leather-bound note pad that I carried around. I was amazed to find the story moved along nicely, seemingly without me. The characters said things I would never have the nerve to say. I daydreamed about the witty banter I'd exchange on morning television during my book tour, took up wearing a tweed cap and even smoked a pipe with a carved meerschaum bowl.

As it happens, one day the words stopped coming. I awoke, partook of my morning ritual, and stepped out into the street, all the while failing to suspect that the world had turned over during my dreamless sleep. The characters were suddenly "ridiculous" and the plot was "paper thin." Rejection begot more rejection and I began to realize that poverty was less humbling. Foraging through a dumpster for a piece of yesterday's pizza proved infinitely more satisfying than watching agents and publishers chew up and spit out your guts.

But then the words don't come because you're driving a taxi and listening to some rich fart from San Francisco who's ticked off at his wife—with the Chanel smell and a three-carat diamond—because the limo driver didn't meet them at the airport. If they lose their table at Gibson's, he says, he'll likely lose the account he came here to steal from his competitor. As a result, they'll have to give up the winter home in Ibiza and, probably, the girls' tuition at Exeter. All this, he says, because she refused to come in contact with the airplane toilet seat before they landed.

Or the words don't come when you finally meet a nice girl in the restaurant where you're waiting tables and you manage to get a date with her along with a righteous tip. Comes the weekend and you put on your only sports jacket that isn't shiny or frayed around the lining, you blow half a month's rent on flowers and wine and dinner and theatre tickets, and you take her to the hottest new dance club where she runs into her chums from the country club. Then you stand around feeling self-conscious, ill-bred, and poor, always poor, while they impress each other with their tales of the LaSalle Street jungle and Porsches and swimming pools and contractors and architectural designs for the summer-house. Always there are architectural plans.

Still, you tell her about your novel. And her eyes glaze over during the ride home, while she sits far away clinging to the door handle like she'd rather be running alongside the car. And she's not thinking about the romance anymore. Gone is that first flirtatious moment when the attraction was pure and unencumbered by the baggage of time. Now she's thinking about where you're from and where you're going. She's thinking about the life you could never give her and she's thinking about the architectural plans.

Finally, when the words don't come, it no longer matters. You've worn the wolf's cold embrace like a badge of honor and you have nothing to show for it. Where is your curriculum vitae? What about your portfolio filled with accomplishments? For God's sake, man! Where is your property? Where are your wife and kids? Which charities and social causes do you support? What is the matter with you? You're approaching fifty and you don't even have a resume?

So there I was, this sorry sack of shit for brains, luxuriating at the foot of Lucien Echo's table, wondering why the words wouldn't come. I stood outside my life playing imaginary footsie with his woman and hoping for a reason to bury him.

"Of course, I'll carry your message to Mama Raspberry," I offered for all the above reasons.

"Say whad?" Mama Raspberry asked, reacting to Lucien's message, which I delivered through her peephole. Mama opened the door and her ebony pinpoint eyes grew large with incredulity. "My Lucien say whad?"

Louise Raspberry folded her tree trunk arms across the tented front of her incandescent pink housecoat. She was past fifty, stood no taller than five-five, and she must've weighed two hundred forty pounds. Yet her dark chocolate skin was smooth and wrinkle-free. Even the fat around her neck and on her arms, pushing through the short sleeves of her silk gown, appeared more powerful than flabby. Mama considered me with the same jive-ass look that she'd used a thousand times before; whenever someone new came to her door searching for crack, hero-in, uppers, guns, designer clothing—you name it. They came to buy and sell and trade and, sometimes, they came to pass the time. But they all needed something.

"That's my Lucien," Mama finally added, laughing, while her face relaxed. "All this time I be thinkin' the truth supposta set you free."

Of course, sometimes they also came to rip off Mama's place. Despite Mama's long reign as High Priestess of her neighborhood, some people were stupid or desperate enough to try to gangster Mama's stash. Countless times Mama had been forced to defend her first floor railroad flat, where she lived with her grown alcoholic son, Lester, her seventeen-year-old daughter, Shawnticia, and Shawnticia's two toddlers. Then there was Mama's man of the month. Lawrence happened to be the most recent drifter who displayed the correct temperament. A some-time lover and armed protector, Lawrence received a roof over his head and a free supply of whatever it was that brought him to Mama's door in the first place.

"Howse my atturney?" Mama asked after she ushered me into a dank-smelling vestibule. She closed the burglar-barred door behind us with a ritual of snapping bolts and chains, and she propped up a steel bar lock against it. For obvious reasons I had chosen midday to come here. Nevertheless, I noticed the windows were closed and heavily draped, shutting out the fresh air and daylight. Only a naked bulb hung from the hallway ceiling next to a no-pest strip. When Mama led me toward the living room I could hear the hum of an air conditioner and a television set blaring The *Flintstones* cartoon program.

"Some niggers don't know," Mama offered, removing a large pistol from within the folds of her tunic. She placed it on a side table in the hallway at the edge of the living room. Her two grandchildren were inside, spread out in front of a big screen TV upon which Barney and Fred, large as life, were peddling along the road in their motorless steamroller car. My eyes followed the peeling green paint on the walls to the far corner of the living room. Three adult males were seated around a battered wooden dining table involved in a card game.

"That's the message Lucien asked me to deliver. I'm sure he's disappointed," I said after much deliberation.

Mama was aware that I was frightened. On weekends, white boys from the suburbs lined up along her block in their daddies' cars, waiting for the runners Mama sent out with vials of crack and bindles of snort. Sometimes they'd come inside Mama's den for a taste before doing business. Mama was used to frightened white boys who wanted to get off on the danger as much as on the dope she sold to them.

"I don't minds tellin' ya," Mama said, "I'm real disappointed, too." She directed me to sit in a brand new soft leather recliner while she groaned and creaked, easing her wide frame down onto the nearby stone ledge bordering the fireplace.

"My atturney and me," she added wistfully. "Lotsa water underneath them britches. Sheit, I remember the first time I intra-duced Lucien to that old Polock judge—Brumski's his name. He dead now. . . . Cept'n, one day, the Rev'rend Clyde Fraser calls me about hiring Lucien after Lester be clownin' with his baby sister, Porcia, over by the Rev'rend's church on Fiftieth and Indiana.

"Y'see, Lester, bless his soul, he not right up here," Mama explained, twice touching her temple with her thick forefinger, which sported a large ruby ring encased in a diamond-encrusted setting. "Lester be liken' his Jack. He not a criminal. He just ain't right, and he's a drunk. . . . Anyway, Lester and Porcia—she live over to the Southside— they was watching the Newlywed Game on cable and Lester gets it inta his drunk fool head that he's gointa marry Porcia 'cause they plays better than the couples on the TV. Porcia, now she an iddy-biddy thing. 'Cept'n, by then, she made thirteen and she been fightin' off Lester so long she ready fo' him. So Porcia, she say, 'Fine, Lester, we goes to Rev'rend Clyde's church and we gets married and then you can have my booty.'"

Mama exhaled deeply and rolled her eyes in a sign that the most caring mother can't protect her children if they're determined to be mischievous.

"Only Lester don't never go anywhere," Mama said, glancing at the threesome around the table. "He already had his license taken away six times 'cause he drivin' intoxicated. But Lester finds my Fleetwood keys, and Porcia swipes my best Jap knife . . . Y'know," Mama says, when it's clear that I don't understand the reference, "them Jinsoo knives they sells on TV, they cut anything. So I's up in the bed and Jacob . . . Was it Jacob who's stayin' with me at the time? Well, I guess them kids escapes my notice."

As I wondered which one of the card players was Lester, I saw two handguns displayed on the table like salt and pepper shakers.

"Then Rev'rend Fraser calls. He say Lester done wrapped my Fleetwood 'round a basketball pole in the church parking lot attemptin' to partake of some prenutuals. Only Porcia cut him bad enough so's Lester might never be the marryin' kind. . . . Well, most natu'lly, I goes over. By the time Lester leaves the emerge'cy room and I get home, Shawnticia and Jacob been arrested and them kids on they way to a foster home. Jacob sold two grams to some undercover brother, Latrelle, who been fixin' to bust my ass since I refused to pay his protection no more."

Mama's story was interrupted by two short buzzer blasts coming from the hallway. She excused herself and returned a few minutes later stuffing some bills down the front of her nightgown.

"Whatchu be lookin' at?" Mama asked, spying me staring through her sheer housecoat at humongous breasts hanging nearly down to her waist. "You tells Lucien, Mama's still a fox," she added before I could respond.

Then she walked around to the overstuffed couch on the opposite side of my chair.

"I's gettin' to it," Mama said, sitting down slowly on the arm of the big sofa. "Rev'rend Williams felt my predicament," she finally continued, "so he tells me to call Lucien. Man, he was sweet the first time we approachin' court. My atturney wearing his I-talian suit and a carnation inta his lapel, and Judge Brumski, he say, 'Mama, whadju doin' here *again?*' . . . Then Lucien, to whom I failed to mention that the Judge and me was on a first name basis, he done caught Officer Latrelle inta' one a his lies, and old man Brumski tells Latrelle not to lets the door hits his fat ass on the way out. . . . That was fifteen years ago and Lucien be walkin' me ever since. Aint nobody better."

"I'm a little confused," I said after Mama leaned back against the sloping arm of the sofa in a sign that she'd finished her testament to Lucien Echo. "Didn't you tell the grand jury that he paid Judge Rotini to throw out your case?"

"Y'means, that's what the guvment told me," Mama drew herself back up again, defiantly. "You don't be tellin' the guvment nuthin.' They gotsa story about a key I bought from a special agent, who be so strung out, his damnself, he don't even count right. Then they talks about them Fed'ral guidelines gets me ten years. . . . The Feds is nastier than police 'cause they aint interested in money. So they tells me they already knows my atturney paid Judge Rotini and they wants me to coop'rate."

Mama rose from the couch and led me back through the hallway, past the front door, until we came to her darkened bedroom. "Dis here's Lawrence," Mama said, indicating the large, middle-aged black man lying, fully clothed, across the unmade bed watching a porno video-tape. "He's a friend to my atturney," Mama said to him.

Lawrence grunted in my direction, rose from the bed, walked over to the TV set resting atop the bureau and stopped the VCR. On his way out Lawrence turned on the ceiling light and cleared off a chair against the wall by toss-ing some clothes onto the floor. Mama motioned me towards the stained upholstery while she sat on the king size bed facing me.

"How is I suppose t'recanize one old white man from the next? . . . But the guvment lawyer, he say, 'Mama, we got yo atturney on tape in Judge Rotini's office talkin' bout fixin' yo case. 'Lessin you admit you done gave Lucien fifteen hundred dollars for the judge, youse outta bizniss."

"They have a tape recording of Lucien in Judge Rotini's chambers?"

"That's what I's told." Mama rose from the bed and walked over to a closet with sliding wooden doors. "I don't even know how much I given Lucien all these years. When Lucien aks, I give it. The guvment wants cancelled checks. Sheeit!"

Mama slid open the closet doors bulging from inside with men and women's brand new designer clothing. "You 'bout a 40 regular?" she asked. Then Mama sorted through the hangers, the old wooden pole across the top sagging from the weight of fine leathers, suedes and wools. "Check dis out," Mama said, removing a sleek, tweed Adolpho sports jacket with charcoal flecks. She motioned for me to stand up and try it on.

I removed my navy blue blazer, one of the two sport coats that I wore whenever I worked in public, and allowed her to slip the stylish garment over my shoulders.

"Ooh. Real fine," Mama crowed, shaking out the sleeves like a tailor. "You aint half bad lookin' once you dress right and learn to stands up straight."

"I can't afford this," I said, figuring it must cost five hundred dollars on Michigan Avenue.

"Since you heppin' my atturney, you gots thirty dollars?"

"Sure," I replied. "The sleeves don't even need to be shortened," I added, handing her the money as though we were in the men's department at Bloomingdales.

"You gotsa wife?" Mama asked, no doubt indicating that she would happily outfit my spouse in case I needed to explain how I scored such a deal.

"No wife," I said, "and no prospects. . . . So it's true that the U.S. Attorney gave you immunity for your testimony?"

"Say whad? . . . They gives me a punk publik defender, they puts me in front of the grand jury and tells me to say `yassir' to whatever they's aksing if I wants to go home. And bizniss aint been better since them city narcs don't come 'round no more. If that's immoonidy, I guess I gots it."

Mama must've sensed that I was uncomfortable with this explanation of how she happened to rat on her attorney. Perhaps, she felt guilty. When I reached for my old sport coat lying on the bed she grabbed my arm. "Sheeit," Mama said, "Lucien done taught *me* the scam."

We stood there silently for a moment, as I noted the slimy underbelly of Lucien's life pulling him down. Mama led me into the hallway toward the door. I thanked her for the jacket and promised to keep in touch, while I couldn't help wondering what Alex must have thought of this place.

"You tells my atturney I be lookin' out for him," Mama said after I exited the apartment and stood on the stained carpet landing. I hurried down the long flight of steps to the street door, into the hot sun, hoping that my CD player hadn't been liberated from the glove compartment of my car.

Less than a month had passed since Annie's return from Asia. Either I missed her or was feeling sorry for her stuck out in Morton Grove, as I agreed to get together downtown following some animation project meeting she'd managed to score. Annie had been tuned in to the dot.com revolution long before it had a name, having spent the bulk of her pregnancy and Jason's first year parlaying her natural computer skills into conquering the sophisticated moviemaking programs available at the time. Following an apprenticeship during the final pre-Pixar days at Disney, right after she left Ray, Annie had moved up the coast to the Bay Area with Jason in order to do a stint at Industrial Light and Magic. Although she hadn't slaved those sixty-hour weeks in years, opting instead for third world travel, Annie had cultivated a peripatetic commercial skill that was in demand for contract work wherever she happened to find herself.

"I don't feel like I belong here anymore," Annie said once we exited the ornate Wrigley Building lobby into the hot sun. I'd waited in the shade for her to emerge from the meeting with some Sony development reps who wanted Annie to animate their new video fishing game with an underwater scene of comely-looking spotted bass chasing aquatic frog bait.

"So many buildings have gone up recently," Annie went on, while we stopped on the wide sidewalk, amidst the Michigan Avenue lunch crowd, deciding which direction to go. "I'm walking around in a foreign city."

"I hate to tell you, but Ricardo's is gone too. There's an Italian restaurant and an outdoor café we can try."

"Ricardo's is gone? You see why I'm freaking out. The reason I idolize Chicago is the grand history of this architecture. LA's cultural contribution is to remain in a state of flux. Chicago has never-changing shoulders to maintain. Jesus, I remember when the Prudential Building was tallest in town. Now I have no idea where the hell we are. I'm not hungry, anyway. Do you mind if we just walk along the river?"

No problem, I thought, as we strolled off. Whatever was bothering her was better than trying to explain my experience at Mama Raspberry's. Annie turned to the family news instead, forcing me to endure her depressing update. We covered Michael's progress on Prozac, and I was amazed to learn that he wants to adopt a Korean baby. Annie brought up our father's refusal to stop drinking despite the gout in his right leg and a spate of blackouts. When she insinuated that I was partially to blame for Dad's old age bitterness, because I didn't see him enough, I barely refrained from bringing up the Lucien Echo story just to change the subject. But that's Annie, a shit-disturber who makes you face yourself. She'd learned more in a fort-night than I'd bothered to find out in the previous six months. So when Annie got around to discussing my life, I couldn't resist expressing my uneasiness any longer.

"I'll tell you what's bothering me," I said. "I'm working on a story involving some big shot lawyer. It's something . . . well, I'm not sure what to do about it."

"That's funny," Annie replied. "What happened to your novel with that dreary dying Doctor Rob and his fanatical wife? What are their names? Oh yeah, Rob and Beverly Stephens."

"I shouldn't send you any more of my book," I snapped. "You didn't like the premise from the beginning, and I didn't appreciate the remark you made in your last letter."

"What remark?"

"Never mind. You made a remark, that's all."

"C'mon, Ollie. What remark did I make? You know how I feel about your writing. If I didn't think *Stuff The Lady* was a worthy novel, I wouldn't have given it to my friend over at Rosydent Publishing. This new book is . . . well, preachy. *That's* what I said in my letter. Isn't it?"

"That's hardly a compliment."

"I'm sorry. I really am. I didn't mean anything by it, I swear. Please forgive me? OK? . . . Based on the chapters you've sent so far, the premise is fine: self-possessed professional transcends time in search of his soul only to find out, first-hand, what an asshole he's been in his life. It's very Zen."

"I wouldn't put it quite that way," I replied. "But, yes, you seem to have the gist. So what gives?"

"You want my objective opinion?"

"I'm a big boy. I can even take an oxymoron from you."

"For starters, there's the chapter where Rob discovers that his malignancy has spread. After he brings Beverly along to the AMA convention in Las Vegas, he degrades himself for having cheated on her by watching her have sex with that male stripper? I dunno, Ollie. Maybe it's karmic justice, as you say. But I don't buy spouting some theory that a person must dredge up their past sexual transgressions in order to release the negative energy from their present relationship."

"It's called *Recapitulation*," I said testily. "It happens to be an ancient form of breathing meditation that sorcerers used for self-purification. By deeply concentrating on the details of past occurrences, we have the power to essentially recall inside, through inhalation, all the bad energy we've expended during our lifetime. While reliving in the mind each experience, these ancient wizards, anyway, were supposedly able to exhale in the same breath the reconstituted positive energy."

"Exactly my point," Annie replied. "Are you writing a novel or a textbook on mysticism?"

"It's central to the story," I said, not wanting her to know that I'd been fretting for a long time over this problem with my book.

At this point, dear reader you've no doubt noticed that the two main characters seem derived from the short story I wrote thirty years ago. I'm told that this phenomenon often occurs in many forms of creativity. In my case, however, not until Lucien Echo reappeared in my life did I have cause to remember my college piece about an immoral young doctor who buries his sins on the way up the ladder. After considering the potential similarities to Lucien's legal situation, I retrieved the story from my eight Bekin boxes filled with expandable folders comprising the completed works of Oliver Wendell Katz.

Leaving aside the possibility of some subconscious reason, it's entirely coincidental that the characters of Dr. Rob and Beverly Stephens in my novel resemble a more mature version of the couple in my short story. For I confess to using only their names because they sounded so much better than "Dr. Morris and Doris Kressman."

I assure you, though, whenever I managed to stick with it, my opus wrote itself. The narrative style, told from Dr. Rob's perspective: heavily medicated and near death, provided the necessary hook for me to retrace those critical moments in his life. While I always hoped to ferret out the means to Rob's redemption, Lucien's timely intervention helped me distill Dr. Rob's motives down to the choice between good and evil.

Then I read *The Floating Opera* by John Barth. The narrator, Toddy Andrews, is a middle-aged lawyer who announces his intention to relive in the novel the events that occurred during the day on which he decided to kill himself. As you can guess, suicide may also be foremost in the mind of a brilliant and successful obstetrician who's barely middle-aged and stricken with a terminal disease. Accordingly, I had produced, at Dr. Rob's behest, many bizarre pages-worth of alternate methods by which my good doctor contemplates his own demise.

In *The Floating Opera*, Barth's lawyer dissects the rationale for his decision as though he's preparing a court brief. He has syllogisms and paradigms and outlines with Roman numerals. There are references to Cicero, Socrates, and Hamlet, the top-notch brains on suicide. I hope this doesn't sound disrespectful because quite the opposite is true. In fact, I'd like to quote, with Barth's permission, of course, a passage that demonstrates the devastating effect his erudite dissertation had on my puny saga of Rob and Beverly Stephens:

I.   Nothing has intrinsic value. Things assume value only in terms of certain ends.

II.   The reasons for which people attribute value to things are always ultimately arbitrary. That is, the ends in terms of which things assume value are themselves ultimately irrational.

III. There is, therefore, no ultimate 'reason' for valuing anything.

In case you want to read *The Floating Opera,* I won't disclose whether Toddy's conclusion did him in or not. But I must tell you that the damn thing nearly put an end to me. There is no ultimate reason for anything. Whew, that's a hot one!

Now you're probably wondering what in the world this has to do with Annie's criticism of the latest installment from my novel? Well, at the time, let's just say, if a person interested in suicide asked me which book to read, I wouldn't have recommended mine. In truth, I had no idea where Rob and Beverly were ultimately headed. What I had then was a series of period sketches, over the course of which our fun-loving couple had survived a tempestuous marriage for twenty-five years, blessed with two rotten kids and a membership in the Grosse Point Country Club formerly patronized by *the* Gerald Fords. Of course, Rob and Beverly had also endured separate, repeat visits to that prestigious detox clinic out west bearing that same First Family name.`

So dismally superficial and spineless was my protagonist emerging that suicide was an option more appropriately suited to the author. For weeks I believed the project might be over, having carried out in my brain the above referenced Las Vegas scenario in which our fatally ill sawbones summons the courage to put a bullet into his own head. For your sake, I shall forego reprinting the actual excerpt and summarize what I'd sent to Annie:

Following a sustained run of luck at the roulette wheel, Beverly amasses a tiny fortune and a heat-on from the free booze. While Rob is supposed to be at a prenatal seminar studying digital monogram images, Bev finally succumbs to the advances of a young gigolo who's been working her up and down with his eyes from across the swimming pool for two days. Unfortunately, Bev has not yet learned that Rob's bloodstream is swarming with deadly cells; Rob's colleague confirmed just yesterday what he's been denying to himself for weeks now. Consequently, Beverly and Rob happen to end up in adjoining hotel rooms rented surreptitiously for entirely different purposes. While Bev strays, Rob has decided to go out swiftly, with all the comforts, and, possibly, head first off the balcony of the Caesar's Palace Hotel.

What could be simpler—or more twisted—than placing Rob in the most degrading position imaginable? Standing on the terrace with a 38 revolver in his trembling hand, Rob accidentally bears witness to his wife on the adjoining balcony as she is being entered by this young hustler on the chaise lounge. But when the moment of truth arrived on paper I couldn't pull the bloody trigger! I found myself crafting another masturbatory fantasy in which Rob puts down the gun and imagines himself joining their sexual encounter. During this inexplicably desperate attempt to save him, I came up with that cockamamie sorcerer's recapitulation ritual. By calling back the bad energy of his own infidelities, metaphorically, of course, Rob rationally accepts his fate.

Jesus, it was putrid! What's worse, Annie busted me for pretending to understand an esoteric mystical concept that I'd learned in my cab from some stringy-haired woman wearing black lipstick and combat boots. And therein resides the point of this long-winded diversion from the story at hand. My novel was failing because of my intellectual dishonesty. I had no call attributing scholarly psychological motivations to these characters when I was stealing from writers who did the research and I didn't possess a clue as to what most of them were talking about, anyway.

"Your prose sounds more comfortable when you're funny," Annie repeated.

"Thanks for nothing," I snapped, refusing to acknowledge that her opinion had confirmed my own determination to shelve the Dr. Rob book for a spell.

"I try to keep your best interest at heart," she replied.

By the time I looked up we were across the river from old Joe Kennedy's Merchandise Mart. Again the opportunity was at hand to discuss Lucien Echo, but I didn't want to further expose myself to her relentless analysis.

"Listen Annie," I said. "I'm feeling vulnerable right now so I'm gonna split."

"Wait a minute. Don't run off sulking."

"Don't worry. I'll call you in a couple days."

"What about the hotshot lawyer?"

"I don't know the true story yet. You'll be the first to hear when I do."

That evening I telephoned Lucien concerning my visit with Mama Raspberry. As soon as I mentioned recorded conversations in Judge Rotini's private office, Lucien invited me to read transcripts that the government had turned over as part of pretrial discovery. The next afternoon, I recall, was an extremely muggy Saturday in August. My bridge had loosened another notch during the night and was bothering me all morning. When I was changing my clothes the window air conditioner began to cough and dribble like an old man. Then the friggin' thing expended a final hot gasp of back-alley stench and just died. By the time I reached the chilly marble and glass lobby of Lucien's high-rise, I was sweating through my shirt and muttering under my breath. The doorman eyed me, disdainfully, while he announced my presence.

Alex greeted me at the door wearing an exotic batik blouse, skimpy shorts, and a forced smile. She explained that Lucien had been called to some board meeting, at which, she feared, he'd be asked to resign in light of pending charges. After relaying Lucien's request that I wait for him to return, Alex led me through the black and white tiled foyer into a medium-sized parlor I hadn't seen before. Richly appointed, it had her distinctive touch. Visible through another doorway at the far end of the room was the carved wood of a four-poster bed. We settled into the brocade cushion of a Louis-the-something loveseat, while Alex prattled on about Lucien's pro bono legal work and his dedication to various foundations.

"People don't know how much time and money Lucien donates to medical research, drug abuse programs and sheltering the homeless," she said. "He flies at his own expense whenever they call, and he never takes credit for it. That's the kind of thing you ought to write about."

Alex must have known that I was aware of Lucien's community largesse. Alex was visible too. Her restaurant charity events were regularly hyped in the social columns. Our young Beantown beauty was recently quoted about the symphony fundraiser she'd helped sponsor, and there was a review in the Sunday paper on Rococo's first anniversary: "Still Chicago's freshest chef," the article had raved about the androgynous T.S.— "initials only, please" —Alex's solitary choice to run the kitchen. Rumors that Lucien financed the venture with underworld partners, along with the mixture of power brokers and other well-heeled glitterati regulars, fueled a tabloid mentality about the place.

"You've been really understanding," Alex added after she probably noticed me scowling over her Lucien Echo commercial.

"Things don't look so good," I said, demonstrating my command of the obvious.

"If Lucien did what they've charged, I'm sure we can deal with the consequences together. Excuse me," Alex added, abruptly rising from the couch and disappearing into the adjoining bedroom. After a few minutes she returned looking pale and uncomfortable.

"Are you okay?"

"I'm tired and stressed out. The place is mobbed every night. People can be ghouls," Alex went on, screwing up her face while she sat next to me. "Lucien won't listen to me. If the situation involved one of his clients he'd demand to hear both sides. I don't get the benefits of a stranger."

"I don't know what I can do," I replied, feeling voyeuristic that she confided in me.

"There's nothing," Alex responded, while she repeated that one-handed joint-rolling number from our car trip. "He's so goddamn cool, I'm beginning to wonder about the times he . . . "Ahh, forget it," she added, tossing the unlit joint on the low table in front of us.

"What's happened?"

"Typical Lucien timing. He wants me to marry him."

"Are . . . are you going to say yes?"

Her eyes were wide and her face was flushed as she shifted her legs and fidgeted with the hem of her shorts. "Why am I discussing this with you?"

"Because I want to know?"

Alex regarded me for a moment without expression. "We met four years ago," she said, deciding to open up. "A couple years after I moved here from New York, at a business dinner for a celebrity line of men's clothes. Lucien represented the professional ball player and I was the marketing manager for Saks Fifth Avenue. Who knows why the ad agency wanted *me* there."

"You were in retail? What a coincidence. Retail is in my blood too. My parents met in my uncle's department store over fifty years ago."

"Retail? No, I wasn't a buyer or anything like that. I started out wanting to be a veterinarian. I think I told you that I was a sickly kid. Well, from twelve to fifteen, I was in and out of hospitals being probed and treated for this blood disease I had. It's okay. I'm better now. . . . So I spent most of my teens healing every creature I saw. When my interest turned to male bi-peds, my vet dream died quickly. I had been to Columbia by then, and I moved to a studio down near Soho thinking I'd become a fine artist—a painter, in fact. In those days you could still afford to live there.

"I guess I was pretty good, but I didn't have the patience to stick with it. It's like singing, which I love. I sing to myself when I play the piano. I'm just not ready to do it in front of people. . . . Anyway, I ended up taking some graduate courses in design and marketing and, eventually, I called Aunt Babbs, my mother's oldest brother's wife. Babbs is a grand doyenne of Seventh Avenue. Now, Aunt Babbs, she *is* retail. She was my connection to Saks. They had an opening in Chicago, I was thirty, single, and growing more cynical about relationships every day. The rest, as they say, is . . ."

"Dinner in Niketown with Lucien Echo."

"Very clever," Alex replied. "Actually, it was elegant casual wear. My challenge was to make Big and Tall pro basketball players look normal-sized, thank you very much. I remember thinking all through dinner that Lucien and I were both pretending not to be attracted to each other. When he didn't call me I was surprised."

"You called him?"

"I made up some question about the contract and flirted with him on the phone. I'd never been so aggressive over a man before. Somehow, Lucien must've known I was acting out of character because he played along; and we went out four nights in a row. We'd meet at a different place for drinks, which would stretch into dinner, and then we'd keep talking until closing. The next day he'd call to say 'hi' or to remind me about something I'd said across the table, and we'd end up planning to meet again that night."

"It must be nice trusting your instincts that way."

"You seem capable to me."

"What does that mean?"

"Nothing," Alex replied. "I just . . . you're an attractive guy in decent shape. You aren't gay, are you? Well, then, I'm sure you've known women."

"No one like you."

"Oh," she said softly.

Obviously, this beautiful bundle of neurotic energy captivated me. Nevertheless, and here's the weird part, Alex seemed vulnerable to my approach. With her tailored yuppie wardrobe and Bohemian sensibilities, she stirred my drink, all right. I'll be damned if she wasn't coming on to me, her eyes promising pleasures that far outweighed the pain. And Alex portrayed her dangerous and fascinating relationship with Lucien in the most fatalistic terms. I don't mean to sound cynical, but the last thing in the world I wanted to hear at that moment was a cautionary tale.

"You have to understand," Alex said, "Lucien doesn't live like most people. As soon as the restaurant project prevented me from keeping up with his schedule, he started sulking about sacrificing opportunities to be with me. The idea was to keep focused on each other. Without Lucien's support I'd . . . I know how lucky I am to have his backing, but it's almost as if Lucien wanted me to succeed to keep me out of his way."

Her words were beginning to hang in the air amidst the wisps of coconut smoke that occasionally drifted across the room. Off in one corner a tiny altar table displayed the bronze statue of Ganesh and the festooned portrait of some spiritual teacher to whom Alex obviously paid devotion. Smaller wood-carved statues, votives, and oddly shaped crystals also rested on the colorful silk table covering. It became impossible to concentrate on anything but Alex's indecision about marrying Lucien. When she let slip her suspicion that he was having an affair because they hadn't had sex in six weeks, I almost jumped out of my skin.

Why must it always come down to sex? She was using it on me to justify rejecting him, and I was succumbing to her shtick despite my own firmly held notions about falling in love. Over the course of my life spent surrendering to mediocrity, my one bastion of inflexibility had always been the pursuit of a virtuous romance. Not a virgin, of course, but a purely honorable love. It's no surprise that I'd managed to stay single. During the pre-AIDS years I was something of a free spirit about sex. That's a euphemism for being a hound. Annie has suggested that my commitment-phobia was a cowardly excuse for running away from myself. I preferred to think, until not too long ago, anyway, that Hollywood dreams die hard, particularly when reality never comes close to catching up with them. And then along came Alex, someone as close to perfection as it ever gets for the likes of me.

Nothing happened. At least, I don't think anything happened. I might honestly plead that my memory of the next several minutes in Alex's parlor is a little hazy, as I've actually retained two different mental pictures of what transpired. On the one hand, I'm certain that we innocently continued our conversation, my libido in check, except for maybe one failed advance, until Lucien came home. Yet, for some reason, and I'm probably just imagining what I'd hoped would happen, I also recall the warm, wet taste of Alex's soft lips and the sound of her heart beating to the rhythm of my tongue darting around the corners of her mouth. With the palm of my hand I rubbed her hard nipples straining through her thin rayon blouse. Forgotten in the milky white folds of her smooth flesh was the absurdity of what we were doing and the reason I came there. The gravity of our sin was lost to the sweet touch of her hair cascading over my face while she hugged me close. The danger of being discovered in the act heightened my resolve to satisfy her at all costs.

Whatever it was, it ended abruptly. A sound coming from the hallway, imperceptible to me at the time, caused her to break from my embrace. Either she stood up and buttoned her blouse with a guilty look on her face or, more likely, I arose first, embarrassed, my advance rejected. After a moment, I heard footsteps out in the hallway and I realized Alex must've sensed that Lucien had come home. There was no mad dash to get our stories together. Instead I seem to recall that Alex waited until the color in our faces returned to normal. Then she led us into the huge living room, where Lucien was standing behind the mirrored bar fixing a drink.

"Ollie, my boy," Lucien said, looking up from the stainless steel shaker that he was filling with crushed ice. "I know we had an appointment. Damage control. Please forgive me. How're you, dear?" he asked as Alex came over to greet him.

"How'd it go?" Alex replied, after they'd embraced and Lucien returned to the martinis.

"For five years I didn't hear the word ethics mentioned when they wanted variances and low interest loans," Lucien said. "The first sign that their political connection might dry up and the assholes can't stop talking about the *appearance of impropriety*. But we'll get 'em."

"You said no?" Alex groaned. "I thought we decided . . ."

"I envy you, Ollie," Lucien said, apparently ignoring Alex. "I wish I could be a writer, chuck it all and live out of a sack. Only I'm not *me* anymore. . . . Y'see," Lucien went on, nodding in Alex's direction, while he took a swig of his drink, "I'm a law firm, a corporation, and a foundation. I'm obliged to all those folks who pay for my boat and my drop-dead view. So when they tell me to bend over I'm supposed to ask, 'How far?'"

"You know I'll always support you," Alex replied while she sat down opposite him on one of the bar stools. "But you're in serious denial."

"Would you like a martini?" Lucien asked me. "Sometimes I'm not sure whose side you're on," he responded to Alex after I declined to join him. "Giving in to those people would be taken as an admission of guilt. We've been through this."

"You have a court appearance in a week and you still don't have a lawyer. Instead of preparing a defense you want to throw parties and attend functions. What're you trying to get everyone to believe?"

"You forgot the wedding. Is that pretend too?"

An awkward silence followed. Their battle was being waged on a communication level incomprehensible to me, like those high frequency whistles only dogs can hear. Alex finally retreated, her eyes declaring that the matter would be revisited. Lucien was his unflappable self, withholding comment until we were alone.

"Unless I've reached the panic stage Alex figures I'm not concerned enough," Lucien said after we no longer heard her footsteps withdrawing across the room. "You can't blame Alex," he went on. "I've seen the routine so many times and I know the players. I'm not freaked out because it's happening to me. Isn't that funny? Before every case I've tried, I was scared to death because I was responsible for someone else's life. Now that it comes down to my freedom, I'm more focused. The idea of trusting my defense to another lawyer seems ludicrous to me."

Lucien downed his drink and I followed him into the office. There he removed a thick manila folder from the credenza, tossed it on his massive desk and motioned for me to sit in one of the two leather pull-up chairs. "The fact is," Lucien went on, now sounding lawyer-like, "I've been preparing my case the same way I'd do it for any defendant. As far as I know, the evidence against me is entirely circumstantial. Here, take a look at the government's proof. If there's anything more you want me to explain just ask."

Lucien pushed the expandable file over to my side of the desk and asked if I'd like to stay for dinner. He claimed that whenever Alex experienced one of her sinking spells cooking was the remedy she'd found. Then Lucien excused himself leaving me to rummage through the details of his pending nightmare. Soon I was lost in the stack of typewritten FBI reports dictated in law-enforcement speak, referring to "special agents," "objects of surveillance," and "cooperating individuals."

There were also plastic covered booklets containing the transcripts of conversations secretly recorded in August Rotini's chambers, pursuant to a federal court order at the special request of the Attorney General of the United States. Often crude and humorous, the dialogue occurred between His Honor and an assortment of visitors covering a three- and-a-half month period. Although many of the speakers were unidentified, some were lawyers discussing their clients' cases. Judge Rotini was often engaged in a game of backgammon with his regular court reporter, Lori McGaughlin, or one of the other attendees. Much of the transcription was inaudible, made no sense, or seemed harmless. Some of the lawyers tossed around prison sentence numbers like they were bidding on auction cattle.

Lucien Echo's voice was identified on five occasions. There was friendly banter over some harbor on the other side of Lake Michigan, where Lucien and "Auggie" apparently docked their boats from time to time. Lucien even joined the judge at backgammon during one of the two relevant excerpts, which included a brief discussion of an unnamed case that, according to Lucien, was coming up the following week. The dialogue went on as follows:

(AR) Double again? . . . . Watch out Mister. . . . What is it anyway?

(LE) Um . . . It's a search warrant with the wrong address. Didn't you see the motion?

(AR) Huh? . . . Uh . . . No, Matty didn't give it to me yet. How much are we talking about?

(LE) There's a whole (inaudible) . . . guns . . . (inaudible) Tommy Goyle has a confidential informant who went in there.

(AR) I remember that Mick bastard. . . . Boxcars, sonny! Put a fork in you. Goyle's the ballbuster . . . I heard the story about . . . vice snitch . . . (inaudible). That's double again. I'll take a look   at it. Remind me when you get here before the hearing.

(LE) I give up. You're too lucky for me, Judge.

* * * (END OF EXCERPT) * * *

The next passage was eight days later. Most of it was underlined, bracketed, and circled with yellow marking pen:

(AR)   Lucien, my friend. Howya' doin'? . . . I don't know if we're gonna get to you today. . . . zoo   time over this viaduct guy out there with the press and the thrill seekers. . . . The State has too many witnesses . . . can't stop that asshole, Carlin, from cross-examining . . . about his shoe size . . . we'll be here 'til the victim gets up from his wheelchair and . . . out . . . courtroom.

(LE)   Your prosecutor. Palmer? He's brought Goyle here. . . . I'd sure appreciate it if you could . . . sometime this afternoon. . . . We're ready on a motion to quash search warrant . . . shouldn't take more . . . an hour.

(AR)   Oh yeah . . . lemme see. . . . I didn't get anything on it, did I?

(LE)   I have it right here . . .

(AR)   How many cases you got in there? . . . Heh. . . heh.

(LE)   Uh . . . You know. . . . There's . . .

(AR)   Yeah, I know. . . . Just put it over there. . . . I gotta get back to that . . . animal sitting in my courtroom. How's my tie?

(LE)   You look fine, Auggie. Distinguished . . . like Caesar addressing the Senate.

(AR)   I keep tellin' ya, Lucien, think about . . . this robe on some time . . . worse ways to die . . .

(LE)   Yeah . . . one day . . . tired of . . . stress
       . .

(AR)   Anytime you're . . . I'll go straight to
       George . . I don't have to tell ya he
       owes me.

(LE)   Thanks, Judge. You're a good man.

* * * (END OF EXCERPT) * * *

After absorbing the government's evidence file, I was persuaded that Lucien Echo and The Honorable August Rotini had privately decided Mama Raspberry's future during a recess in the viaduct killer's trial. Or so they thought at the time. For there was something wicked about seeing these important men reduced to the black and white police blotter exposition usually reserved for 7-Eleven stick-up men. By the time Lucien appeared in the doorway to fetch me for dinner I remember feeling empowered thinking that he was a common crook.

It probably wasn't a coincidence that Alex had returned to Rococo when Lucien and I stood over the butcher block island in the center of the kitchen, inhaling her arugula salad with raspberry vinaigrette dressing, pounded breast of veal sautéed in tomato, garlic and basil sauce, with spaetzel. We ate out of those silver-colored hard plastic doggy bag dishes retrieved from the restaurant. In between bites I brought up the transcripts. But Lucien calmly dismissed them. He made a point of saying that the crucial passages did not contain specific terms of the alleged payoff.

"The government admits those tapes are inconclusive and that's their best evidence," Lucien said. On the other hand, he conceded that he'd violated the rules of professional conduct prohibiting private conversations about cases on the judge's docket.

"It's one thing to have your license suspended," Lucien responded to my suggestion of ethical impropriety. "That's a stretch from a felony prosecution based on innuendo and questionable evidence. Did you read the FBI statement from Detective Goyle? He admitted writing the wrong location on the search warrant based on his confidential informant's description as the *east* side of the building. If Goyle's informant had been in Mama's apartment three times before, as he claimed, how could the guy not know the correct address?"

"I wondered about that too," I said, remembering that Lucien's cross-examination of Detective Goyle had apparently led to the dismissal of Mama's charges on this point. "The FBI report says the informant disappeared before they could confirm Goyle's story. Does anybody know where he is?"

"Chillum Hoskiss was Goyle's snitch," Lucien replied. "By the time the Feds got a court order requiring the states attorney to reveal his identity, Chillum was gone. How convenient? . . . Jeesus, Ollie. Why would I commit bribery when the case was defective to begin with?"

"By the way," I pressed him, "I noticed a summary of the statement taken from Lori McGlaughlin, the court reporter, and there was a report of Mama Raspberry's statement to the DEA agent who arrested her. I saw their grand jury subpoenas in the folder and a subpoena for Matthew Wachowski, the clerk who worked in Judge Rotini's court."

"Lori didn't say anything damaging because she didn't remember whether I was in the Judge's chambers that day."

"I've seen Wachowski's name before," I replied, "in the *Tribune* stories about your indictment. Isn't he the guy who accused Rotini of soliciting a bunch of defense lawyers in the city?"

"Matty Wachowski? He's the reason they got a wiretap in the first place. . . . Matty used to work in a courtroom that heard a hundred cases every day, like a maître d'. Lawyers sometimes waited from nine-thirty 'till four PM just for their case to be called before the bench unless they gave Wachowski a twenty-dollar tip. After one prosecutor blew the whistle, Matty apparently saw God and offered to go undercover. Wachowski and the prosecutor were both transferred to Auggie Rotini's courtroom, two months apart, and the government began listening to the private conversations of a circuit court judge like he was a mobster."

"Yeah, but wasn't Judge Rotini indicted along with three other lawyers in another case based on those tapes?"

"They recorded him five days a week for a hundred days and Auggie didn't have a clue they were listening. Then the FBI paid him and his wife a visit in Kennilworth during the middle of the night and made both of them listen to the tapes. Auggie told me he shoved one of the agents through the glass patio door, ran downstairs to the laundry room, and threw up in the utility sink. In between deciding whether to resign or sneak off to some country without an extradition treaty, Auggie warned me that they might come after me, too. I'm an afterthought who didn't become viable until Mama rolled over."

"What did Wachowski say about you?"

"They put him on administrative leave just before Rotini and the others were indicted, so they've kept close tabs on him. From what I've heard, though, Matty told the grand jury that he remembers walking in on the judge and me just when I was leaving his chambers. According to him, we overreacted like we were hiding something. Wachowski claims that I was standing next to the coat rack, where the judge's suit jacket was hanging, and Matty thought I had touched or brushed it in some way. Wachowski waited until Rotini also left the room and then he found a wad of one hundred dollar bills in the outside pocket. He said he flipped through them in a hurry, but it was a 'wad,' whatever that means."

"So that's what 'Put it over there' refers to in the transcript?"

"You think I did it, too . . . Don't you?"

"Well, I . . ."

"I put a copy of my legal brief on the judge's desk. Everyone else thinks the same thing; everyone except Auggie. He knows the money didn't come from me. What's he supposed to say? 'Echo didn't bribe me, it was John Jacob Jingleheimer Schmidt who left a roll of hundreds in my suit?'

"People always want to believe the worst," Lucien went on. "You were there, Ollie. Do you think the case was fixed? It doesn't seem to matter that the government didn't charge me when they first indicted Rotini and the other lawyers. Even with those tapes and Wachowski's statement about me, the evidence was so weak they weren't going to risk blowing their other cases against Rotini. Then Mama was arrested selling a pound of cocaine and all she had to say to stay out of prison was, 'Oh yeah, I remember that hearing, the one where my attorney told me he bribed the judge.' C'mon, Ollie. You talked to her. D'ya honestly believe she recalls anything about this case as opposed to all the others she's had? Why would I be stupid enough to tell her if I was going to fix it?"

"That's pretty much what she said. That you asked her for fifteen hundred dollars for the judge."

"She did? When we get to trial, I'll bet, Matty Wachowski will suddenly remember the wad in His Honor's pocket added up to about fifteen hundred dollars."

"Last time we talked," I nervously challenged him, "you said the case wasn't going to trial."

"Ollie, I'm gonna say something nobody knows." Lucien led me through the kitchen onto the terrace wrapping around the corner of the skyscraper. "I'm not trying to influence your opinion," he added. "I want you to hear the facts. Soon after Auggie warned me about the tapes, the government came to me as he'd predicted. Except, they asked me to testify against him. I was offered immunity to swear under oath that Rotini had demanded a payoff from me for throwing out the case against Mama."

I stared off at the distant lights on Lake Shore Drive gleaming through the gauntlet of tall buildings stretching up before me. It was one of those clear, starry summer nights when the sounds and smells made living in Chicago worthwhile. No longer did I believe that Lucien Echo owned this town.

"Last Thanksgiving, the United States Attorney, himself, stood right here and made that promise to me," Lucien continued, growing animated as he leaned against the terrace railing. "They had Rotini on so many tapes, and lawyers were naming other judges in their bribery club who were extorting a piece of the action for dismissing cases in their courtrooms. You have to keep in mind, Ollie, I was friendly with Judge Rotini, but I had no control over how Mama's case was assigned to him. I haven't been in criminal court for years. I'd heard things about Auggie. But seeing as he never asked me for money, I couldn't bring myself to swear that he did. So I declined the government's offer."

Lucien was at his best when he was pinned in a corner. Still, I wanted to believe him. It wasn't surprising that the government would sacrifice the truth in Lucien's case in favor of the bigger political splash involving judges on the take. That was the way sharks operated.

"I'm not sure I wouldn't have chosen the easy way out," I replied.

"When your reputation's trashed and people you care about start to look at you funny, Ollie, I hafta say, being noble isn't what it's cracked up to be."

I sat on the Art Institute steps waiting for Alex in the afternoon sun with the tourists, young art students, and office workers. My heart and mind were in a race to assume control when Alex arrived. I wondered whether she'd seen through my invitation to discuss Lucien's case and decided not to show up.

Earlier that morning I was inside the *Sun Times* morgue going through the database on Lucien Echo. I ran into Walter Karlito, the investigative reporter from Channel 5, who'd followed the criminal court corruption scandal by cultivating snitches and other media whores. According to Karlito, one assistant US Attorney told him that orders to bring down Lucien had originated in Washington. Walter opined that Lucien was getting a raw deal for refusing to cooperate against Judge Rotini. Armed with this opinion, corroborating what I'd heard from Lucien, I called Alex to deliver some encouraging intelligence for a change.

There was also Lucien's decision to retain in his defense Professor Effram Abrahamson, Esq., esteemed appellate lawyer and constitutional expert from the University of Chicago. When Abrahamson had appeared at Lucien's trial setting conference, I thought that the professor was an odd choice. He was highly regarded by the federal bench and his name was associated with many legislative bills and scholarly treatises. But he hadn't tried a case in years. He was in ill health, and you had to wonder whether the professor was up to taking on the collection of snakes the government lined up against Echo.

"I guess it's smart to take the high road," I'd told Alex on the telephone earlier that day, "when your morals are on trial."

"I'm happy Lucien hired someone he trusts."

"There's a Hopper exhibition I'd like to see. Can you meet me at the Art Institute and I'll tell you what I found out from the press."

"I'm going downtown this afternoon. Maybe I can get over there around two."

At two-thirty, I finally went up the marble steps in the rotunda searching for Monet's "Haystacks" and "The River," which hung within the labyrinthine gallery of rooms permanently housing the Impressionist and Post-Impressionist paintings. I usually begin there, in the mid-nineteenth century, strolling the floor on a chronological tour of the most important and celebrated examples of modern art in the world.

That day I was stuck on Henri Toulouse-Lautrec's famous 1888 painting of Cirque Fernando: "The Equestrienne," which depicts a female horse rider performing under the direction of a mustachioed, tuxedo-clad ring-master wielding a bullwhip. During previous museum visits I'd discovered that Renoir frequented the same circus in Montmartre. In the next room was his painting: "Jugglers at the Cirque Fernando," a portrait of Francisca and Angelina Wartenberg, young gymnasts who happened to be the daughters of Fernando Wartenberg, owner of this family circus.

What struck me was the contrast between Lautrec's sinister portrait of the ringmaster, who was certainly Fernando himself, and Renoir's beautifully compassionate representation of the two pre-pubescent saltimbanques. For it turns out that the children, like Lautrec, were deformed in life, their limbs being too short. In consolation, however, Renoir painted them with elongated hands and filled one child's arms with succulent oranges.

I was sitting on the backless bench in the center of the room when Alex appeared next to me. She wore a cream-colored business suit and her hair tied up in a bun. At her side was a sleek leather briefcase, its dark chocolate color matching her shoes. Alex was nervous and distracted. She barely looked at me after I smiled at her for catching me in my daydream.

"I'm sorry I'm late," she said.

"I'm glad you decided to come."

"Well, it's lucky I found you here. Couldn't you tell me this information over the phone?"

"I suppose so. . . . I . . . I wanted to see you again."

"Hmm. I thought you wanted to see the Hopper exhibition."

"You see the Lautrec over there? I've been toying with a screenplay about that guy with the whip. Imagine Paris before the turn of the century, featuring the performers and prominent attendees of this little circus, as told through the eyes of Fernando the impresario. The cultural elite mingle with circus commoners. It's *Moulin Rouge* meets *Freaks*. Did you know that Monet, Degas, Cezanne, Renoir, Seurat, and Cassatt took part in the Paris Impressionist Exhibitions from 1874 to 1886? What a time it must've been. They even had this guy, Le Petomane. I swear to God, he used to get up on stage and fart songs through a hole in his pants.

"So I figured you tie the two segments of society together with a love story between Fernando's lame daughter and some young stud from the rich, artsy crowd. They meet at the Eighth Exhibition, which is particularly huge, because it's the first public event in Paris history illuminated by electricity."

"Ha! Ha! Ha! The sparks literally fly between them. I love it, Ollie. What a great idea."

"You think so?"

"I'm not kidding. Are you really writing this? You have a fertile mind, Mr. Katz."

"Does that mean you think I'm full of it?"

I thought her smile told me what I needed to know.

When Alex rose from the bench I took her hand and felt her pulse quicken. However, as we walked among Kandinsky, Kirchner, and Kokoschka, she seemed distant and uncomfortable again. I had to be getting to her if she was trying so hard to deny it. A pang of conscience struck me and I mulled over the consequences of pressing her further. We silently waded through the Motherwells, Pollocks, and De Koonings, while I contented myself with the notion that Alex might be struggling over the same realization. Instead I grew sullen and ushered her down the stairs, past Chagall's stained glass windows, and outside into the blazing afternoon sun reflecting off the L tracks above Monroe Street.

"I guess you must have another tour waiting?" she cracked.

"I made a mistake," I replied. "I'm really sorry."

"Don't say that. It was a lovely first date."

"You want to get some coffee?"

"I'd better not," Alex said. "I have to go to the restaurant. Walk me to my car and I'll drop you off."

That night Annie left Jason with Dad and convinced me to take her for Alaskan king crab legs at a tiny joint near my apartment. I owed it to Annie, anyway, after running out on her the way I had the last time we got together. And I couldn't wait to spill my guts over the Alex dilemma that seemed to be developing.

No tables were available so we ate at the crowded bar bisecting the narrow room. Rock and roll tunes blared out of the overhead speakers, emanating from a tiny satellite jukebox within flipping distance on the bar. Throughout most of dinner Annie spared me her intense probing, concentrating instead on the meal. Then she reached into her paper-lined wicker basket, cracked open her largest shell, which she'd saved for last, popped the whole succulent piece into her mouth, and turned to face me. "How's that new story about the hotshot lawyer you mentioned the other night?" she asked, torturing me again.

"Yeah. Well, right now, I'm digging out the facts. But I think I'm about to do something stupid and I figured that's your department."

"All right, Ollie! It's a woman. Isn't it? I've been wondering about you for a year now. I never pictured you and Sally together."

"Yes, there is a woman involved," I eventually admitted. "Unfortunately, she's the fiancée of my subject who happens to be in a lot of trouble."

"What kind of trouble?"

"Legal trouble. But the thing is, I can't tell if she's coming on to me because she's trying to save him. Not to mention that the guy trusts me with some heavy stuff. I feel like a heel."

"How do you feel about her?" Annie asked, peeking at me while she waited to catch the bartender's eye for the check.

"I was nuts about her until she started behaving like she was available. How can you respect someone who's willing to cheat on her lover?"

"You haven't changed," Annie said. Then she pulled a hundred dollar bill from her black leather knapsack and waved it in the bartender's direction. "I love you dearly," Annie went on. "I don't want you to end up a lonely old pervert, but if you don't set any realistic goals . . ."

"The guy could have me killed if he found out," I interrupted. I think he's connected," I added, sotto voce, as Annie handed the money over to the bartender.

"Who is this person?" Annie asked once we'd exited up the narrow stairs and were out in the hot and sticky nighttime air.

"Some rich lawyer who went to Madison at the same time I did. Until a couple months ago, I've only seen him once since the 80's. I don't think you . . ."

"You're doing a story about *Lucien Echo*?" Annie nearly gasped.

"How the hell did you know that?"

"Oh Christ, Ollie. Lucien Echo? Don't you remember? You introduced us at Butch Maguire's when I came home after Mom was diagnosed."

"No, I don't remember. That's twenty years ago. What's the big deal, anyway?"

"It was the winter of nineteen eighty-two," she corrected me.

Annie fell silent as we walked up to the intersection at Clark and Broadway, where the nightly parade of humanity's weirdest was in full bloom. Transvestites, drugstore cowboys, and chicken hawks strolled among the strait-laced restaurant crowd heading back to Lake Shore Drive. The breakneck pace of summer energy had not changed during all my years in the neighborhood. The clothes were remodeled, staccato electronic music blared from ghetto blasters, cruising cars went up and down on hydraulic lifts like parade floats, doorway mendicants displayed hand-scrawled signs and everyone was armed with a deadly weapon.

"What's so special about the winter of nineteen eighty-two?" I asked, wondering why I'd forgotten that they'd met.

"I'm not surprised you blocked out the experience," Annie replied. "You were totally off the wall for a while when Mom died."

We walked past my street and continued along the Parkway toward the harbor entrance underneath the Lake Shore Drive overpass. I *had* recently mulled over my encounters with Lucien during that time, including some recollections of another situation involving a woman. However, Lucien hadn't asked me about April Stewart—that was her name—nor had he seen fit to bring up my sister. But then I couldn't tell whether it was more the matter of my denial or his manipulation that prevented our getting around to rehashing yet another experience between us with a strange twist.

The question dogged me as Annie and I made our way through the dim, tunnelled catwalk of concrete and meshed wire running alongside the powerboat channel out to the lake's rocky edge.

"My mental condition is not the question here," I said. "Anyway, why are you so interested in Lucien Echo?"

"I didn't expect to hear that you're doing a story on him after all these years. Is he really a gangster? I mean, were you serious about hit men?"

"I don't think so. But he represents these people for a living. Who knows how they pay their fees? Country doctors take chickens and vegetables for their services. The guy is facing trial for bribing a judge on behalf of a drug dealer."

"Sounds like you've made up your mind that Lucien did it."

Her words stung me like the mosquitoes sucking our blood before we felt their presence. It was my own fault. We were sitting on the seawall of jagged rocks, above the shoreline, where those pesky little buggers proliferated in the sultry low-tide air. From our perch we watched a small flotilla of pleasure boats motoring through the underpass into the harbor. Most were returning from one of the towns dotting the shore across the Lake along Indiana and up through Michigan.

"What difference does it make to you whether Lucien did it or not?" I asked.

"It doesn't sound like something Lucien would do."

It doesn't sound like something Lucien would do? Can you believe this crap? Where did Annie get off accusing me of being biased? I was pouring my heart out to her while she was concealing from me intimate things that she obviously knew about him. And so what if I *had* thought Lucien was guilty. The bad ones always make better stories, anyway.

I tried to cast off my anger by staring out at the long line of boats slowly gliding in through the channel. That's when I saw him again. There was that damned little fellow in the surgical gown, up on the bridge of a forty-foot Magnum cruiser, piloting his way past us into the harbor. The same tiny doctor that I'd seen on Lake Minona at the hull of the crew team shell with a megaphone in his hand.

"Pl . . . eeease!" I barked at Annie. "How could you know what Lucien would do?"

"Well . . . at the time, we were close."

"Don't tell me you screwed him?"

"Don't talk to me that way," she replied angrily. "I didn't say we were lovers. I said we were close. Whether we screwed or not is none of your business. Better you worry about getting your own story straight."

End of discussion. All right, I confess, the reappearance of the little man in the boat was a cheap trick devised to alert you to another flashback coming up. It is no less true, however, that I'd been oblivious to Annie's prior association with Lucien; just as I'd spaced out on most of the events that took place around the time my mother died. As Annie was quick to point out, I'd recently become more concerned about rubbing shoulders with Lucien—other body parts in Alex's case—than discovering whether he was guilty or innocent. Since the answer might exist within those missing puzzle pieces out of the past, with your indulgence, then, may we search a little deeper for reasonable grounds to judge Lucien Echo?

AUTUMN 1982

"Screw this bullshit car!" Lucien Echo slams his hand against the steering wheel, wondering why in the world he bought a Scorpion. Never mind all the lies about the electrical system, there are only two Lancia mechanics in the area and neither one of them has figured out how to service the damn thing. Forget about Rolando, Lucien's auto thief client, who offered to get rid of the piece of crap after the fuel pump blew out for the third time. Lucien curses himself, mostly. The Blue Book value has dropped like a rock. If he allows Rolando to strip it and dump the buzzard in the Calumet River, he'll still lose on the insurance.

Lucien looks through the open doorway of his garage, into the alley, checking for anyone who might be watching him. He removes a small glass vial from his suit coat pocket, bends over in the leather bucket seat, and snorts into each nostril a tiny spoonful of cocaine. Half a

172

gram remains from the eighth he picked up Saturday morning, following Diane's telephone call.

Diane is a dancer in one of the Cicero strip clubs. Last time the club was raided Diane was charged with "keeping a house of prostitution" just because they found a key to the place on her. The owner had prevailed upon Lucien to represent his three employees and five dancers arrested during the vice round up. That translated into two grand up front, one court appearance, nine hundred more in bail bond receipts, and nobody went to jail.

Lucien and Diane hit it off right away. She was grateful to her white knight with the slick tongue, the shiny sports car, and the never-ending supply of schmoo. Lucien is thrilled that she likes to come to his townhouse late at night, sit naked in his hot tub, listen to his music, do his drugs, and engage in sexual adventures. This weekend Diane enlisted Lucien's help with a new dancer at the club: Snow, a curvaceous, light-skinned black beauty with peroxided collar and cuffs. Diane had been working on Snow to share her first lesbian experience. Thinking Snow might respond in a ménage a trois, Diane suggested that they come over to Lucien's for a Saturday afternoon debauchery. At sunrise this morning, when Lucien sent them off, nobody had slept or eaten the delivery food for two nights. But they were sated and delirious from exploring each others' various orifices.

Now Lucien will be late for court. He puts in the key again, and grinds the accelerator. Mercifully, it sputters, catching hold long enough to turn over.

"I can't do this anymore," he thinks to himself. Not bothered so much by the professional risks he keeps on taking, Lucien's overwhelmed with emptiness when he awakes from a bender. Tanking up and letting go was exciting at first; somehow it washed from his mind the dirt and slime of the streets. But, in the haze of crashing, Lucien wonders whether he isn't becoming like the people he represents. He's riding a roller coaster of titillation and despair fueled by drugs and some deep self-destructive urge that he can't quite put his finger on.

"Never again," Lucien promises himself as he drives out of the alley behind the cluster of townhouses, heading south on Larabee toward the Ogden corridor. The cold gray morning contributes to his funk. During this amorphous time between fall and winter, when the wind blows dead leaves off the trees and the ground turns hard and brown, Chicago is as brutal as it gets. Lucien speeds by the dirty concrete high-rises of Cabrini Green and traverses the flat open spaces of the industrial compounds. Fearing another electrical short, he refrains from using the heater and switches on the radio. Out comes that infernal "Love lift us up where we belong. Where the eagles fly . . ." All day long, on every station, Joe Cocker and Jennifer Warnes for months.

If Lucien escapes to Southern California—he's been pondering this option lately—he has enough money to start over. But the L.A. scene would be weirder, and things are going so well that he's taken on a hungry young ex-public defender to cover for him when he's scheduled to be in two places at once. Lucien's expanding client contacts, inside legal connections, and hard work are generating a profitable and enduring power current. In a few more years, he thinks, his image will be indelible, he'll delegate a lot more responsibility, and then he'll split for as long as he wants, whenever he chooses.

Lucien parks in the crosswalk near the courthouse entrance on California Street and hurries up the granite steps. His "catch of the day" is a murder case involving an electronics firm burglary that went sour. After a security guard had surprised the three culprits loading their van with equipment, he wound up shot to death during their escape. An elderly woman walking her dog in the alley next to the loading dock managed to get a look at two of the men and the license number of their Ford panel truck. When the abandoned vehicle was recovered a few days later, police lifted the fingerprint of D. S. "Toothless" Murray, convicted burglar and drug addict. Following two shaky nights in custody, he admitted his participation in the caper and further implicated Cotton Bradley as the shooter.

Lucien's client is Cotton Bradley's older brother, Abel. Considering the criminal defendant demographic, Abel is an anomaly; a white family man with a job who might actually be innocent. Unfortunately, Abel owns the panel truck. When the police asked him how it ended up on the other side of town, he maintained that it had been stolen on the day of the burglary. Suspicious of Abel's failure to report this alleged theft, the detectives made him stand in a police line-up, where the dog-walking lady positively identified him as one of the burglars.

During his initial meeting with Lucien, Abel admitted that he'd lied about the truck's being stolen to protect his brother Cotton who'd taken it. But Abel swore he was home with his wife and kids on the night in question.

Owing to the physical resemblance between the brothers, Lucien thinks Abel might be telling the truth. The old lady could easily have confused Abel for Cotton. Cotton Bradley is a second-story man with a long record and no apparent redemptive qualities. After his last stretch in a Tennessee prison, Cotton had drifted here following Abel's migration from Nashville many, many years ago. When Cotton was apprehended at the Greyhound station he was savvy enough not to make any statements, thereby failing to exculpate his brother.

Despite the woman's acknowledgement that Abel looks like Cotton, especially from thirty feet away, she stuck to her story that Abel and Toothless Murray were the two men she had seen running from the dock into the getaway van. In light of Toothless's admission that Cotton shot the guard, the detectives simply deduced that they'd nailed the three people involved. Under the felony-murder rule, if one defendant kills somebody during the course of a burglary, they can all be convicted of murder. But if the woman has made a mistake, as Lucien believes, the third burglar is at large.

Inside the old gothic courtroom Lucien finds the chaos up front more daunting than he anticipated. While walking down the long center aisle he spies the three defendants sitting in the jury box next to a sheriff's deputy. Lucien assumes that their preliminary hearing has been announced and passed over by Judge Palmetto on account of Lucien's tardiness. The spectator sections are packed with family and friends of those on the docket, as well as witnesses, police officers and a cross-section of usual courthouse groupies. But the sketch artist and the gaggle of reporters filling up the front row make Lucien nervous. The dead guard was a moonlighting police officer and press heat has built since the crime scene was suspiciously opened to reporters.

"They're in Chambers on your case," Millie says, as Lucien approaches the clerk's desk alongside the judge's tall bench.

"Have I missed much?" Lucien asks, staring at Millie's lacquered helmet of pink-tinged hair contrasting her mustard-colored county smock.

"Not really," she replies, fidgeting with the reading glasses hanging over her tabletop bosom. "You know how fussy the Judge gets when reporters are here."

"You look stunning, Millie," Lucien says, walking past her toward the padded door into Judge Palmetto's private kingdom.

"I don't care if Woodward and Bernstein are out there. This hearing won't begin until the conflict of interest is . . . Well, Mr. Echo," Judge Palmetto interrupts his own tirade, "so nice of you to grace us with your presence. Maybe you can explain to Mrs. Frumpkin that this is a critical stage in the proceedings. Our esteemed prosecutor doesn't seem to understand that Cotton Bradley is entitled to independent counsel because one of the public defender's clients has implicated the other."

"Car trouble, Judge," Lucien says, gesturing to the other lawyers in the room. From the look on the assistant states attorney's face, and Mrs. Frumpkin's physical appearance is amply suggested by her name, Lucien surmises they're discussing whether to grant a postponement in order to throw Cotton Bradley to the wolves. By process of elimination, Lucien figures that Bill Grillio must be the lawyer His Honor intends to appoint to take over Cotton's defense. Roger Murphy and Ed Sternberg, the two assistant PDs who appeared at the arraignment last week, are standing over in the corner near the window while Grillio and Frumpkin are toe to toe in front of Palmetto's cluttered desk.

"I wouldn't presume to tell the prosecutor how to present her case," Lucien adds. "But I certainly won't object to a continuance while Mr. Grillio prepares for the hearing."

"The people do object," Mrs. Frumpkin protests.

"It's a reasonable request under the circumstances," Judge Palmetto responds firmly. "The defendants are in custody and they don't object. Mr. Grillio has just been handed the file, graciously accepting this appointment, pro bono, I might add. Since the witnesses are available to return you'll have to put off the reporters for another week. D'ya understand? No leaks from any of you."

That's a little too much protesting, Lucien thinks. He looks at Ed Sternberg, who raises his eyes in a sign of resignation that they're mere players in the political orchestra for the prosecution of high profile cases. Lucien and Sternberg go way back together. As far as Lucien's concerned, Ed is as sharp and honest as they come. Normally he'd fight for the preliminary hearing to go forward in order to cross-examine the witnesses before trial.

Lucien figures there won't be a preliminary hearing this time. The prosecutor has undoubtedly made a deal with Toothless Murray. Lacking any other eyewitnesses to the shooting, Mrs. Frumpkin needed Murray's testimony against Cotton Bradley. Sternberg made the easy choice to stick with Toothless, the talking rat, and withdraw from representing the client whose head everybody was clamoring over. With an extra week to put their case before the grand jury, the state will have a murder indictment against Cotton and Abel just in time to avoid the rescheduled preliminary hearing.

Now Lorraine Frumpkin and Judge Palmetto were pretending that they hadn't set up the scenario in the first place. They discuss seventy-five cases a day, sometimes until late in the evening. They are overworked, underpaid, and knee-deep in human waste to which nobody usually pays attention. When the cases come along that affect how people vote, they're determined to do "what's right for the community." Even if that means calling in His Honor's buddy, Billy Grillio, the lawyer most likely to sacrifice Cotton Bradley's worthless hide in favor of the publicity. By copping a swift guilty plea the killer will be punished and justice will be served in Judge Palmetto's courtroom. If Lucien keeps his mouth shut, Abel Bradley could receive his own bonus gift from the prosecutor just for being in the studio audience.

Sure enough, after everyone appears in the courtroom to put on the record the continuance and the gag order, Lucien and Sternberg linger in the back hallway outside the judge's chambers. "What did she offer you?" Lucien asks him.

"Fourteen to fourteen and a day," Ed replies. "Murray is ecstatic he could be out in seven years. With the fingerprint evidence they have against him, Toothless figures the minimum is a great deal. And Frumpkin's boss needs a murder conviction."

"Has your client realized that he has to give up the fellow they haven't caught yet?"

"Good luck on that one," Ed says. "Frumpkin is so jazzed on frying your client's brother, she didn't bother to ask about your guy. I'm sure she'll offer you the same deal."

"Is Toothless gonna tell the truth?"

Sternberg looks at Lucien like he's crazy. It was a stupid question, Lucien decides, inquiring after Sternberg's wife and kids instead. He listens patiently to Ed's proud daddy rap about piano recitals and little league baseball. Yet, Lucien's stomach turns at the veiled confirmation that Abel Bradley is indeed innocent and nobody cares. Frumpkin is willing to coddle Murray as long as he helps their case and Sternberg isn't rocking the boat. If the charges against Abel are to be dismissed, Lucien must convince the states attorney to coax the whole story out of Toothless Murray. While the prosecutor's office has been trying to cover up its mistakes, Lucien's client has been sitting in a filthy jail cell for ten days, away from his family and his job that no longer exists, and they're standing around the water cooler swapping office gossip.

"How can anyone get used to trading people like crop futures?" Lucien wonders, as he walks into the dingy fourth floor corridor. The wide hallway has plaster walls covered with drab green paint and tall wire-meshed windows. Once grand and shiny, the gold and bronze elevator details are dulled beyond recognition. Lucien spots a group of reporters comparing notes on the proceeding. He waits until the committee breaks up and Jim Dudgeon from Channel Two walks over to the stairwell for a smoke.

"Hey Echo," Dudgeon says after Lucien pretends to walk past him in order to descend to the floor below. "What's the story behind the delay?"

"You know I can't talk to you, Jim," Lucien responds, motioning for Dudgeon to follow him down the stairs. "But you could break the case wide open," Lucien adds when they're halfway between the fourth and third floors.

"C'mon, Lucien," Dudgeon says, while he sucks on the nub of a filterless cigarette and then grinds it out on the dirty marble step. "They got an eyewitness and a confession. I happen to know the grand jury is scheduled to hear it tomorrow morning."

"Tomorrow everybody's gonna be looking for the third burglar, 'cause D.S. Murray is about to name him for the prosecutor. Unless you get to him first."

"If you're jagging me off. . . ."

"You want to help an innocent man go free?"

"Sure, Lucien."

"I'm tellin ya' Murray knows where the third guy is hiding. You'll be saving his life. Hell, you might scoop the cops."

"All riqht, the third burglar's still at large," Jim Dudgeon says, flipping his checkered cap onto his curly mop of gray hair. He shakes Lucien's hand, searching his eyes for any signs of duplicity. Although Echo has been square with him in the past, Dudgeon senses that Lucien's balls may be bigger than his stomach this time. In the end it's impossible for Jim Dudgeon to resist. "My confidential source," he says, "is someone close to the court proceedings in the case. That okay?"

Lucien hurries outside where the day has grown grayer, colder, and more depressing. He removes a parking ticket from the windshield and the car won't start. While calling his secretary from the corner bar, Lucien pledges to buy one of those newfangled mobile telephones that plugs into the dashboard cigarette lighter. After Robin phones for a tow, she informs Lucien that the mail contains the government's brief in the Gardenia appeal and a long-awaited settlement check for Wilma Brown's broken hip suffered during the crush of bodies when Marshall Field's opened its doors for the midnight madness sale. Miguel Sanchez is waiting to see him and his young associate, Gail Novitzky, wants to discuss her court appearance this morning on the Friedlander Trust case. Robin finally reminds him that he's late for a lunch meeting with Gordon Traeger, senior partner in the personal injury/medical malpractice firm of O'Connor, Traeger & Hayes.

"Another day in paradise," Lucien now says to the cab driver, who just muttered "hoity toity" under his breath when Lucien told him to go to Binyon's restaurant. Lucien wants to go home and sleep for a few hours. He wants to be fresh for his dinner engagement with April Stewart, redheaded tootsie of the Youngstown, Ohio sheet metal Stewarts. She's been playing hard to get for two months now, Lucien realizes, since they met during Sol Fazil's tax audit.

Sol Fazil's World of Pants is being threatened by his long-time competitor, Abdul Rahmeen, owner of the Pants World chain of haberdasheries. For years they've followed each other into the same locations, copied each other's design, inventory, and pricing. Sol Fazil hails from Syria, Abdul Rahmeen is Lebanese, and they hate each other. By securing a prime lease at the new mall in Hinsdale, Fazil demonstrated again his domination of the European polyester and gold chain look in DuPage County. It's believed that Rahmeen took revenge by alerting the IRS to a phantom inventory scheme practiced by Fazil.

Lucien is spearheading Sol's defense along with the bright and beautiful auditor, April Stewart, dispatched from Arthur & Amberson Company. Not long out of graduate school, April is an aspiring financial planner for the Big 8 accounting firm. During their first coffee date, following Fazil's grilling by the revenue agent on his case, April guardedly told Lucien that she'd asked for a transfer from the Youngstown office. "For reasons I don't care to discuss," she said.

Lucien was fascinated by her seeming unavailability. He prevailed upon April's hardy midwestern appetite for rich food and music, while he minded his manners and refrained from interrogating her like a witness. He drew her out slowly, until last Tuesday night they ended up swapping spit at the front door to April's condominium.

"Tonight's the night," Lucien thinks, as he checks the cabbie's eyes in the rear-view mirror and bends down over the hump for another tootsky. Lucien has known how to use sex to manipulate women since he was thirteen, when he was seduced by the married lady living in the two-flat building next door.

"There's a lesson in there some place," Lucien now says to the cabbie, hearing him coil prices. They eventually stop in front of Binyon's marquee. Lucien peels off another dollar, adding it to the tip, and he escapes into the tiny reception area.

After wiping away all outward signs of dread, Lucien searches the room for Gordon Traeger's booth. However, when Lucien approaches Gordon's white-linened table, sparkling with crystal and silver in the overhead light, he looks worse than Lucien imagined. Normally pink, pudgy, and strong, Gordon's fifty-seven-year-old face is gaunt and sallow, and his thick, white main of well-trimmed hair is disheveled. In less than a year this distinguished former president of the Trial Lawyers Association and high muckity-muck of the Standard Club, whose name strikes fear in the boardrooms of insurance companies throughout the country, has deteriorated from the ravages of diabetes.

Following Lucien's hasty departure from the states attorney's office, Gordon Traeger took him under his wing. Although Lucien managed to survive for only two years in the pristine environment of O'Connor, Traeger & Hayes, he learned things from Gordon that no professor could teach him. Now the legendary barrister's hearing is fading and his memory fails him with increasing regularity. Gordon's denial, perhaps his death wish, is fueled by Stolichnaya and the belief that his partners are trying to screw him out of the firm that he started during Eisenhower's second term.

"Jeesus, Gordo," Lucien says after he sits down and points at the glass of vodka on the table. "You know that stuff is taboo."

"I'm already dead, my friend. Just ask Jim Hayes or that pimp, Barry Schiff, or any of my other so-called partners. Now they're fighting over my bones like mongrels in an elephant graveyard. I want you to sue those pimps for every file that's mine."

"I heard you lost the Pinto class-action referral from Ralph Nader's people. Look, Gordon, you have to take care of your health. That's what matters. Slow down and forget about the business for a while. What does Joyce think?"

"Now that David's in medical school . . . Did I tell ya' he goes to Georgetown? . . . My wife doesn't care what I do as long as I don't mope around the house all day. I can't stand this. They've taken most of my files away, they tiptoe around like I belong in a rubber room, and I have to clear the piddly shit I do handle with that pimp, Schiff!"

Gordon stops talking while the waiter sets down two bowls of turtle soup. He uses the opportunity to take another swig of his drink. Lucien sits by, helplessly, wondering why he ever chose to be a professional dumping ground for people who get fooled by life. Lucien certainly feels for Gordon. After all, though, they aren't friends. They've talked on the phone maybe five or six times a year since Lucien left the firm. Unless they run into each other in court they seldom socialize. Hell, he's seen Joyce four times in nine years.

"It's the indignity that makes me . . ." Gordon chokes on his words. He sobs softly for what seems an eternity, until, embarrassed, he tries to regain his composure. He ends up blubbering out of control.

"I'm sorry," Gordon adds, finally getting hold of himself. "You're somebody who understands it's not the money I want back. They're afraid of you, Lucien."

What Gordon is proposing snaps Lucien to attention. Being recommended to Traeger's clients and their connections is worth millions in future business. Lucien excuses himself for a bathroom run, using the stall to take another snort. While standing before the sink mirror he savors the notion that the crème de la crème has come to him for advice and counsel. He's delighted to be screwing with O'Connor, Traeger & Hayes in the hourly pursuit of restoring Gordon Traeger's good name.

"Karma," Lucien resolves, catching one more approving glimpse of himself in the mirror before he returns to the table. "Too bad Gordon doesn't have much of a case," he adds under his breath. Based upon Lucien's cursory examination, anyway, Gordon's partnership agreement has an ironclad termination clause. Even if the case turns out to be a simple baby-sitting job, that's okay with Lucien. He can buy a 450SL with the retainer and have something impressive to drop on April Stewart.

"Can I do the Latin Hustle?"

April Stewart's query is rhetorical. Lucien isn't big on cutting the rug, but it beats talking to the collection of losers sitting at his table. Whenever he comes to Faces, Lucien reserves a booth in the over-crowded room and a crew of men and women vie for the empty seats. If the mix is palatable Lucien doesn't mind buying the champagne. Tonight the first wave of squatters includes Jimmy Leverage and Arlene Galenska. Jimmy is a wholesale gem and drug dealer currently operating out of his tony Oak Street boutique. Arlene is Jimmy's latest assistant manager, sales rep, and coke whore.

"Sometimes I attract these people on account of my work," Lucien says to April once they're bobbing and weaving under multicolored flashing lights to the piped in sounds of the Human League. They look marvelous together, reflected in the mirrored walls surrounding the dance floor, among the tightly packed, well-heeled crowd of double-breasted hipsters and ersatz debutantes.

"That's some dress on her," April replies, referring to Arlene's beaded tubular mini. "Do you enjoy it when women show their business like that?"

"Their business? Are you kidding?"

"Just because I don't use foul language. . . . I've been around."

"This is Chicago," Lucien replies. "The only thing people around here understand about upper crust is on a deep dish pizza."

"Well, at least *you're* not trying to look like fashionable Mafiosi."

"I got the guy out of trouble once. He wants to show his gratitude."

"Are you going to share the vial he gave you?"

"I thought you didn't approve?"

"I don't. I suppose it's a lucky coincidence. I'm not going to be a party pooper."

April Stewart is determined to change her life. That's why she's allowed herself to go out on the town with Lucien. That's why she lobbied to transfer here from Youngstown in the first place. Two and a half years in Arthur & Amberson's satellite office had hammered home to April many quality-of-life differences that never mattered to her before. Despite the privileges afforded her growing up, April had escaped her parents for Ohio State at the first opportunity. While she profoundly misses her three brothers and two sisters—April's five siblings and curly red hair are the result of Irish blood on her mother's side—April's continuing struggle with her uptight parents remains tolerable because of the healthy distance between them.

Maybe that's why she thinks she has insight into Lucien Echo's psyche. If she goes to bed with him tonight, April figures there won't be any commitments. Lucien said as much to her already. On the other hand, during the year she's lived here, April has seldom socialized and made few friends, preferring instead to stay home and practice her music on the piano. April is shy, the insecure youngest child who suffered from everyone's lack of attention and interest in what she did. Considering how infrequently she steps out, April is baffled by the small-world coincidence that befell her earlier this evening. While waiting for Lucien at Butch Maguire's bar, she happened to run into the only other man in town who has caught her attention so far.

April met Ollie Katz this summer at the Old Town Art Fair, when she absent-mindedly walked away from the souvlaki stand without her change and Ollie retrieved it. They merely shared some pleasantries and a walk among the fine art displayed on A-frames along Orleans Street. From time to time, April found herself thinking of Ollie's sense of humor and his eyes. Consequently, at Butch's bar, April recognized Ollie standing with an attractive lady who, it turns out, is his sister Annie. They chatted amiably while April couldn't help feeling Ollie's attention fixed on her.

Lucien arrived and the energy changed. Ollie and Lucien barely spoke to each other. April had to pry from Lucien the fact that he'd known Ollie since college. Suspecting that Lucien might be jealous, April tried to make him feel comfortable with her. Instead Lucien lavished attention upon Annie, inviting Annie and Ollie to join them here at Faces after dinner. When April asked Lucien why he'd changed their original plan to be alone together, Lucien apologized for not consulting her and suggested they cancel by leaving a message at the door. Lucien was so slick about the whole thing, April wound up insisting that they stop here for an hour in case Ollie and Annie showed up. Now she's dancing in Lucien's lair and sniffing cocaine, practically promising to sleep with him.

"There they are," April says, spotting Ollie and Annie wandering through the noisy, crowded room. April points behind Lucien's head and they move back over to their table. When Jimmy and Arlene don't budge, April and Annie must squeeze into the wall side of the booth, leaving Ollie to search for an additional chair. Lucien sits on the outer edge of the group, makes the remaining introductions, and deftly secures the promise of additional champagne glasses from a passing hostess.

"So you live in California?" April asks Annie.

She nods, smiling.

"Which part?"

"California?" Jimmy Leverage cuts in. "I been to California, up in gold country. Grass Valley it's called. Only they wasn't growing that kind of grass, if y'know what I mean."

"We live in Santa Monica," Annie says to April, ignoring the comment. "My husband and I took off together after high school and wandered around most of the warm spots. For now, we've settled in Southern California."

"Annie works in the movies," Ollie interjects, having returned with a chair. "Did you see *Come Back to the Five and Dime, Jimmy Dean, Jimmy Dean*"? Well, my baby sister was the producer."

"Very funny, Ollie," Annie replies. "I was a lowly production assistant. Something my brother loves to make fun of. I don't think Mr. Altman would appreciate sharing the credit."

"You work for *the* Robert Altman?" Arlene Galenska asks. "Julie Christie was too hot in *McCabe and Mrs. Miller*."

"It's not very glamorous learning the business," Annie goes on. "I get lunch a lot. On location I'm the advance interior scout. I talk people into letting the crew destroy their house."

Lucien revels in the unfolding scene. There's nothing like female competition to stimulate the libido. Whereas April and Annie are about the same age, April is fair-skinned, freckle-faced and slender while Annie is dark-haired, meaty, and voluptuous. Lucien already senses that April may be predisposed to brooding. On the other hand, during his brief encounter with Annie at Butch Maguire's, he definitely felt a spark pass between them. Now that he knows Annie is married Lucien wonders where her husband is.

Lucien also can't help wondering how a mope like Oliver Katz could be related to such a fox. In college, while Katz used to refer to his family in those stories he was writing, Lucien doesn't recall hearing about anyone like her. Since Lucien decked Ollie in Burgerville, almost fifteen years ago, they've suffered only two brief and uncomfortable encounters.

At a Bulls game, when they first ran into each other during the halftime social parade under the stadium, Lucien was happy to see him. Ollie was standoffish, pretending he'd forgotten the confrontation. Rather than simply accept Lucien's apology Katz inexplicably started pressing for details of the incident again. Feeling embarrassed and confused, Lucien excused himself from his own social group, leaving Ollie standing there to avoid any further confrontation with him.

Why must things ever come down to cliché? The next time they met Lucien got an earful of Ollie's failed attempts to publish some story about the experiences of a substitute teacher at an inner city high school. It was only a year ago, on St. Patrick's Day, at the Four Farthings, where they bought each other a couple of rounds and Ollie drunkenly romanticized his inveterate writer's life. Alas, according to Katz, anyway, the network had stolen his idea for The White Shadow TV series. And while Ollie maintained a good-natured veil of prosperity concerning his future, Lucien sensed a more urgent financial instability underneath.

Ollie boasted of living over a pizza joint on Clark Street with no savings account or serious plans. Yet he asked Lucien for advice on forming a corporation to do some secret business with the city, and he babbled on about making a killing importing silver jewelry and religious artifacts from northern Thailand. Although Lucien didn't say so, he admired Katz's strength of character despite his lack of business acumen. Ollie had seemingly transcended the need to be accepted. He claimed to be motivated by the process instead of the fame and fortune that could accompany the regular publication of his works.

Such freedom from co-option is merely academic in Lucien's profession. While the concept of jurisprudence remains pure, the art of advocacy, to Lucien, anyway, grows increasingly inconsistent with the practice of law. He has no practice without clients who twist the truth and ignore justice in pursuit of their money and power. Making matters worse, in the eyes of so many clients these days, Lucien is just another business vendor told what the company thinks he needs to know. There really isn't a client anymore, only the company position.

"I can't afford to be a poet," Lucien thinks to himself. It's easy wallowing in obscure seclusion to escape compromise. Lucien's reputation depends upon selecting the proper cases, good packaging on the street, and kissing the right asses at the right time. If Lucien is morally accountable for those things, he wears his whore label in style. But that self-righteous phony, Ollie Katz, has no right lecturing him about artistic integrity while he stares at Lucien's lizard skin cowboy boots and asks how much he paid for his townhouse.

"Annie and I oughta be going," Ollie says over the crowd-chattering din and Thelma Houston wailing, "Baby . . . my heart is full of love and desire for you. Please don't hurt me this way."

Annie wriggles out of the booth with a hand from Lucien. "So early?" he asks her, managing to make eye contact.

"It's late for me," Annie replies. "I'm usually in bed by ten."

"Thanks for your hospitality," Ollie says to Lucien, shaking his hand. After waving at Jimmy and Arlene, Ollie puts his hand down as soon as his eyes reach April across the table.

"What a nice surprise running into you again," April responds, smiling broadly. "If you're in town for a while," she then says to Annie, standing behind her brother, "maybe we'll get together for lunch."

"I'd love it," Annie answers. "So long everybody."

"The way Lucien flirted with you is disgusting," Ollie says to Annie when they're outside in the early December chill. An arctic blast coming off the lake has dumped on Rush Street a sleazy mixture of rain and snow. Traffic is snarled amidst bright neon signs and the Christmas lights decorating the way. The clubs and restaurants along State Street are emptying as the two of them tread on the icy pavement toward Ollie's car. "He was rude to April," Ollie adds.

"I think he's handsome. You're jealous because I got more attention than you."

"Yeah." Ollie says. "What was that lunch bit, anyway?"

"Sometimes you are dumb, big brother. It's not me she wants to see again."

"April was nice to me because that jerk was coming on to you. You'll never hear from her again unless you call her."

"Why are you so negative?" Annie chides him. She's on the passenger side of Ollie's car while he attempts to unlock the driver's side door. The lock is frozen. Ollie eventually heats it with a plastic cigarette lighter retrieved from Annie's purse.

"I'm not being negative," Ollie finally replies when they're creeping along in a single lane of traffic, plowing through the cover of new snow on the street. "Don't forget why you're here," Ollie goes on. "Mom is in the hospital dying. You shouldn't be out flirting with another woman's date because Ray isn't around. Shit! I really burned my thumb."

"What a hypocrite! You're the one who dragged me down here in the first place."

"That hospital was so depressing. It's no wonder people go in there and don't come out again. . . . The doctor said it could be hereditary. D'ya think we ought to get brain scans to be safe? I mean, I never said anything about it but, sometimes, I get this numbness in the fingers of my left hand. Other times my left leg throbs for no discernible reason."

"Poor Daddy. He looks so afraid to be left alone."

"He won't be alone. Michael's there and I'll be better about going out."

"To lose your partner after all those years of depending on each other . . . must be like cutting off an arm, or worse. Makes you wonder whether it's worth getting that attached to anyone."

"Stop talking about her in the past tense, fer Chrissakes! It's a tumor. Sometimes they shrink as quickly as they came. Maybe that radiation thing will work."

"Relationship is a fragile flower," Annie says, seemingly about their parents; on the other hand, though, maybe not.

Ollie doesn't respond until they're lumbering along the Edens Expressway toward Morton Grove. "One wrong word ends the love affair of the century," he says as they pass a salt truck, its spray of slush buffeting the car. "I suspect that our reward must exist in the doing. Y'know? Unconditional love stuff. That's why I expect a shitty deal and I'm never disappointed."

"You don't really think I'd cheat on Ray? Do ya?"

* * *

"She's married," Lucien whispers playfully into April's ear, while they relax in the plush cushions of his leather sectional couch. Disheveled and mildly sweaty, they're advancing beyond the petting that commenced after they hit the front door to his townhouse. "You've nothing to be jealous about," Lucien adds, running his lips down the side of her neck and across her shoulder. "You have the greatest ass I've ever seen."

"Oh yeah?" April shivers at the heat of his breath on her body. She turns to him in the dim light exposing her breasts from beneath the undone folds of her blousy Halston dress. "Is that my best part? `Cause I don't mind if you're attracted to her," April says, brushing her hand over his open zipper. "She's beautiful. Hell, I'm attracted to her. . . . That's a joke," she adds, seeing his reaction. "I know what you want, you pervert," April goes on, now resting her hand on his swollen penis. "You'd like both of us together, wouldn't you?"

"I want to make love to you. That's for sure. Are you trying to find out whether I'm monogamous?"

"Easy does it," April says, sitting up and sniffing another line of cocaine off the glass cube coffee table. Wall-to-wall carpeting and a mountain of electronic entertainment equipment complement the living room pit arrangement. "I'm horny," she goes on. "I haven't had sex in a year. So don't worry. My interest is purely hedonistic."

Lucien takes April by the hand, helping her step out of her dress, and he leads her to the carpeted staircase. Following her up to his bedroom, he watches thigh curves meeting buttocks beneath her brief panties. Lucien's thinking about the other times he's taken this walk with other women in circumstances that make his head spin. Oh yeah, he'd hesitate if they couldn't make it up the stairs under their own power. Then they got dunked in the hot tub for a spell. If that didn't work he'd drive them home, cruise the bars, and pick up a hooker.

If Lucien now begins to massage April's damp crotch, which she's revealing to him from her reclining position on the bed, he'll wind up making love with her all night. Tomorrow he'll take her home and, he figures, probably never see her again. As soon as Lucien gives her everything she claims to want tonight, she'll have nothing more to do with him. He'll no longer be the type of guy with whom she'd have a relationship.

"Oh, Lucien, yes. . . . Right there. . . . Yes. . . . Oh, yes," April moans, grinding her glistening hips under his probing tongue.

For in the end Lucien decides to thrust it into the fray, so to speak, despite the odds against tasting the nectar again. It's not a question of morality. Mutual gratification without recourse is all he can muster these days, anyway. Lucien's mind is cluttered with Writs of Mandamus, the likes of Abel Bradley and Gordon Traeger. Assignments are waiting to be handed out, options need to be exercised, and appointments are already in place for many months to come. He's a barrister, a modern day Palladin, paid to flap his jaws for the highest bidder.

"You're a thoughtful lover," April declares, after they've finished and they lie back relaxing, side by side, underneath a tangled corner of his thick tartan comforter. "I must've come three times," she says, sitting up and twirling her finger in the hairs on his chest.

Sometimes April amazes herself. She can structure a tax- free municipal offering that has the S.E.C. eating out of her hands and she knows that Ron Guidry won the Cy Young Award four years ago. Yet, she couldn't avoid having meaningless sex with this man. In light of her long dry spell April tells herself that she's overreacting. But giving in to temptation because it's acceptable these days is hardly an excuse.

"Where are you going?" Lucien asks, watching her gather her clothes off the carpet and pad toward the bathroom.

"I didn't leave any food for my cat and . . . Anyway, I have an early day tomorrow."

"Okay. I'll take you home whenever you want."

"You stay right where you are. You earned it. Really, it's fine. . . . I'd prefer to take a cab," April says, sounding a bit more final than she intended.

Weakness of the soul, that's what her mother would call this. Whatever it is, April intuits that she must get away from here. She desperately needs the warmth of her flannel pajamas and her own bed, nestled under the covers with Anne Beattie, or John Irving, and a quart of rocky road ice cream. If today was indeed the first day of the rest of her life, there is nowhere else to go.

"You're so vain. . . . You probably think this song is about Chuuu!" Ring croons loudly enough for Ollie to hear from the adjacent shower stall in the men's locker room. Jerry Bell is the sole Phi Pho brother with whom Ollie maintains regular contact, and during the winter months they play tennis indoors at Ring's health club.

After Jerry took an extra semester to earn his bachelor's degree, he hung around Madison through the summer. Ring abandoned any hope of pressing on to graduate school at about the same time that he decided clown school wasn't really for him either. He returned to Chicago and tried to make a go of it in his father's chain of discount drugstores. Five years, two wives, and two kids later, he begged Daddy Bell to buy him a seat on the Board of Trade.

Ring has always gambled on just about anything, and he never worries over money. Consequently, he's been thriving on the options floor ever since, where his motormouth delivery and ceaseless energy are perfectly suited for the daily madhouse in The Pit.

Ring was such a screw-off in college. When his first marriage failed and he announced his plan to go "long in bellies and short on beans," Ollie thought it would become a self-fulfilling prophecy. Now Ollie is stunned by the ease with which Jerry continues to succeed under such pressure. Every weekday morning Ring hits LaSalle Street ahead of the sun. Following several cups of coffee and a jelly dough-nut sugar rush, he's on hyperactive overload, the condition required to complete his trades by noon. Ring takes his midday meal consisting of a polish sausage with mustard, relish, pickle, and fries at Irving's on Wells Street. With half a quaalude and a diet Coke to wash it down, he's back on earth in plenty of time to count his chips, check his orders, and plan tomorrow's attack before the closing bell sounds.

Then it's a short drive here for a workout, or a ten-nis match and a schvitz, where Ollie just nearly skunked him in the second set. Ring blames his loss on some attrac-tive redhead who slinked off a nearby court and spoke to Ollie between games. She stuck around to watch them vol-ley and Ollie played way over his head. Now that Ollie is being less than forthcoming about this wench, for whom he obviously possesses the hots, Ring is compelled to sing that Carly Simon song into his ear until he cracks.

"I told you all I know about her," Ollie says when they're standing in the locker room alcove before a row of marble sinks brushing their hair in the three-cornered mir-ror. The counter is covered with the club's favorite brand of sundries, blow-dryer contraptions, and those sanitized combs swimming in the ubiquitous blue jar.

"So what if your sister wouldn't call her? You should've called. I would've."

"That's not my style."

"Oh, yeah, I forgot. You get 'em by osmosis."

Ring's reply hangs in the sweet, sweaty air as they amble out of the locker room toward the main lounge inside this converted brick and steel warehouse complex.

"How's your hot little spinner—I mean, sister—anyway?" Ring presses him sarcastically. "Too bad she moved away when she did. 'Cause, I remember, that summer after she graduated high school and hung out with us there was chemistry."

"I'm sorry to have to tell you this but Annie wouldn't fuck you with my dick," Ollie says when they're sitting in the club restaurant on the second floor and he's examining those little red hearts on the healthy choice menu. The dining room is situated on a carpeted pod without walls in the center of the running track, which circles the tennis courts below.

"No . . . wait," Ollie corrects himself. "That's not what I meant. I'm certain Annie doesn't think about you at all. But if she does, I'm sure she thinks you're a putz."

"You probably won't believe it," Ring replies, bushy eyebrows scrunching his dark little eyes into a serious stare. "These days, with everybody running around shtupping each other, I'm glad to be married again. I know you think I'm narrow-minded and petty because I make a lot of money and don't give a shit about world peace or anything more stimulating than the Bears. I happen to accept my limitations. Don't put me down for it."

"I'm sorry, Ring. You're doing what you want with your life."

"You know what your problem is, Ollie? When you quit law school and ran off to Morocco, or wherever the fuck-else you went, you came back a different person. You began attaching moral significance to your anti-establishment stance, thinking you were some neo-Bohemian stud hanging around Bughouse Square, writing poetry, and smoking a goddamn pipe. Remember? . . . That shit is fun when you're twenty-two and looking for a way to avoid the cold reality of supporting yourself."

"Is this your way of saying you're not interested in my idea for the driving range island in the lake? Hey, Ring, I understand."

"I'm saying that you still regard success in any form as corrupt. You're either too lazy or too afraid to commit to a profession. What's worse, you look down on all of us sell-outs who have the nerve to enjoy the fruits of our compromise."

"A poverty snob? I don't think so," Ollie responds. "I'm not too proud to beg. Hell, I'll let you get the check if it'll make you feel better. I'm not very good at taking orders. That's all. That's why the driving range is a perfect deal for me. Only three years remain on the existing lease and it already makes enough to pay for the expansion down to the sea wall within a year. All we need is the astro turf, the wire meshing, and the pontoons. I'm tellin' ya, sixty thousand is a steal."

"Why will the city go along with this?"

Ring asks the question halfheartedly, keeping an eye on the TV set mounted above the juice bar. Johnny Morris is reporting on the health of John Riggins for the Super Bowl game with Miami in four days. Ring has a "dime" on the Redskins, but neither one looks like a champion after the strike. Ring figures that the Dolphins' rushing defense is suspect, so Riggins should be able to run wild.

"The property extends down to the lakefront," Ollie goes on. "I've been told that if we meet certain restrictions under the lease, the city will approve exclusive use up to five hundred yards out into the water. We can put the floating green two hundred thirty yards away and, even with twenty-five tees operating all day long, nobody is ever gonna get a hole in one."

"You're nuts, Ollie. Y'know that? You can't just give a Cadillac away every time somebody hits a lucky drive."

"All right, make it a 320i. Who cares, anyway? Don't ya' see what I'm talking about? You publicize the hell out of it now, in the dead of winter, and when summer comes we've got a hit on our hands. By this time next year we're franchising the idea to every resort in the country with a stretch of beach or a lakefront. Ollie's Tropical Island Driving Range can be easily installed anywhere in the world."

"I dunno, Ollie. I got this court thing to think about. I'll have to get back to. . . . Hello? Is that your mysterious babe coming out of the locker room? Don't turn around she's coming this way."

"Like I said, maybe you should call Lucien for advice."

"I'll see," Ring replies; he isn't thrilled to share with anyone else the embarrassing details surrounding his recent arrest for driving while intoxicated. "Lucien and I never had much to do with each other," Ring says instead. "He's probably too expensive these days. . . . Hi there," he goes on, standing to greet April as she reaches the table. "My name's Jerry."

"Nice to meet you, Jerry."

"Would you like to join us?" Ollie asks, having turned around at the touch of her finger on his shoulder.

"Well, I was just . . . Sure."

Ollie inhales the scent of April's freshly washed hair as he gestures to the chair nearest him. April smiles at him, capturing his soul in her eyes. While Ring regards them both with a mixture of amusement and nostalgia, April focuses on the broiled chicken breast sandwich that the waiter had served to Ollie only moments before she arrived.

"Take some," Ollie says to her. "It's pretty good."

"There's mayonnaise in that dressing. I better not," April replies, putting down the fork she had instinctively raised from the place setting in front of her.

She's hungry, all right. But now is not the time to gorge herself or reveal any specifics about her latest purging incident. Today April has fallen off the wagon for the umpteenth time this young year. She hasn't been on the wagon since New Year's Eve. Oh, April's been good lately, in Chicago, anyway, compared to some of her other relapses over the years. At first she was positively stimulated by the big city excitement and her new professional responsibilities. Simply stated, that was a trick. April learned long ago to transfer schools or take off on extended holidays whenever her self-destructive compulsions surfaced. During this recent stretch April fed off her honeymoon period at the office, gathering enough courage to attend the company Christmas party.

Maybe it's boredom from the routine that's creeping back into her life. Nevertheless, that clawing sensation in her stomach returned, like she was jumping out of her skin, and she's fallen into the old patterns. Feeling trapped and unable to enjoy any aspect of her life, April needs to push herself beyond her present state. So she eats in order to feel better. Instead she feels fat and that makes her feel worse. Then she throws up in order to feel skinny, and she's hungry all over again. The current cycle happened to begin on New Year's Eve, a few hours before Lucien Echo came to collect her for their date.

April knew something was up at lunchtime, as she'd craved an oatmeal raisin cookie. By the time she came home from work her mind was racing everywhere. Then she broke into tears. But while she was trying on her backless velvet evening dress, wondering whether she'd make it till they dropped that stupid ball in New York City, she realized that she'd guzzled nearly an entire container of chocolate chip cookie dough. April gave in with hardly a whimper, though she'd been dry, pardon the pun, for a year. Within minutes, however, she was elated, an enormous weight having been lifted from her shoulders. Lucien arrived in his tuxedo, looking like James Bond, and together they wowed them at the Traegers' sit-down dinner for eighteen in their Streeterville pied-a-terre.

Among the stuffy crowd of jeweled professionals and their pouffed-out society wives, April and Lucien were the youngest couple. They sat at a grand table covered with fine crystal and china, silver-flocked candlesticks in fresh flower centerpieces, golden-flecked, party top hats and elaborate noisemakers. They ate caviar and squab, drank Dom Perignon and stood outside on the terrace in the freezing cold listening to the whoops and hollers and the firecrackers exploding at midnight. Following a late night snack on Rush Street, where they gaped at all the post-party crazies parading around, they had hot sex on all three levels of Lucien's townhouse. April went home the next afternoon and—just like that—they've been avoiding each other for the past three weeks.

April can't bring herself to believe that Lucien is capable of loving her unconditionally. And she can't deal with that. Not with the trouble she's having believing in herself. April Stewart isn't ready for a mate. At her recent annual review she was commended by the Executive Committee and given a sizable raise. But she was informed that it would be four more years, at least, before she'd be considered for partner. Things were bad enough in Youngstown, where the hicks pretended to be sophisticated. Here she's a "chick" and the competition is overtly sexual. Today, in fact, April was playing ball with Chuckie Dodman, the freshly divorced senior partner above her. That's when she first spotted Ollie, two courts over, in his cute little tennis shorts.

Now April's pretty sure that Ollie's interested, as she sits next to him on her living room couch studying his concerned brown eyes. After they spent an hour talking in the health club restaurant, punctuated by a Caesar salad and Ring's dirty jokes, Ollie offered to drive April home and he wound up stopping in for a nightcap.

"Beowulf," Ollie says, seemingly out of nowhere.

"What in the world does Beowulf have to do with your favorite song?"

"Beowulf? . . . Did I say Beowulf?"

"I asked what your favorite song is and you said Beowulf."

"I meant Steppenwolf," Ollie corrects himself. "My song is 'Born to be Wild.' Yesterday, on 'Jeopardy,' I learned *Beowulf* is the earliest known piece of modern writing translated into Old English. Like the Rosetta Stone. I have no idea why I said that instead. I'm distracted by your beauty."

"I see," April replies. She leans back into a puffy cushion on her white sofa and plops her stockinged feet onto the coffee table. "You're trying to forfeit those points you got for honesty a minute ago."

April's ninth floor condo is a pristine one-bedroom box of modern amenities including beige shag carpeting and floor-to-ceiling windows overlooking The Farm in Lincoln Park Zoo and Lake Michigan beyond. The sub-zero air temperature condenses on the glass obscuring the view tonight.

"What's wrong with flattering you? If I didn't mean it I wouldn't have said it."

"Well, as long as you meant it," April says, trying not to blush.

"I am distracted," Ollie goes on, deciding to confide in her. "My mother's in the hospital, dying. She has inoperable brain cancer and every day they have to drain fluid that builds up inside her head. Some days, usually in the mornings, she's lucid and we can talk. Other times she's barely awake and seems to drift in and out of consciousness. The doctors say there's no hope; that she can go at any time. I guess she's not dying fast enough for them because the hospital has been putting pressure on us to make her bed available."

"How awful."

"The other night we were together—my father and my brother and my sister—and we wound up discussing the doctor's suggestion that we take her off the respirator. Everyone agreed we should try to speak with my mother and see what she thinks of the idea. My father, who is normally not an emotional guy, was too devastated to talk about it with her. And, for reasons that remain unclear to me, I was selected.

"So it's early yesterday morning, one of those times when my mother recognizes me, and she presses my hand gently with her skeleton grip extending out from under the sheets. After fumbling around for the right words, I ask her if she's thought about the possibility of not getting any better. My mother looks at me and says, 'I see him over there at the foot of the bed.' . . . 'Who do you see?' I ask. 'Who's over there at the foot of the bed?' . . . 'The Angel of Death,' she replies with absolute clarity. 'He only comes when I call him.'"

April doesn't know how to respond. She can't understand what Ollie must be going through. Nobody close to her has died, excepting one of her grandparents, and then she was too young to feel Ollie's innermost kind of sorrow. How beautifully sad, April thinks.

By the time he rises from the couch to go home their chemistry is percolating. Ollie's managed to turn her on by spilling his guts. He takes April's hand when she delivers his coat from the hall closet and she lingers over the softness of his touch. April thinks about reading his palm and searching his eyes for the ever-elusive, deeper understanding. Their attraction is strong despite their excuses. When they kiss it is warm, moist, and deep; their separate longing runs together like a river dam bursting in the moment's desire.

For the next five weeks, anyway, they seem to be building their own bridge of pleasant bewilderment, helping stave off the cold, damp bowels of February. In between vigils at the hospital, and tending bar three nights a week, Ollie practically moves into April's high-rise. They discuss how macabre it must appear that their relationship is happening at a time like this. Ollie's sadness is subsumed in April's attention, which allows him to accept the inevitable without some grand plan. So much so, in fact, in the hallway outside the ICU one evening, Annie is moved to remark that Ollie's peculiar behavior points to a state of denial.

On Sunday morning, their sixth weekend together, there's a break in the weather. They wake up in April's queen-sized bed, which is also inhabited by fuzzy, nattily dressed stuffed creatures. A moment of mutual uncertainty evaporates in a reassuring kiss, as the scent of their naked bodies mingles under the down comforter. April tosses off the covers and bounds out of the room to the front door.

She retrieves the Sunday *Tribune* from the hallway, tosses it onto the bed, and modestly sidesteps into the kitchen area. Soon the sound of dripping coffee brings Ollie out of a daydream in which they are lying in the hot sun, side by side, on a large redwood deck overlooking the Pacific Ocean.

"The sun is blazing," April says, as Ollie realizes that it's pouring in on him through the open blinds. April is showered and rosy-cheeked in a silk dressing gown and towel turban wrapped around her hair. "People are walking around in shirt sleeves."

"What if I take you out for brunch?"

"You sweet man," April replies, coming over to the bed and kissing him on the mouth. "You can tell a lot about a person from their skin. You, for example, your skin smells fresh and pure. I love the smell of your skin. It's so smooth. . . . Almost virtuous," she goes on, now nibbling on his bare shoulder.

"Stop that," Ollie responds playfully, as he gets up shivering. "Maybe it's a subconscious fear of intimacy," he quips, walking into the bathroom.

* * *

"Your subconscious fear of intimacy?" April repeats his remark later when they're sitting in a booth at the Belden and she is sufficiently stuffed with Nova Scotia lox and cream cheese on wheat toast. "I asked what you meant when you said that before."

Although the comment had bugged her, April didn't intend to bring it up. Then Ollie wanted to come here again. She doesn't mind a delicatessen, except it's his neighborhood hangout and the same crowd shows up on Sunday morning to see who spent Saturday night sleeping with whom.

"I suppose I was only half-kidding," Ollie admits.

"Now we're getting somewhere," April says, leaning back in the Naugahyde booth and looking around the noisy dining room, smelling of fried onions and feta cheese. Fluorescent ceiling lights reflect off the booths covered with pink and blue neon upholstery, and April swears she can see particles of chicken fat glistening on the walls. "Pardon me for saying this," April goes on. "Please don't allow the pressure you put on yourself to make you neurotic. The other night it bothered me to hear you say you have too many choices without an honest-to-God belief the world will be a better place no matter what you do. They're all just missed opportunities unless you do something."

"Some risks are better not taken. I'm holding out for something I can lose myself in."

"You could make a difference."

"Is this the boyfriend test? If it is, let me say up front that when the moment of truth comes I'll be ready. It's a no-brainer, my dedication to truth, justice, and the American way. Is that the difference you mean? `Cause no matter which way it goes, after the dust settles, what's left is a miserable little life of integrity with the same unanswered questions."

"You're just lazy," April responds after some reflection. She has a way of distilling the most complex issue down to whichever one of the Seven Deadly Sins happens to pop into her mind at the time. Things in her life are rarely more complicated than that: sloth, pride, lust, anger, gluttony, envy, and covetousness. The basic temptations are readily available and not altogether unknown to her whenever April flirts in the path of spiritual demise. Nevertheless, she's firm to demand from her partner the kind of honesty that stands the test of time. April ponders this anomaly while she stares longingly at the remains of Ollie's salami omelet. "Are you going to finish those fries?"

"We're talking about an on-going inventory shortage," Lucien says to April over the telephone. "The amount is significant, yet Arthur & Amberson failed to recognize it."

It's office-to-office and Lucien's tone sets off alarm bells in April's head.

"Your firm prepared Sol Fazil's financials for two of those years," Lucien goes on matter-of-factly. "You should have known from the sales figures that his inventory was grossly overstated by enough to trigger this audit in the first place."

April is skeptical, to say the least. Being on the receiving end of Lucien's legal opinion that her firm was negligent is tough enough to swallow. For him to imply, rather smugly, that they *conspired* in Sol Fazil's tax fraud is way too cold. "You don't really think," April calls him out, "that the IRS is going to let you blame this on us?"

"Let's say, they're interested in my proposal if it ends the matter for all parties."

"How could anyone here possibly have known that Mr. Fazil was unloading his merchandise off premises and not reporting the cash?"

"You're so right," Lucien responds, leaning back in his executive recliner and propping his polished Italian wingtips atop the clutter of papers strewn about his desk. Lucien loves the thrill of commerce and his power to influence another person's destiny. Lucien especially enjoys the sexually charged atmosphere that April's creating with her competitive response to his assault.

"If the Service doesn't care where the missing income went," Lucien goes on, "why should you? The government's willing to treat this as a civil case with interest and penalties. Sol's willing to release your bosses from liability for professional negligence if they pay the tab."

"Fuck you, Lucien!" April's voice rises on the second syllable of her outburst. "You're not talking to one of your criminals. My firm will insist on disclosing Fazil's scam and I resent the idea that you think you can use our friendship to pander this proposal."

"You're so right." Lucien replies, repeating "the mantra that made Milwaukee famous," as Gordon Traeger used to say. In those salad days Lucien would dutifully meet Gordon at Mayor's Row to digest pending matters and an afternoon shot. "During negotiations, agree with them whenever they go off on personal shit," Gordon preached. "They'll have to give up the next relevant thing you ask for." Over the years it hasn't made any difference to Lucien whether *they* were women or opposing counsel. It works just the same.

"Look April, if you press this, maybe you can refer Fazil toward highway roadwork. Big 8 firms didn't get big by turning in their clients. Don't believe for a second that your executive committee won't submit Sol's claim to your firm's own carrier. I appreciate your integrity. But they'll pay the claim to avoid the litigation and the partners will approve the settlement to avoid testifying before a grand jury."

Although furious at his condescension, April is confused by Lucien's trust in the lurid scenario that apparently awaits her. She's never faced an attack on her professional judgment before, let alone such a tawdry charade delivered by a man whose cock she has sucked with a clear conscience. "If you're so sure of yourself," April hears herself respond, "Why didn't you bring this to Tad Jalenko instead of involving me any further?"

"I'm sorry to offend you. I thought you'd understand this has nothing to do with us. If that's what you want . . ."

"I'll discuss it with him," April interrupts. In an attempt to regain her composure she looks up from her desk through the open doorway of her tiny office. Her secretary's humming electric typewriter obliges April to react professionally, while she struggles to free herself of him.

"Are you sure?" Lucien persists. "I'll give up the case if that's what you want. Can we talk about it tomorrow evening? I'll pick you up after work and we'll go to Yvette's for a drink."

"Impossible," April responds, not wanting to tell him about Ollie. Not now, when she's suspicious of anything Lucien says. "I'll need a few days to check this out and get back to you. It's better this way."

What a load of horseshit that was, Lucien thinks, as he disconnects the line and punches Robin's number on the intercom. "Tell Novitzky to come in here," Lucien says. "See if you can find the telephone number for Mister Benjamin Katz in Morton Grove," he adds, glancing at the obituary notice that he's been saving for several days now. "It's K - A - T- Z . . . No, I don't know the address. Try information," he barks, replacing the receiver.

Lucien gets up from his desk, walks to the door, and locks it. From inside the hollowed-out base of a metal sculpture on the credenza he retrieves his emergency vial and neatly doles out two lines onto the edge of his Plexiglas desk blotter. If April's fucking some other guy, Lucien wonders, why doesn't she admit it? "It doesn't matter to me," he reflects, inhaling one line through the sawed-off Mc Donald's straw he keeps in his desk drawer.

After replacing his stash and unlocking the door, Lucien barely has time to Hoover the other queue before Gail Novitsky knocks once, opens the door a crack, and peeks her head into the room. Having left the public defender's office five months ago, Gail walks tentatively to the padded straight-backed chairs facing Lucien's desk. Not that Gail hasn't already tried some tough cases on her own. But from what she's seen of Lucien so far, he's given to moods, subtle sexual references, and uncanny judgment predicting human behavior. Every judge and lawyer she's run into, who finds out that she's working for Lucien, speaks admiringly of his skill. Seeing as Lucien's paying her salary, benefits, and a third of the business she brings in, Gail is determined to mind her manners like a pliant sponge.

"Tell me again," Lucien asks, motioning Gail to sit in the nearest chair, "Why can't we force Treager's partners to dissolve the firm and auction off the clients like any other asset?"

It's no surprise to Gail that Lucien wants to discuss Gordon Treager's alleged damages again. He's been bugging her every day for a week since Gail gave him her draft complaint seeking an injunction against Traeger's law firm. Lucien refuses to accept that Gordon's contract unequivocally grants the remaining partners exclusive rights to buy out the interest of a partner who leaves for any reason. Now Gail's patience has worn thin and, despite Lucien's superior experience in these matters, she can't help wondering about his motives.

"I know you don't want to litigate a frivolous claim," Gail responds, uncomfortably twisting her body in the chair. "If you subpoena their client files, they'll counterclaim for Intentional Interference and come after Gordon for Malicious Prosecution when it's over."

"Don't get hysterical," Lucien says, shuffling through some xeroxed pages Gordon supplied, listing his firm's cases and their projected revenue. Traeger made it clear that he's unconcerned about the money at stake. He's convinced that the surreptitious manner by which his partners assumed control has caused the diabetes to infect his liver. These same men who Gordon trained and took into battle with him over the past thirty years have assembled a dossier of transgressions and personal butt-saving excuses with which they are formulating his ruin, piece by piece, unless he thankfully exits on his knees.

Now Lucien's trying to teach his own protégé that the way to deal with O'Connor, Traeger & Hays is to threaten a public fight for their clients. Ethical potholes, embarrassment over invading the privacy rights of important executives—not to mention scrutiny of the firm's billing practices—are worth millions more than what they're offering under the buy-out formula in his contract.

"They can't stop the clients from leaving," Lucien insists, getting up from the desk and walking to the paneled closet in the corner of his office. "Once they discover they're getting ripped off by the firm they'll go with Gordon," he continues, unzipping his pants and tucking in his shirt without turning away.

Gail Novitzky knows when she's being dismissed out of hand. Still, what she doesn't understand would fill those oversized C cups she's worn since law school. Ample evidence exists of Gordon Traeger's present unfitness to practice law and Lucien wants to set him up in a new office. "Heap on those legal fees," Gail says, sotto voce; and "God Bless pre-trial discovery." That's the dominant theme of the litigation cases she's working on. She watches Lucien put on his gray wool suit jacket and straighten his tie in the mirror on the back of the closet door. "How long will I be able do this?" Gail Novitzky wonders softly, removing her tortoise-shell-framed bifocals and squeezing the bridge of her freckled nose.

"Stop muttering to yourself," Lucien says, and he exits with a phony smile of encouragement and a wave. It's Thursday afternoon and he's ready for the long weekend search to satisfy his decadent cravings. What remains of Lucien's conscience cries out to take responsibility for unleashing evil forces into the world. But Lucien is only one man and most people think the Constitution is just a piece of paper, anyway. So he drowns his desire to do good work in a sea of underworld friends and seedy sexual adventures.

"Frivolous claims my ass!" Lucien still stews when he crosses the LaSalle Street drawbridge above the icy, dark green river, cruising in his new XJ6—he found the 450SL ostentatious. Miguel is waiting at the cafe with an eighth, but Annie Katz returned Lucien's call and agreed to meet for a drink. Dinner was also possible. Annie said that they buried her mother yesterday and, while she didn't know whether she could taste food right now, she needed to get out of the house. How considerate of him to call, she said. Why don't they meet at that new diner near Ontario Street?

Lucien pulls into the parking lot and hands the keys to a baby-faced carhop wearing a satin club jacket and one of those soda-jerk hats. Fifties' nostalgia for people who weren't even there? Every decade we run out of ideas so we repeat ourselves, Lucien laments, unable to suppress the sarcasm as he negotiates a maze of flashy retro counter-tops, vinyl and chrome-covered booths and barstools. "She Wore Tan Shoes and Pink Shoelaces" blasts from the overhead speakers. Warehouse windows cast an eerie glow in the twilight and Lucien spots Annie waiting at the counter, toward the rear of the vast, loud room. She's dressed in jeans and a heavy ski sweater, while her radiant eyes fix upon Lucien curiously.

"I wasn't sure you'd recognize me," Lucien says, observing that Annie's skin is pale; she's thinner and more fragile than he remembers.

"How many men can make a pass in front of their girlfriend and get away with it?"

"April's not my girlfriend."

"My brother will be glad to know that," Annie says, managing to be direct.

"April's a wonderful girl. We aren't on the same page. Ollie should go for it."

"I think he's on the case," Annie replies, gulping down the glass of beer she was nursing when he arrived.

"I didn't call you to discuss your brother's love life."

"I know." Annie considers playing along but she's in no mood for bullshit. "You want to comfort me in my grief," she blurts out instead. "To offer your condolences and help me understand God's will. Never sick a day in her life. How can she just . . . disappear?" Her eyes water over as she catches her breath. "I'm sorry. I can't express myself in front of my father or my brothers."

"What do men know, anyway?"

"Please order me another beer," Annie says, "I'll go put on my stolid Midwestern face."

Lucien Echo doesn't often think about dying. He's convinced that when his time is up, it's up. He'd rather have a tombful of exciting stories keeping him company for eternity than some whiny remembrances from a life spent in terror of today. According to Lucien, the great truth about death is that it's something you can't know until it happens.

Uh oh! That's how it starts, Lucien now reflects, as he watches Annie expertly pull her father's Chrysler into the cramped extra space in his townhouse garage. Could this woman get to him? Pepper a spirited discussion with sadness and susceptibility, add poignant personal insights, a dollop of sensitivity, and Annie agreed to follow him home. Lucien also spent considerable time listening to her problems. It seems that things come down to Annie's worthless husband, Ray, who's jealous of her modest success, while he can't get arrested. Lucien speculates that Ray can't get a hard-on either, because Annie has the look of someone who hasn't come in a long time.

Annie Katz-Arness glances around Lucien's romantically lit living room; she wonders how many other women have stood here wondering the same thing. Annie is depressed and feeling like she might as well be boxed in formaldehyde too. Despite the welcome distance from her husband, Annie's dreams of freedom are proving better than the event. She's horny and itching to succumb to the stress. Though she knows it's wrong to think about herself at a time like this, being back in Chicago with her family has served to bring up these emotions again. Annie senses that she's failing miserably at her marriage and she longs to do something definitive.

Her gloom is overripe. From the beginning, Ray's self-hatred has remained unchecked to the point where Annie's convinced that her husband is star-crossed. They were so young when they took off together. Annie has stuck it out thinking that Ray will grow up one day. Now Ray's fate seems a spreading stain that threatens everything else in her near perfect life. Maybe it's not such a big deal.

But in three weeks they'll be at the Oscars, invited by one of the producers of *Tootsie*, and Ray will get drunk, feign some illness, or find some other way to destroy the evening. Annie never thought she would think such a thing, yet she's begun looking for ways to avoid going home when Ray is around.

"Who could fault me for my weakened state?" Annie asks Lucien, half-kidding, while she relaxes on his cushioned recliner.

"Once in seven years is a pretty good record," Lucien counters, bringing over two glasses of scotch. He sits down on the edge of the glass cube between her chair and the leather sectional. "If you avoid penetration," he adds, handing Annie a drink, "Technically, it's not cheating."

"You and my brother have more in common than either of you would admit."

"I'll bet Ollie's seen you naked."

"On the way over here I thought about you and me," Annie replies, taking a good-sized swig. "You're desirable and, God knows, I've been looking for an excuse. But I dunno, it does almost seem incestuous. I know this sounds ridiculous."

"I don't think I've heard that one before." Lucien walks over to the high tech turntable in the middle of his wall of audio-video equipment and flips over the record. "I'll try to control myself. You must tell me all about your fascinating life."

"After my dead mother and my shitty marriage, what else can I tell you? Anyway, you're the celebrity. Didn't I see your picture the other day in the *Sun Times*?

Posing on the golf course with some big shot county commissioners?"

Lucien can't remember when he's had a lousier day woman-wise. First it was April slamming his professional ethics. Then it was Novitsky and her implications about his predatory nature. Now Annie exposed his egocentric lust for fame. Lucien won't deny taking pleasure in being recognized. He still gets a kick from replaying those television interviews, back in December, when Abel Bradley's murder case was dismissed. Live segments on the networks covered the third burglar's dramatic surrender to Jim Dudgeon. People called for days with praise and new cases they hoped Lucien would look into. Why shouldn't Lucien get off on what he does? His trials and tribulations make up the fabric of society. It's no surprise Lucien's rush is intensified when people pay attention.

"You really are beautiful," he says to Annie. "Too bad you're spoken for."

"You're full of it like my brother," she replies, relieved the sexual tension between them has passed.

It's midnight when Annie shuts off their discussion. Tonight her cheating heart remains unsatisfied while her head is pounding from Lucien's intensity and Dewars White Label. Despite two cups of coffee, Annie decides to stay at Ollie's rather than drive back to Morton Grove. She's feeling sweaty with self-examination and surprisingly resolute about finding some new common ground with Ray. She's managed to gain some personal insight from her exchange with Lucien. If, God forbid, she ever found herself in trouble, Lucien Echo is the first person she'd call.

"I've been driving around for forty minutes looking for a parking space," Annie says to Ollie, who waits for her at the top of the stairs leading to his studio apartment. The odor of bread dough, garlic, and tomato sauce fills the tiny hallway as Annie climbs to the second floor landing.

"You called an hour ago. That must've been some goodnight kiss."

"Why're you home, anyway?" Annie asks, pecking him on the cheek. They traverse Ollie's long narrow hallway and enter his sparsely furnished living space. Visible through the lone window is the blinking neon "Always Open" sign across Clark Street. "I thought you were going to leave the key and stay at April's."

"So did I. Well, what did the great Lucien Echo want?"

"Why do you dislike him? He's interesting and incredibly perceptive. I learned something about myself that . . . Anyway, I think I want to have a child."

"With Lucien Echo?"

"With Ray, dummy."

"Since you got here you've been talking divorce. One night with Lucien and you want to save your marriage by having children?"

"How's Dad doing?" Annie changes the subject while she inspects the flannel pajamas Ollie produces for her from his dresser. She doesn't mind facing his question; Annie didn't say she wanted a baby to save her marriage. She's going to do her best to make things work, all right. Fatherhood might cause Ray to feel needed and self-important. Ray hasn't had adult responsibilities before so there's no telling what effect parenthood will have on him. But she doesn't want to do this for them. Annie wants to mother a child. She wants to challenge herself through innocent eyes and, in some small, positive way, extend her grasp on the world.

"When I called the house at eight-thirty, Aunt Sally was still there," Ollie says. "Dad was blubbering. He was so drunk Michael had to take the phone away from him. It's Dad's lone Catholic trait; he's using the wake to stay drunk because he knows he can get away with it. D'ya believe everybody encourages him? Mom's not cold yet and Aunt Sally's already moving in."

"What a disgusting thought," Annie replies, retrieving extra pillows from the hall closet, as Ollie hovers near his own warm and waiting sofa bed.

The floor and an uncomfortable stuffed chair are the only other alternatives. Annie was five years old the last time she crept into Ollie's bed, pleading for sanctuary from the frightening sounds of the night. Annie wouldn't think of sleeping with Michael. It seems natural with Ollie after all these years.

"If you don't want to talk about what happened with April," she says, "I'll understand."

"Would you prefer that I sleep on the floor? It's a lot more peaceful than the bed at April's right now," Ollie starts blabbing immediately. "I don't know what it is with her, Annie. She's completely possessive about her stuff. Everything, and I mean everything, is separated and accounted for. Groceries, household expenses, tapes, records, books, laundry. That's cool. But whenever I'm at her place she turns into a slob. Dishes piled up in the sink, business papers and other stuff lying around everywhere and tampons growing a beard in the waste basket."

"It is her house, y'know."

"I know it's her house, she knows it's her house and she's never going to let me forget it's her house."

"You're embarrassed about tending bar three nights a week."

"No. You don't get it. Instead of dealing with a thing directly women must deal with the psychological and emotional reasons for the thing. It doesn't matter whether it's wallpaper or wedding rings. April gets defensive whenever I don't blindly accept her choice of anything. 'You *always* disagree,' she says. Never mind that she asked for suggestions in the first place. Suddenly I'm criticizing her taste or her body. Who knows whether it's insecurity or control? Before you know it we've escalated to 'You're angry with me' and then the dreaded silence, which often turns into a crying jag where the subject doesn't ever get discussed."

"Gimme a break, Ollie. April isn't like that. Tonight Lucien even blessed it. You're so paranoid."

"Paranoid, huh? Three weeks ago we went out to some fancy-shmancy restaurant with her buttoned-down boss and his wife. Well, Freddie orders two big-ticket bottles of French wine, and when the check comes I kinda wait to see what Old Freddie's gonna do. April blasts out of her chair like a shot. She grabs the bill and announces to the table, 'Oh, it's my turn isn't it?' While she gives me a look that says, 'Schmuck, you haven't taken your turn since the day we met.'"

"Ollie, last year, I got stock tips on California new technology companies, and there's money in the bank you could have. Like a loan. I'll charge interest if you want."

"From my baby sister? No thanks. Anyway, that's not the end of it. On the way back to April's place I called her on the dinner check thing. At first, April insisted that she told *me* to grab it before we went out and that she'd reimburse me later. When April realized she hadn't warned me at all, she apologized and I thought, okay, fine."

"Then what's the problem?"

"Tonight she's at her writing table paying her bills. I'm in front of the television set, trying not to think about Mom, and April says to me with a straight face, 'Here's the receipt from The Bakery restaurant. You haven't paid me back yet, have you?'

"I'm tellin' ya, Annie. April knows she's pushing my buttons. It's emotional terrorism; any deviation is met with serious retaliatory consequences. Or she's nuts. . . . How can I live with someone who spends that much on a meal and then comes home and throws it up?"

On this warm March day April Stewart obsesses over a tiny wrinkle that appeared this morning on her forehead midway between her eyebrows. She should be enjoying the afternoon sun, the smell of fresh budding trees and defrosted soil. But April is fretting over whether her mother's advice to stretch a piece of scotch tape over the crease when she's alone could possibly work.

The downtown exodus began after lunch when the temperature reached sixty for the first time this year and most of the managers didn't return to their offices. April went home, changed into jeans and put on one of her tight-fitting knit tops. She's meeting Ollie near the sea lion pool at the zoo and she intends to clearly announce her smallish, proud-standing breasts. April's been distracted by the specter of Lucien Echo hanging around until recently. She hasn't slept with him since Ollie became her lover. But Lucien's remained in her life, and she hasn't been straight with Ollie about him.

Calling it quits with Lucien over sexual politics wasn't exactly what April had in mind. All the same, a week ago, she was required to inform him that her boss supported his IRS proposal. Just as Lucien predicted, the US attorney was essentially accepting her firm's hush money paid through a confidential civil agreement with the IRS. Although April was dismayed by the ease with which unethical judgments were being embraced, she took the final papers to Lucien's office intending to resolve the lingering issues between them. What in the world was she thinking? "It's a gray area," Lucien had said, trying to reassure her. "A perfectly legitimate settlement," her boss Tad Jalenko confirmed in his smarmy way.

"In a pig's eye," April now mutters to herself as she strolls over the concrete footbridge leading to the zoo's rear gate. She didn't need a lecture about prudent business decisions from Jalenko. And the last thing in the world April wanted to admit to Lucien is that she's no better than him. That's why they couldn't make it together and she was too chicken to say so. Instead April became emotional and wound up disclosing how seriously immature she is. To his credit Lucien was a gentleman to the end, gracefully allowing her all the rope she needed to hang herself. Exactly what she lacked in the matter--grace. Something April seeks desperately yet seems more elusive to her with age.

It's near feeding time at the lion house and three, loud, successive roars echo throughout the old stone building. The tiny tension band across the base of April's skull drops into her shoulders, runs down her arms and out her fingertips. "Two separate hearts," April decides. That's what she wants to say to Ollie. She continues along the paved path past a row of empty monkey cages, relieved to discover this new approach for maintaining a healthy relationship. Low pressure, mutual maintenance, that's enough for now.

"What a day!" Ollie exclaims when April approaches their prearranged meeting spot next to the popcorn cart. He kisses her and slips his arm around her slender waist. His face scrubbed, Ollie appears tranquil in Hawaiian shirt, blue jeans, and knock-off topsiders. Today Ollie feels the way he wishes he always felt, sensing exciting promise in the moment. Today he's experiencing a rare state of limitless energy out of which dreams emerge. Or could this be another one of his mood swings?

Most of the time Ollie puts on airs for everybody. In truth, he thinks that a simpler existence has less chance of turning tragic or producing other dreaded complications. He can't help getting lost in the minutiae of the moment. Something always goes wrong. Ollie frets about the weather and the White Sox, he worries about his haircut and his love handles. He stews over his neighbor's leaving her car on the sidewalk in front of his apartment building whenever she can't find a parking space. Ollie gets nervous and excited a day in advance when he realizes that he's going to run out of coffee. He's awash in this sea of trivial obstacles to accomplishment. How can he take any action when it's always one step forward and two steps back?

Ollie knows that his writing suffers most from this spiritual atrophy. He expected to be well established by this time in his career. Maybe a regular contributor to *Esquire* or *Rolling Stone*, or even those entertainment weeklies springing up lately, such as—dare he say it? —*People* magazine. For God's sake, Ollie isn't talking about the Pulitzer Prize. But will he ever get beyond the idea stage for his novel? And does he really expect Hollywood to option his screenplay? The fact is that Ollie's recent article about "au courant" all-night dance clubs and eateries, for which *Chicago* magazine paid the princely sum of two hundred dollars, remains his claim to fame.

Who in the world cares whether Ollie Katz languishes in the futility of it all? Or if Ollie's concentration wanes in the face of things more mundane than those worldly topics about which he struggles to write? Don't we all suffer the same, private, paralyzing dread? Not today. Today Ollie believes in himself. He's reborn in the warm afternoon sun, remembering to become that attractive person others can't get enough of. Here in these rare moments of clarity, when Ollie's fear of rejection is consumed by delusions of grandeur, he realizes the essence of his dreams.

Ollie confidently stares into April's bright eyes and the transformation begins. Separate beings mysteriously rubbing up against each other in search of common ground. April kisses him back lustily and, grinning, she takes his hand in confirmation of their special dance. Who knows what gives with new love in springtime?

Arm in arm, they join the flow of passersby along the zoo's main thoroughfare over to the glass-domed great ape house. A baby gorilla was born this morning and, luckily, they observe the mother nursing in her straw nest assembled atop the environmentally controlled jungle cliff. Father proudly leaps about and pounds his chest, guarding their faux cave from the human voyeurs. Watching April watch this marvelous scene of primal domesticity, Ollie can't help but think that the Gods of Coupling are conspiring against him. So far, anyway, Ollie's managed to drift in and out of relationships with sufficient frequency to avoid using those three little words. Nevertheless, by the time they walk a few blocks away from the zoo, Ollie plunges headlong into their future plans. The topic surfaces when they're sitting at an outdoor patio table in a Clark Street restaurant.

"It's a Far East assignment for six weeks," April says while they sip tea and watch the rush hour traffic. The sun is setting behind them and soon the air will be too cool to comfortably make the short walk home. "I'll be auditing a manufacturing plant near Hong Kong and I can bring you along. Maybe if you come up with a local tourist angle you can publish something in the English-speaking newspapers there."

"I'm not wild about foreign travel right now," Ollie hesitates. "They're threatening to kill Americans abroad again. But two months is a long way off. It's a generous offer to consider, for sure."

Then Ollie suggests dinner at a romantic bistro, and April is exhilarated. She tingles with anticipation at the thought of making love in the shower, after a nap. Before you know it they're lost in another kissy-face game at the patio table. It's a moment of truth. Ollie knows that a commitment will soon be required to sustain them. For as perfect as things are, relationship is akin to Heisenberg's Uncertainty Principle. Like the fragile electron, stimulated by the heat of the microscope's light, a relationship remains in motion and can't be measured. Born in that tide pool of mutual love, it must be fed and encouraged to grow unchecked by doubts or labels. Otherwise it sputters and stalls and, eventually, will shrivel up and die. So Ollie isn't shocked when April says that maybe it's time to tell her parents about him.

"They're coming to visit this summer," April goes on. "Four, five days . . . max. If you behave yourself you might get some great meals out of it. Hey, Ollie, what's with the look? I'm not asking you to move in with me."

"What look? I wasn't giving you a look. I was thinking about what you said. I suppose that means I can't move in `till after your parents leave?"

"First it's a look, then it's a remark."

"So I made a remark."

"You're always making remarks. Don't be a smart aleck, Ollie. Be thrilled that I want my parents to meet you."

"I am. It was a bad joke. I don't know why I said it."

"Maybe you oughtta talk to that therapist I met over the winter," April says. "We connected again and I'm considering seeing her. She helped me understand something interesting about myself recently."

"Yeah, like what?"

"Well . . . I used to think my food addiction confirmed the abandonment issues surrounding my family. After a while I believed I'd never amount to anything so it was easy to sabotage opportunities. Now I've realized that my parents' approval is basically irrelevant. I'm the one being sabotaged."

"You learned this from one conversation?"

"The point is," April replies, screwing up her face and casting a peculiar look in Ollie's direction, "A terrific person doesn't set priorities or adapt beliefs to please other people. Good things happen when you accept responsibility for what's honestly in your own separate heart."

"Why do I smell a rat?"

April hesitates for a full five seconds and finally comes out with it. "If you want to be a bartender for the rest of your life that's fine with me."

* * *

Two months later, Lucien Echo shifts his buttocks on a wobbly old barstool, facing Ollie Katz, who happens to be tending the other side of the polished wood plank. Lucien feels no pain after the scotch and whatever else he ingested before wandering into The Bulls jazz club half an hour ago. As Lucien leans across the bar to emphasize his point, Ollie strains to hear him over the sounds of Ahmad Jamal's trio filling the tiny, cave-like room.

"You understand what I'm talking about," Lucien goes on. "I don't care how beautiful, smart, talented, or rich they are. Every woman has a friggin' defect. Each and every single one of them has some goofy thing that eventually drives you crazy. Y'know what I'm saying?"

Ollie's been bartending here three nights a week for a year, but it's his first encounter with Lucien. They haven't seen each other since that fateful night at Faces, when Ollie's mother was in the hospital, and Lucien was out with April.

"Someone better will come along," Lucien expounds without encouragement from Ollie. "Another relationship that's either unattainable or impossible to maintain. I don't bother anymore."

Ollie doesn't know why he told Lucien that he broke up with April. Technically, it isn't true. April broke up with him. Moreover, Ollie has the most exasperating habit of shooting his mouth off whenever something happens to him. Never mind that he can solemnly keep the confidence of others. Ollie can't stop confessing the embarrassing personal details of his life, from every boring angle, to any perfect stranger willing to listen

"Place any woman in a new relationship," Lucien goes on. "Within ninety days she'll shift gears along the exclusive road to marriage. The `L' word comes up, or three months, whichever comes first. But the fun is over and the `C' word surfaces, which inevitably turns into the `M' word."

"Oh, c'mon."

"Consider the initial attraction," Lucien replies. "There's laughter and excitement because nobody is thinking about getting serious. 'Fess up, Ollie, aren't most men perfectly happy to maintain the status quo? Yet, after three months, questions spring up about what you're doing when you're not with her, suggestions surface for improving your wardrobe and your grooming habits, the discussions about monogamy become personal, and your future plans are subjected to solemn scrutiny."

"Maybe it's the nurturing instinct," Ollie suggests. "Or believing that relationships must be complete. Maybe women don't want to waste biological time with a frivolous partner."

"Maybe I haven't been slapped with an ultimatum on the ninety-first day in every relationship I can remember."

Ollie doesn't usually do male bonding. Lucien's effortless maneuvering through life astonishes Ollie, and he can't resist challenging Lucien about being a lawyer. "Not to change the subject," Ollie says. "How do you depersonalize the crap associated with representing your clients?"

"Some people insist that when you lie down with dogs you get up with fleas," Lucien replies, rising from the bar stool as if to leave. "I don't agree. I try to remain a cipher for the ever-elusive truth, always able to recognize when I'm lying to myself. That's the spark I need. . . . Hey, I'm sorry. You're catching me at a bad time. I just lost one of my best clients."

"No, I'm sorry," Ollie replies. "I thought you looked a little weird when you came in. I shouldn't have brought up the subject. Did you say you lost one of your clients?"

"If you pour another one of those," Lucien says, sitting back down on the stool and pointing at his glass, "I'll tell you the whole sad tale. It's already in the papers . . ."

Long after Lucien finished recounting the circumstances of Gordon Traeger's demise, and for the rest of the night, Ollie couldn't stop thinking about it. Lucien genuinely cared about the man, growing emotional as he gave a vivid report of Traeger's last fling in Las Vegas. The next morning, while Ollie sits at his broken down roll top desk, it occurs to him that the episode makes one helluva short story:

"Blackjack! . . . And Blackjack again!!"

Gordon Traeger excitedly drew in a deep breath of cigarette smoke, alcohol, and stale air conditioning. "Holy balls," Gordon muttered, sotto voce, as he watched the dealer casually turn up a blessed Five of Diamonds beside his already uncovered Jack of Spades. "It's the most I've ever won on one hand. Two Blackjacks doubling down!"

Again Gordon sucked in the jet-fueled atmosphere upon which so many inveterate gamblers thrive in this satanic town. "Just look at those," Gordon mused on, referring to the ten-thousand-dollar plaques the dealer was pushing at him. "They waived the bloody limit just to let me split em. Holy balls," Gordon muttered once more, while his ears rang and his pulse raced. Perspiration beads on his forehead, only seconds ago accumulating in a warm puddle of fear, cooled and dried up with the realization that he'd crossed the threshold into a new dimension. Gone was the little voice that always caused him to hesitate exactly when he was about to plunge over the edge. Finally, Gordon Traeger was a winner!

"I'm gonna savor this moment," Gordon thought. Instead he rose too quickly from his upholstered leather stool, its stilt-like wooden legs catching in the plush, plumb-colored carpeting. Undaunted, Gordon pushed firmly against the baize blackjack table, managing to free his expanding middle-aged belly. Then he scooped up his magical ebony casino markers, a la James Bond, and cast a sneering eye toward the other players sitting around the table.

His gaze fell upon the Librarian, as he'd mentally referred to her throughout his incredible run of luck. Probably in her sixties, the woman was barely visible behind her tall stacks of five-dollar chips. Adorned in turquoise jewelry and sporting a brand new, pink-tinged, permanent wave, courtesy of the Desert Spa and Beauty Parlor, the Librarian will sit quietly betting the minimum and sucking down sloe gin fizzes all night. Until a few minutes ago, when he won seventeen hands in a row, Gordon was a loser just like her.

Gordon reached into the right front pocket of his country club trousers, pulled out a one-hundred-dollar chip, and pushed it across the table toward the dealer. He couldn't remember possessing such savoir-faire before. Yet, he was exuding a worldly charm and sophistication heretofore unknown among the other Polish immigrant families hailing from the northwest side of Chicago. Gordon wasn't living under a rock. He'd been to Vegas before. Hell, Gordon Traeger walked tall among the movers and shakers on LaSalle Street. Still, he knew that everything he'd accomplished in life had come off somebody else's dime until that magical black-jack moment.

"Hey, curly," a husky female voice said into Gordon's ear. "You plan on spending that booty?"

Gordon turned, thinking that he must not have heard the woman correctly, while her slinky perfumed arm definitely brushed against his shoulder. "Pardon me?" he said, looking into the sparkling deep blue eyes of the same gorgeous young woman who'd earlier stopped to watch the action at his table. She was stylishly thin and her straight platinum blond hair was cropped short. The lady had smiled at him provocatively while his pile of chips grew, and Gordon had construct-ed a fantasy of parading around town with her on his arm. It had been twenty years since he had thought such things for more than a fleeting moment.

"I guess you're bringing yourself home to mama," Verna Von Zell said with appropriate dis-appointment.

"My wife is up in the room doing her nails and probably talking to her mother long distance."

Verna thought he wasn't entirely unattrac-tive. Given that she'd been forced to ditch an afternoon date, who turned out to be worse than her service had promised, Verna was already dressed up and out on the town. When she hap-pened by Gordon's table, on her way to another

sleepless night in front of the television, Verna
had quickly sized up the situation. The man was
desperately trying to have a good time and, she
figured, he was married.

"Well . . . then," Verna responded to
Gordon's honesty, "you can't call her for permission to buy me a drink."

"Joyce knows what I'm doing," Gordon
answered. He ushered Verna up the steps at the
edge of the casino and led her through the well-
dressed crowd waiting on line to see the dinner
show. Surrounded by the constant jangle of slot
machines, they reached a bar decorated like
Cleopatra's barge on the Nile and Gordon sat
down in one of the gaudy purple velvet booths.

"Wait a minute," Verna said. "I don't
think I want to get into kinky stuff."

"I didn't mean Joyce was going to join us.
Is something like that out of the question?"

"Boy has this ever been a day," Verna
replied, sliding next to Gordon in the booth and
flashing her beguiling smile again. Then she fin-
gered the single strand of milky white pearls dangling from her suntanned throat. "You little
devil," she said. "I'm not a lesbian or anything,
but I have partied with a woman before. Under
the right circumstances," Verna added, letting her
sequin stockinged knee brush against him under
the table. "It's my choice, of course."

A toga-clad cocktail waitress suddenly
stuck her semi-exposed bosom in Gordon's face

as she leaned across him to replace some Keno cards from the table stand.

"Say, darlin'?" Gordon said to the tired-looking, pretty, young woman. "You think an old fart like me has a chance? I'm offering her diamonds but all she wants is love."

"Who're you?" the woman asked through sunken cheeks covered with too much rouge, "Flippin' Howard Hughes? I'm sure the lady knows a real diamond from a fake one. Don't ya honey?"

"By all means, let's see the real thing," Verna countered, good-naturedly, while hooking her arm through Gordon's in a conspiratorial gesture. "I'm sure we'll know what to do," Verna whispered in his ear. "Won't we, darlin'?"

"Ladies," Gordon responded unashamedly, "Think of me as your genie. We'll take a walk through those fancy shops downstairs. You get a wish and you get to wish whatever your heart's desire."

"Oh yeah, Mister?" the waitress replied. "Okay . . . I'll play along with this crazy old bastard," she added for Verna's benefit. "I suppose he gets the third wish?"

"We'll take the best suite in the hotel," Gordon replied. "With a hot tub and maybe a sauna. We'll have a massage, take a bubble bath, drink champagne and eat caviar and oysters."

"I could use a new coat," Verna piped in, "or one of those new video decks. What about your wife?"

"It's our anniversary. Joyce already saw something she liked."

"No Mother, I won't forget to wear a hat," Joyce Traeger said, sighing into the telephone while she checked her figure in the mirrored closet doors of their hotel suite. "You should see what they walk around in at the pool," Joyce went on, frowning at the sight of her ever-so-slightly sagging breasts. "This morning, I dragged the poor dear into every shop and couldn't find a thing . . . of course, Gordon hasn't been drinking. . . . Sometimes I don't think you realize how serious it is. . . . Well, 'terminal' isn't a word anybody likes to hear. . . . Yes, Mother, they have our room number in case the doctor calls. . . . What's to understand? Someone with a healthy liver dies and they put it into Gordon's body. First they did it with monkeys and now they can do it with humans. . . . No it isn't morbid to talk about. It's hopeful. . . . Honestly, Mother, I wonder about you sometimes. Hold on a second, will ya' . . . these hotel cords don't reach. . . ."

Joyce put down the receiver and walked over to the desk phone, stopping by the mirrored doors long enough to tuck up her boobs the way they were soon going to look again. If her mother thought that discussing the transplant was gruesome, she'd go nuts if Joyce disclosed her agreement with Gordon to exchange operations. Joyce had never been obsessed with beauty. Being a shade darker than forty, she kept herself in good condition. She attended aerobics class on Tuesday and Thursday and played tennis on Friday. Ever since Gordon had had the beejeesus scared out of him, he's been amorous as hell despite all the medication he was taking. How could she tell her mother that their relationship had actually improved?

"Mother? . . . Are you there?" Joyce asked, while she sat at the ornate writing desk and absented-mindedly flipped through the room service menu. "Anyway, you probably won't believe this," Joyce went on. "Gordon's been a different person."

Then Joyce noticed the manila envelope containing important financial papers that Gordon had unpacked for her to peruse this afternoon. "Just in case," Gordon had said, knowing that Joyce knew what they owned. They had the brick Tudor in Riverwoods, the snowbird ranch house in Scottsdale, the stocks, his partnership annuities, and she had a key to the safety deposit box with nearly two million in cash squirreled away. While it was sweet of him to reassure her this way, Joyce couldn't bring herself to think of their twenty years together boiled down to a dog-eared envelope full of stuff.

"Yes, Mother I'm fine. . . . No, that's not it. Gordon is no longer frightened by the uncertainty over how much time he has. . . . Of course he still cares! . . . He claims that it's liberating. I've never seen him so attentive and passionate about things. . . . Don't you think he's entitled to enjoy every day as if it's the last? . . . Down in the casino. . . . Oh please, Mother! That's what people do in this town. . . . Don't worry, he would never do something that stupid. . . . That's right. We have reservations for the Dome of the Sea restaurant at the Dunes and then we're going to see Ann-Margret. . . . Yeah. I guess they reconstructed her whole face. . . . Well, she never did have much of a voice. . . . What time is it there? . . . Jeez, there's somebody at the door. Maybe Gordon forgot his key. Hold on again, okay?"

Joyce walked through the bedroom hallway to the door. A handsome young man in a dark suit handed her a small gift box from Tiffany's in the promenade downstairs. After she confirmed that the man had no idea whether there was a card inside, Joyce found her purse and sent him on his way with a generous tip. She hurried back to the phone while she excitedly tore at the expensive foil wrapping on the box.

"Mother? . . . Oh my God!" Joyce gasped once she opened the rectangular velvet case. "This is incredible. Gordon just bought me the most exquisite diamond bracelet I have ever seen. . . . It must be ten carats. I thought he was kidding around today when he asked the salesperson to take it out of the case. . . . I can hardly catch my breath. . . . I know, Mother. . . . My heart won't slow down. Well, of course I'm not going to leave it in the room. . . . Look, I better get going. I've got to get dressed. Gordon should've been back by now. . . . All right, Mother. That's very considerate of you. . . . I promise, I won't tell him you sent an anniversary gift too. . . . Goodbye Mother."

The digital clock on the marble table read 9:17 PM when Gordon Traeger and Verna Von Zell entered the foyer of the Emperor Nero suite. Gordon watched Verna remove her black lace shawl exposing her bare shoulders. She dropped it behind her on the thick white carpet and strolled off in search of the bathroom. Gordon went over to the enormous round bed and stretched out on his back, looking up at his fully clothed image in the large mirror above his head. He removed the heavy ebony casino plaques from the left pocket of his sports coat and placed them on his chest. From his other pocket Gordon withdrew a .38 caliber snub-nosed revolver and fired a bullet through his right temple.

PART III

I'll always wonder why Lucien went ahead with his annual Christmas party six weeks before his own trial was scheduled to begin. He told me that most of the charitable foundations and employees who depended on his parties for years had opted to go ahead. I'm sure that Lucien wanted people to continue thinking his life wasn't coming apart at the seams. Though it seems sordid to me now, I'll admit, at the time, I was excited to be hobnobbing with the interesting and powerful people around town. A few judges and some other local bigwigs didn't show up. They weren't missed since two hundred people must have flowed through the soiree while I was present. Alex's personal touch was everywhere from the holiday decorations to the ornamental presentation of food prepared and served by her restaurant staff.

Mainly there were hip swells dripping with haute couture and willing to engage in the requisite three minutes of superficial social drivel. More fascinating were the weirdos, the artists, and the old-time hangers-on who knew

Lucien when. Sitting on my coveted roost at the mirrored bar, I snatched juicy tidbits off the procession of squatters on the adjacent stool while I could hear the jazz quintet playing from across the parlor.

"He doesn't look the part but Murray's a mogul," Bobby the Halsted Street poet informed me about the diminutive, olive-skinned, middle-aged man walking away from the bar. Sporting an off-the-rack tweed jacket, and a mad scientist grin, Murray was touting his latest consumer gadget invention. "Murray hates lawyers," Bobby went on. "All of them except Lucien, who he probably paid more this year than I'll make in my lifetime. . . . See that nubile beauty over there?" Bobby pointed at one of two anorectic fashion plates, wearing DKNY black leather and matching nose piercing, jitterbugging on the dance floor. "She's Alderman Blum's lesbo daughter. Y'know? Ritchie's new guy from Lakeview?"

More couples were soon grooving to "Duke's Place" and I noticed Alex standing next to the piano player. It was almost ten o'clock and I hadn't caught her alone. Earlier we'd made small talk, as I watched her gliding through the pretentious social enclaves scattered around the maze of rooms without showing any strain in her eyes or on her neatly glossed lips. Whereas the über–hostess role seemed natural to Alex, by that time, I knew nothing could be further from the truth.

We hadn't seen one another for three months, since our museum encounter, yet we'd ended up having long telephone conversations. At one point Alex confirmed her shyness, saying she would rather spend the day in her pajamas, alone, without a sound from the outside world save a

Tori Amos record. She'd never gotten past the idea that people are basically phony. She learned this lesson early on, she confided. When she turned thirteen she had to face a childhood blood disease, a form of leukemia called A.L.L. "Imagine thinking about your remaining moments," Alex said, "confined to the well-intentioned silliness of the people around you." There and then Alex recognized that the lives of others would always seem more important than hers. Especially since it was her life forever in danger.

Acute lymphoblastic leukemia is a curable childhood cancer that's one of the major medical success stories of the last two decades. Over seventy percent of children receiving optimal treatment are cured. Along with a powerful chemotherapy cocktail, the regimen consists of many phases: central nervous system preventatives such as cranial radiation, consolidation, reinduction, reconsolidation, and maintenance. When Alex went through three years of it all, most currently accepted drugs and procedures were wildly experimental. She was one of the early lucky ones who achieved remission and has maintained normal cells in the blood, bone marrow, and cerebrospinal fluid.

Alex told me that without her father's scientific knowledge, and constant pushing toward the cure, she wouldn't have made it. There will always be the risk of relapse, she said. And she was far too young to have learned how to rely upon complete strangers and please adults who literally controlled her life. But after walking around in high school, bald-headed and skinny, like a concentration camp refugee long before Sinead O'Connor, Alex felt she'd earned her Ph.D. in socializing. Given her insecure nature, Alex admitted that dealing with the public was the one part of her life where she'd stopped being afraid.

The music ended and I watched her conversing with the piano player. She glanced in my direction and I was about to wave at her when Lucien's voice came from directly behind me. Alex may have seen the two of us in close proximity, as she disappeared into her parlor through the door nearest the bandstand. When I turned around Lucien was speaking with his lawyer, Effram Abrahamson.

Lucien was a man under siege, on trial for his life and no doubt consumed with worry. As his judgment day drew nearer the pressure increased. By Halloween he'd gone into seclusion. "He's meditating," Alex had said sarcastically, when I called to speak with him about potential character witnesses. Then she'd halfheartedly made another excuse during one of our recent conversations. Despite those signs, I remember being surprised to see Lucien appear so anxious at his own party.

"Hey, Ollie," Lucien said, eyeing me on the stool. "I was just coming for you. . . . D'you know Effram? Why don't you walk along with us?"

"Lucien, I don't think you . . ."

"Don't worry, Counselor," Lucien interrupted the older man. "Ollie understands the importance of confidentiality. Right?"

I nodded my assent, following Lucien and his hired conscience across the wide living room. Touring the crowd was the ultimate party experience for me. Inside all the schmoozing I discovered the texture of Lucien's power. Illustrious names and glorious stories behind faces I'd been observing all night made up the core of Lucien's business and political connections. People who stopped him to offer holiday wishes or a clever anecdote lifted his spirits. By the time we reached Lucien's den, he'd gathered enough information to take a public perception poll. This kept him composed long enough to focus on some alarming information that Abrahamson was apparently conveying when I'd joined them.

"Effram has wind of a deal in the works between the government and Auggie Rotini," Lucien said to me as we paused on the Oriental rug in front of his desk—exactly where I stood when Alex first asked for my help. "If that deal happens," he continued, "the prosecutor also wants to spare me a trial if I plead guilty and accept eighteen months in prison. . . . Here's the best part. The Justice Department in Washington couldn't care less that the US Attorney in Chicago was willing to clear me when the FBI wanted my cooperation."

"It will come up if there's a sentencing," Abrahamson interjected while his schlumpy frame descended into the overstuffed chair in the corner. "The prosecutor can't deny that immunity discussions took place," he added calmly. "Your sentence is up to Judge Plunkem's discretion. I told you, Lucien. Nothing has changed."

"So it's still a year?" Lucien said. "Maybe nine months on a particularly good morning," he went on, not mockingly, per se, but in a distressed tone. "Nobody knows Plunkem better than you, Professor Abrahamson. That's what you told me when I hired you, isn't it? . . . What d'you think, Ollie? How much time should I do?"

"Look here, Lucien," Abrahamson replied tersely. "You wanted me to advise you on what I think the man will do. Don't insult the messenger because you don't like the news. . . . I didn't want to interrupt your party," he added, more cordially, while making a show of rising with dignity.

"I'm sorry Effram," Lucien implored him, rushing to his side. "I know we're going to win. I feel terrible dragging you over here and dumping on you this way. Please forgive me. . . . Here, how 'bout a cigar? No? . . . Well, some champagne then? I'll bet you could do with more of those fabulous barbecued oysters. Tell me, Professor. What can I do to make it up to you?"

"All right, Lucien," Abrahamson responded with a wave of his bony hand. "You can be unctuous with me, but a jury will see through it. On second thought, though, I think I will stick around for a few minutes. Wasn't that Senator Marrow's aide I saw in the hallway earlier? His office screwed up the language for a sentencing bill I drafted and it's the perfect time to . . . Oh, I almost forgot. Here's the report of my investigator's interview with Detective Goyle," Abrahamson went on, glancing disdainfully in my direction while he pulled some folded papers from inside the breast pocket of his blazer. "Status quo, Lucien," he said. "Chillum Hoskiss is still missing and Tommy Goyle's story hasn't changed."

The professor certainly didn't covet my company during confidential discussions with Lucien. Being hypersensitive to that unwanted feeling, I would've declined Lucien's invitation to join them in normal circumstances. But Lucien had made it clear to me that as far as he was concerned I was his investigator, bound to remain silent. No matter how imprudent his conduct might have seemed, I was entangled in Lucien's trust in me. Finding Lucien humbled in this fashion for the first time in thirty years, I concluded, selfishly perhaps, that I too had reached the point of no return.

Since those early 80's, it seemed, I was stuck in my ill-conceived dream world of haughty purpose and unmarketable prose. I was withdrawn from the world, remaining unencumbered by the practical and moral choices accompanying responsibility. I had carried my denial to the point where I'd managed to block out my relationship, albeit short-lived, with April Stewart, and who knows how many others? It wasn't hard to understand why I felt compassion toward Lucien. While I was asleep, he was wallowing in society's afflictions and being judged for it every day. I began to understand how Lucien could have spun such a big fat web of self-sabotage. I also couldn't help thinking that here was the hook I needed to write Lucien's story.

So I decided to talk to Mama Raspberry again. Not because of anything Professor Abrahamson had said. After all, I knew that Detective Tommy Goyle was Lucien's star witness. Goyle's testimony during Mama's search warrant hearing had been the legal springboard for Judge Rotini to throw out the case against her. It wasn't surprising that Abrahamson was keeping an eye on Goyle, making certain he stuck to his "wrong address" scenario. Still, something had bugged me about the way Abrahamson said, "Chillum Hoskiss is still missing." It sounded like Chevy Chase's old "Saturday Night Live" newscast "Generalissimo Francisco Franco is still dead."

"What's the matter, Ollie?" Lucien asked after Abrahamson had departed and we were standing near the tall library shelves stretching around his den. "You have a weird look on your face."

"I hope it's just a coincidence that Chillum Hoskiss disappeared within a few days after the US Attorney approached you to cooperate in the Rotini investigation."

"You sound like the prosecutor," Lucien replied coolly. "Of course they think I had something to do with Chillum's failure to surface. Pardon my choice of words, but it's a little desperate, don't ya think. Some junkie splits town before the prosecutor confirms what he told Goyle and they're supposed to believe one of us tipped him off?"

Lucien walked around his desk and sat in his smooth leather chair. He was distracted by events unfolding around him, not the least of which was the eerie sound of holiday revelry coming from the other side of the wall.

"It doesn't matter what Chillum would say," Lucien added without emotion. "The police got a defective search warrant for the wrong address. That issue is a red herring," Lucien went on more wearily, leaning back and raising his eyes to the ceiling. "Listen to me, will ya? Tip-offs and red herrings. This cops and robbers stuff must be getting to me. Forget about it, Ollie. Go enjoy the party, all right? I have a call to make."

I made my way through the apartment in search of some food. In the hallway outside the dining room, I straightened the lapels on my snazzy new sports coat and sauntered over to the impressive seafood buffet. While reaching for the green-lipped mussels, I felt a hand on my arm and I realized that Annie was warning me to be careful; only she knew I sometimes get a rash from clams and mussels. I snatched some jumbo shrimps instead, feeling empowered by my inside connections at such an opulent spread. I was rarely invited to these high-class affairs. Annie, on the other hand, was used to Hollywood parties and "A list" people.

Annie had decided by then to move back to Chicago. She and Jason had settled into a two-bedroom cottage in Glenview, allowing Jason to attend Evanston High School the following year. Annie had wrangled a cushy deal out of those folks at Sony. By then they'd been paying her top rates for three months to develop six minutes of fish footage, and they purchased the hardware and programs she needed to set up her home office. Annie earned every dollar putting in long, monotonous hours to the final approvals and causing her to remember why she gave up animation in the first place.

When Annie first got wind of Lucien's party she must've been feeling social again. In addition to the hours she was spending on the project, Annie claimed that she'd been turning down overtures since her return on account of Jason's need for stability against his too rapidly unfolding adolescence. It was bad enough that Jason had dropped out of band class. My father nearly croaked when he learned that Jason and two of his buddies were busted one night, outside the community rec center, playing poker for money under the fluorescent lights in the vestibule. I could go on for days about my enterprising nephew, but I'm sure you get the point.

Annie and I had arrived together around eight-thirty. Lucien greeted us, and within minutes they were reminiscing about their encounters during the time our mother died. By my account, anyway, Annie did not discourage him, their chemistry appearing as strong as ever. When Annie and I ended up standing at the sideboard, eating out of gold leaf china plates, I told her, half-kidding, that I wasn't convinced everything was kosher between them.

"Oh please," Annie replied. "The years *have* been kind to Lucien. You look fine, too. Did I thank you for bringing me along?" she went on, sweetly, coaxing away any remaining jealous feelings I might have harbored. "I haven't been to a party like this in years. You should tap into these heavy hitters. I recognize some of them from high school."

"Maybe you'll stick around and gimme some pointers. . . . Uh-oh. Here comes the queen of the circus," I added, gratefully changing the subject as I spied Alex walking through the hallway on the far side of the dining room. "Please don't humiliate me by disclosing something about her that I shouldn't have told you."

"Ollie. I'm sorry, I haven't given you any time," Alex said, coming over and kissing my cheek. "I've been wanting to meet you," she went on, smiling warmly at Annie. "Girl, you don't know how many people have asked me about the beautiful dark-haired woman in the exotic dress."

"It's so nice to meet you, too."

"I'm afraid I couldn't discourage a couple of the handsome, rich ones," Alex responded in mock conspiracy.

"Thanks for the plug," Annie replied. "I've reached the age when it's more likely that I'll be taken hostage than find a husband."

"You're kidding?" I broke in. "You're not stressing on that again?"

"You barely look thirty, Annie," Alex said. "You have the most beautiful skin. What do you use?"

"I take Chinese herbs . . . and vaseline."

"You swallow vaseline?" I asked her.

"No, you idiot," Annie replied. "I put it on my face at night. Imagine putting up with this your entire life?"

While I pondered whether Alex might take Annie literally, it also occurred to me that Annie was testing her.

"This is such a lovely place," Annie continued, shifting her assault to flattery.

"Lucien's great about letting me do whatever I want here," Alex replied. "It's his personality, though. Just between us, I wouldn't mind if we gave up this lifestyle. C'mon, Annie, I'll show you around."

Alex led us down the main hall through a tangle of perfumed bodies with high hair and angora sweaters draped over slinky evening gowns. I felt self-conscious about listening to Lucien in confidence and then resolving to investigate further on my own. My best move was to play out the role of Alex's ally and go-between. Unless Alex already knew the bad news, there wasn't any reason to repeat Lucien's latest disclosure about a prison sentence. On the other hand, any more attempts to personalize things, or encourage the slightest suggestion of nookie between us, had to be frowned upon.

After shepherding us along on her rounds, Alex left us to fend for ourselves amidst, as it turns out, a number of Republicans. Despite discussions over socio-economic and geo-political issues, I'm sorry to report that most people were really exchanging their infomercials. It was soon after midnight, and the high-spirited crowd had given way to a boozy afterglow. The remaining guests were formed into small clusters, recounting harrowing tales about the social-climbing wars, or discussing the latest scandal revealed in the tabloids. The music had become sporadic, relegated to the subdued pacing of a jam. Annie was making sounds like she wanted to go home and Lucien was darting from room to room like the Energizer Bunny. I followed Alex into the kitchen on one of her clean-up missions. The servers had done their bit and gone so the opportunity was at hand to set the record straight with her.

"I apologize for coming on to you," I said, leaning on the counter next to the double sink. "It was stupid."

"Whoa," Alex replied. She was placing glasses into the dishwasher and she looked over at me with disbelief. "What's come over you?"

"I guess I've decided to be responsible. With Lucien up against the wall you don't need silly distractions."

"Did something happen I don't know about?"

"No. But if things do get worse . . . Anyway, I should support both of you right now."

Alex closed the dishwasher and came over to me. "Thank you," she said softly. "Oh, Jeesus, Ollie. I swore I could accept this. If Lucien's been lying to me all this time, how can I trust him again?"

"Isn't forgiveness a necessary part of love?"

"Maybe. But this thing is hanging over our life. I'm powerless to stop it and can't put it out of my mind. The waiting . . . imagining the most horrible possibilities . . . questioning what I've done," Alex went on, touching my arm.

She stood close enough to sense my enchantment with her, as I resisted the urge to take her in my arms and kiss her moist lips. This was hopeless, I thought. The flirting ended, replaced by the timeless calm of something far more compelling.

"As long as we're being honest here," Alex said without looking at me, "I need to get something off my chest. I've avoided you since that day at the museum, when I realized I was becoming attracted to you."

Well, what do you think I did next? I got the hell out of there as fast as possible. I mumbled something like, "Oh great," and I hugged Alex for a long time. One of those spiritual, deep breath, touch-all-of-you hugs that people in California like to do. Annie came up with that comparison in the car driving me home. But then Annie must've realized I was in a bad mood because she kept her mouth shut the rest of the way. "It doesn't get any better than this," I uttered to nobody in particular, after Annie dropped me off in front of my apartment building and I was heading inside. Alone, I faced my long-neglected novel on the one hand and a less complicated form of self-gratification in the other.

"Sir Rabindranath Tagore was a Hindu poet who lived from 1861 to 1941. Tagore met Albert Einstein in 1926, at Einstein's summer villa outside Berlin. During the next five years they got together at least four more times in Berlin and New York, where they engaged in discussions about the nature of the universe. Einstein was committed to realism. He had faith in the existence of the physical world, of truth independent of man. Einstein is often quoted as having said the moon was *there*, whether one looked at it or not. Tagore, on the other hand, fundamentally disagreed with Einstein's view of realism. In his book *The Religion of Man*, Tagore states, 'We can never go beyond man in all that we know and feel."

I stopped reading from the latest chapter of my novel, which I'd decided to call *Dr. Rob's Journey*, and looked over at Annie. "Tell me if you've heard this before," I said a little sarcastically, while she sat stone-faced on my living room couch. Annie was in the city for a business lunch and popped over to say hello. By then I'd taken another stab at Dr. Rob's much maligned march toward the great beyond, and I'd nagged her to let me read it aloud rather than sending her home with the new pages.

This newest installment found our good doctor in the upbeat throes of a remission. The combination of drugs, vitamins, herbs, and dietary restrictions gave Rob enough strength to leave the hospital and go home to Beverly for the time being. Forced to give up his medical practice—and the associated stress—Rob intends to enjoy his remaining days in the Stephens' family nest created over their twenty-five years together.

Although Beverly isn't a devout Christian, she doesn't question the divinity of this last opportunity to fulfill their lives. She gives up her book club, the teen mentoring, and her other community work. She arranges Rob's professional affairs and sees to it that the children, who are grown and long gone, return to their old rooms for extended visits. For his part Rob is exalted by the realization of inner peace under critical conditions. As a life-long student of science, Rob would normally be aligned with Einstein rather than Tagore. More than ever, though, he's convinced that his hallucinatory journeys back to the past are settling some old scores. Rob's personal exploration of unknown reaches in the face of death has caused time to collapse for him, allowing a spiritual view of the universe. One night Rob explains this discovery to Beverly, in part, by quoting dialogue from a conversation between Einstein and Tagore, published in 1930 by the *New York Times*:

> Einstein: There are two different conceptions about the nature of the universe – the world as a unity

dependent on humanity, and the world as reality independent of the human factor.

Tagore: This world is a human world – the scientific view of it is also that of the scientific man. Therefore, the world apart from us does not exist, it is a relative world, depending for its reality upon our consciousness.

Einstein: Truth, then, is not independent of man?

Tagore: No. Truth is realized through men . . .

Einstein: The mind acknowledges realities outside of it, independent of it. For instance, nobody may be in the house, yet that table remains where it is.

Tagore: Yes, it remains outside the individual mind, but not the universal mind. The table is that which is perceptible by some kind of consciousness we possess.

Einstein: Our natural point of view in regard to the existence of truth apart from humanity cannot be explained or proved, but it is a belief nobody can lack – not even primitive beings. We attribute to truth a superhuman objectivity. It is indispensable for us—this reality that is independent of our existence and our experience and our mind – though we cannot say what it means.

Tagore: In any case, if there be any truth absolutely unrelated to humanity, then for us it is absolutely non-existing.

Einstein: Then I am more religious than you are!

I put down the draft again and glanced at Annie, who looked like she'd swallowed something rotten.

"I'm sorry Ollie," she said, following a long pause, "I don't get it."

"Whaddiya mean?"

"Well, what do *you* mean? . . . I mean, what's the point?"

"Whaddiya mean, what's the point?"

"Stop saying that. Will you?"

"Annie, haven't you grasped by now that Rob is beginning to understand the truth about himself? When the greatest minds in the world can't agree on whether science is based upon faith in something beyond our consciousness then who is Rob to argue? He's obviously becoming enlightened to the cure from within."

"Jesus Christ!" Annie was surprised. "Where did you say that? . . . I don't know, Ollie, maybe it's because nothing seems to happen in your book. Rob takes imaginary trips to the past and spouts aphorisms about the meaning of life? Don't ya see?"

"Some of the best stories in history were based on characters who never got out of bed," I replied, pissed off. "Wounded soldiers in hospitals waiting to die, or people spending their lives in prison. What about *Johnny Got His Gun*? Or *Papillon*? Or *Kiss of the Spider Woman*? And don't forget *Siddhartha*. He crossed the same damn river every day for forty years. Nothing ever happened to him? Right?"

"Okay, Ollie," Annie relented, as she got up from the couch and headed toward the bathroom.

As soon as she returned, though, Annie started in again. "I have no business telling you how to write," she said. "You've worked hard to create a compelling story. When it's done I pray it's not doomed to commercial oblivion for trying to interest people in literature.

"I have to get back to my computer for a few more hours," Annie added while retrieving her coat from inside the hall closet. "Then I pick up Jason from swimming practice after school—at least he acquired one good habit from me. I still have to make dinner and work on another new project tonight. . . . Rats. I won't make the gym today."

I understood exactly what Annie was *kvetching* about. I'd spent more than two years working on my saga. If I finished it and a miracle occurred some publisher would offer me the standard first time fiction deal: an advance roughly equivalent to half a public school teacher's salary without benefits. So I tried thinking of satisfactory excuses to diffuse Annie's concern about the potentially puny pot of gold at the end of it all. However, as far as I was concerned, being doomed to obscurity as a purveyor of literature didn't sound like such a terrible fate at the time.

Annie didn't know that I was a lot more nervous about meeting Mama Raspberry at the Uptown Theatre later in the afternoon. I'd stalled for nearly a week following Lucien's party. Then I gathered the courage to call Mama and prevail upon her to meet somewhere we weren't being watched. Forget about whether her phone was tapped or if she might turn me in. Here's something else I did that was really stupid: I lied to Mama by saying that Lucien asked me to call her again. . . . Well, I was convinced that she knew where Chillum Hoskiss was hiding. In the excitement of being devious, however, I wound up disregarding some dire consequences in order to convince Mama Raspberry that I meant Lucien no harm.

From my vantage point across the street, I watched her black Fleetwood pull in front of the movie theatre and stop beneath the old-fashioned marquee promoting the Holiday double feature *Blood Simple* and *Fargo*. Mama struggled out the front passenger seat into the gray afternoon and Lawrence drove away. She bought a ticket, ambled inside the vast, empty lobby, and headed for the snack counter. After waiting at least ten minutes, I was satisfied nobody had followed her and I hurried indoors. Mama stood off to the side of the brightly lit lobby next to a winding marble staircase up to the balcony. She was turned out, for lack of a better term, in a black suede suit with fringe and a floppy gangster hat. To my relief, our face-to-face evoked a rather underwhelming reaction, as Mama was busy shoveling popcorn into her mouth from one of those huge wax tubs.

"This sista' grabbed the Acadmee Award," Mama said, pointing to an old poster of Frances McDormand wearing her police uniform and leather cap with fur earflaps. "She done married the director. . . . I been to all them Conehead Brothaas' movies. Raisin Airzona, Bartin Finkus, and The Big Lewinsky. Some funny sheit hap'nin'. Cept'n, Hollywood gottsa bunch a crap out these days."

"I didn't know she was married to Joel Conehead," I replied, unable to think of anything else to say. When Mama glared at me,' I added, "Y'know, we could watch the movie if you'd like."

"My man, Denzel. He shine," Mama went on, seemingly ignoring me. "Better than that skinny-ass bitch, Jewya Roberts and her sappy sheit. . . . Lemme get this straight," she suddenly added, regarding me severely for the first time. "You wantsta company me to the movies? Boy, what's on yo' mind?"

"I think the government has evidence that Lucien was involved in Chillum Hoskiss' disappearance," I blurted out. "I believe . . . if you know where he is that will help Lucien."

Mama Raspberry nearly dropped her tub of popcorn, while her powerful body clenched into a large suede bowling ball. For one terrible moment she stared right through me. Then I followed her toward a red velvet loveseat in the dark passageway opposite closed double doors leading to aisle three.

"Lucien aint sent you here," Mama said after we sat down next to each other. "This here's some nasty sheit. You hear what I'm sayin?"

"But if the government finds Chillum first . . ."

"You aint liss'nin," Mama interrupted and moved closer to me. Then she offered some popcorn, which I couldn't refuse, and we remained silent for a few moments. "Don't get involved," Mama said in a more maternal way. "You might not like whatchu find out. . . . Best you don't be sniffin' around, you heppin' Lucien." Our eyes met again and my hand trembled as I found myself reaching into her buttery tub. "S'poze I know something about Chillum, anyway," Mama added, leaning into my face. "If I aint told the Guv'ment, why am I gonna tell you?"

I'd anticipated this question the moment I realized Mama Raspberry might lead me to Chillum Hoskiss. I figured that she believed I was stumbling around trying to prove Lucien's innocence. She was protecting her lawyer in ways I would never know. The problem with getting Mama to tell me the truth was, if my suspicions were right, I was about to become involved in obstructing justice. Once she informed me of something the government wanted to know I would indeed be in a heap of "sheit." Mama was leaving it up to me.

"You can trust me," I said, spouting the magic words. "I don't want to do anything to hurt Lucien. Simple as that."

Mama bored into my brain with a chilling look. "Chillum Hopkiss restin' in Mis-sippy," she replied softly. "He gone near a year already, the ashes spread over his Granddaddy's swamp farm near to Greenville."

She looked away momentarily, searching the narrow, dimly lit hallway that stretched around behind the lobby. Then Mama stared into my chest. "Cept'n if anybody be hearin' this from me," she said. "They be dead too."

"He's dead?" I patted my midsection in an absurd gesture that I was clean of any wires. "How'd he die?"

"Now whatchu want to know that for? Sheit, boy. You is stupid," Mama said, straightening up and beginning to chuckle. "Whatchu thinking? . . . Chillum's death certif-kit say natchel cawses," Mama added, commencing to laugh hilariously, until she suddenly began to choke on a popcorn kernel lodged in her throat.

I wondered how to accept this, while I watched Mama Raspberry coughing and gagging in between trying to catch her breath. She was apparently laughing herself into a coma over the fact that Lucien Echo had murdered a witness. It couldn't be true. He wouldn't do something so evil. Even

Lucien's lawyer had agreed that Chillum's testimony wouldn't hurt Lucien's defense. The mistake had afforded Judge Rotini a legal reason to void the search warrant. At worst, Tommy Goyle looked a little foolish and Mama Raspberry got off the hook.

Lucien had no reason to do it, I thought, as I slapped Mama's back until she raised her hand in a sign that the offending seed had passed through her gullet.

"How do you know Lucien was involved?" I asked after she'd resumed breathing normally and we'd walked over to the water fountain.

"We done conversin'," Mama replied. She took a drink, extracted a mother-of-pearl compact case from her Vuitton bag, checked her makeup, and straightened her hat. "I'm waitin' on Lawrence any minute. But since you heppin', you aks Lucien why Chillum got a hot shot after I tell Lucien where he stay at? And Chillum be afraid of needles. Sheit, boy," Mama added, laughing again when she saw my reaction. "You messin' witch yo' life."

I don't mind admitting that I'd reached a defining moment in my consciousness. It would've been much safer to walk away as Mama had urged. If I was able to confirm Chillum's death, my darkest fears about Lucien might be realized. I'd love to say I recognized that the time was at hand for me to gather my courage and follow the justice trail wherever it might lead. Under the rubric of responsible reporting I would crack the case, step out of the shadows, at last, and claim my rightful place in the world. But, if the truth be told, there I was again, contemplating the worst-case scenario.

Despite Mama Raspberry's warning, a few days later, I found myself exacerbating a risky situation. First, I maxed-out my credit card on a plane ticket to Memphis and a rental car. From there I drove south for hours, through a freezing rain, to the Bolivar county seat in western Mississippi. Believe it or not I schlepped to the boonies by way of some fascinating terrain, along the Mighty River, in search of Arthur Hopkiss's death certificate. That particular government spelling mistake proved to be another interesting piece of news Mama gave me at the movie theatre. Chillum's surname isn't "H-o-s-kiss." The FBI reports that I'd read had spelled it with an "s" instead of a "p." Whether this was innocent, or not, the Law Enforcement National Computer search had failed to turn up any out-of-state death record.

I should write a separate piece about my two days on the road between Greenville and Cleveland, Mississippi. It's enough to say here that I ran into many weird and helpful people along the way. From the roundelay of pimply-faced desk clerks at the Red Roof Inn, to the wisecracking old ladies working at Denny's on the other end of the strip mall. Still, I'm obliged to give specifics concerning Ethel Strubley down at the Bolivar County Recorder's office. Ethel came to the information window with hand-painted reindeer on her bulky wool sweater and battery-powered Christmas tree earrings twinkling off the sides of her bleached blonde wig. She sized me up, grading my request form like a chatty teacher. After disappearing for several minutes, Ethel returned with the first nail in Lucien Echo's coffin.

"Youse right, Mister. I sure found it," Ethel drawled, handing me a xerox copy of official proof that Arthur Hopkiss died three weeks after FBI agents had reported their first failed attempt to locate him in Chicago. "This here says he passed a year ago over in Rosedale," she went on, as the tiny green and red tree ornaments attached to her pinkish earlobes blinked on and off. "Prob'le cause is listed as a' accidental drug overdose."

So it was that I next found Deputy Sheriff Oswald W. Kreamer eating a sandwich in the Rosedale Town Hall. Oswald Kreamer was a tall, skinny redneck with a huge purple nose that he kept wiping with his handkerchief. Deputy Kreamer certainly remembered being called to the Motel 6, out on the interstate, after the maid had found Chillum's cold, naked body on the bed. "The little bugger was stiffer than a minister's collar," Kreamer said, taking a liking to me once he figured out that we possessed the same initials. Moreover, by the time Deputy Kreamer brought me into his office and allowed me to read his homicide report, I'd become so adept at lying that Kreamer didn't flinch when I told him I was looking into a death benefit claim for Chillum's kids in Chicago.

According to the deputy's formal account: "Arthur Hopkiss was a routine heroin overdose by hypodermic needle in the arm." Kreamer had tracked down a female witness named Clarisse Powell who admitted that she'd left Chillum in the motel room alive and "totally wasted" a few hours before the coroner's estimated time of death. Kreamer had also interviewed Arthur's next of kin: grandmother, Myrtle Batts, who informed the deputy that Chillum had recently returned from Chicago's South Side, and that was about it concerning the details of his life.

In sum, nothing had appeared suspicious to Deputy Kreamer, and he advised that the coroner found no reason to convene a formal inquest. Cremation was authorized at the grandmother's request and the ashes released to her. As far as the deputy knew, nobody else from Chicago had inquired about Arthur Hopkiss' death during the year. "Hopkiss was just another faceless Boogee messin' up the landscape," Kreamer added.

The matter might have ended there. Except, the next day, acting on a nagging hunch, I drove over to Myrtle Batts' ramshackle river house, along the east bank, and quickly learned some things Deputy Kreamer hadn't found out. For starters Mrs. Batts is third cousin to none other than Louise Raspberry. It turns out, nearly every afternoon for sixty years Myrtle Batts has drunk whiskey on the same old creaking front porch where she divulged to me that her whiny, weak-minded grandson, Arthur, had been a problem from the day he was born until the day her daughter died when Chillum was only ten.

I was chilled to the bone sitting on mildewed vinyl lawn furniture, somewhere in the bog, while Mrs. Batts let it be known that Arthur's acquisition of a heroin addiction was no surprise to her. She'd seen so much hatred and disrespect in the world that she often wondered why God chose her to live through it all. When I asked her to explain what she meant, Mrs. Batts demurred, insisting that she'd known little of Chillum's recent and, as it happened, his last affairs. Yet, she'd managed to gather that Arthur was a "snitch." And despite thinking that his demise was unfortunate she apparently hadn't grown too agitated over it.

Myrtle Batts was slack-jawed and slight-framed. She wore a flannel housecoat and walked with a wooden cane throughout the clapboard house her daddy had built with his porter's salary from the Rock Island Railway. She told me about her church Bible readings and meetings at the elders club, her crossword puzzles and Matlock on television. Mrs. Batts' routine wasn't going to be interrupted over her worthless grandson. After I pressed for more details, she divulged the rumor she'd heard that Arthur was chased out of town for informing in a drug deal. When I asked if anyone had investigated, she told me a Chicago policeman came looking for Arthur a couple days before he died.

"I remember the coincidence, all right," Mrs. Batts said. "But the local deputy who informed me about Arthur's death, he wasn't interested and I didn't want no trouble. So I never did talk about it. Arthur deserved a decent service with his ashes spread over the property, God rest his soul."

When I asked Mrs. Batts if she recalled what the police officer from Chicago looked like, the man she described was Tommy Goyle.

* * *

Scarcely forty-eight hours later, I was wandering down Michigan Avenue talking to myself in the chilly windless night. My options had dwindled. I'd outsmarted myself in a serious public mess, and I was experiencing the loneliest Christmas Eve in my life. I watched the snow falling under the florescent street lamps outside Water Tower Place. A noisy crowd filled the wide sidewalk, obscuring the elaborate window displays and separating me from the folding tables stocked with genuine silk ties, wool scarves, and other knock-off sundries. Every Christmas Eve since my mother died Michael and I had respected her memory by going to Dad's. That night, according to Annie's account, anyway, the festivities would prove gratifying to the attendees. I couldn't handle it.

I'm told that my father announced his decision to turn over the store to Michael. It seems my brother had swung a deal to convert it to a Men's Warehouse franchise, including a shoe department Dad could putter in whenever he so desired. Michael's sexual appetite had apparently returned—he must've gone off his Prozac—as Annie said that Michael's new girlfriend, Sara, kept touching him under the table during supper. What with my sister back home, plus my father's beloved grandson to carry on tradition, this version of the Katz family holiday was the one not to miss. Still, Dad didn't want to hear cab-driving stories or bartending tales from me. The thing my father wanted to discuss at the time—the thing everyone wanted to hear about—was the Lucien Echo scandal.

Having recognized Lucien's name in the media from somewhere in our past, my father had prevailed upon me for developments in the case. Although Dad stopped trying to read my short stories long ago, he seemed mesmerized by Lucien's predicament and encouraged me to exploit the situation. I couldn't bring myself to let him know, or any of them, for that matter, how I'd screwed up blindly pursuing Lucien. Moreover, how could I go to the prosecutor with my discovery if I couldn't tell my family about it?

I understood that remaining silent was not a legal option. At first, I thought I'd mail Chillum's death certificate to the authorities, anonymously, thereby allowing the news to break on its own. No doubt the FBI would locate Myrtle Batts and make the same connection to detective Goyle. But Mrs. Batts would tell them about me and they would know who sent the proof. In any case, one conclusion seemed more and more inescapable to me: after the US Attorney had confronted Lucien over the August Rotini wiretaps, Lucien and Tommy Goyle conspired to silence Arthur Hopkiss forever.

Within the two days following Goyle's encounter with Myrtle Batts, in such a tiny place Goyle could have easily found Chillum and followed him to the motel room. Then he had waited for the girl to leave and lethally injected Hopkiss, making it look like an accident. Keep in mind, when the Rotini and Echo corruption investigation started, Tommy Goyle was a friendly government witness who might have perpetuated their simple misspelling of a confidential informant's surname. If that was the plan, it was working until Mama Raspberry disclosed to me that Lucien had asked her for Chillum's whereabouts. Maybe it was Mama's way of doing equity, as she'd handed me the definitive evidence against Lucien. Since the FBI hadn't managed to locate him, how else did Tommy Goyle find Hopkiss so quickly?

If I kept silent I'd be charged with Obstruction of Justice after Chillum's death was eventually uncovered. And would I ever be safe? At that point, I hadn't told anyone. Yet, I hadn't slept for more than a few hours during the previous three nights. I'd changed forever the course of my life while I no longer had control over it. Resolving to uncover the truth, I didn't bother considering whether I could endure its consequences. Well, *hard cheese* for me. Exposing the facts seemed a whole lot more important than my measly hide. I'm oversimplifying things, I know, but considering the way I'd used my relationship with Lucien we weren't that far apart. That's really why I roamed Michigan Avenue on Christmas Eve unable to show my face to my family. Who in their right mind would be proud to become an informer?

At Superior Street, I turned the corner and ducked down the steps into Gino's East. Despite further internal debate, I called Rococo from the pay phone, expecting to find it closed or Alex not there. Instead, she answered and before I knew it I was on my way to the restaurant. I didn't want to tell Alex what I was going to do, but I wanted absolution for what I was also doing to her. My connection with Alex was the biggest impediment to busting Lucien, although I'd given up hoping she would care for me in the same way. As I walked beneath the Franklin Street L tracks, a thin blanket of virgin snow covered the deserted sidewalk. How painful it was thinking that I might never see her again.

Inside the boxy shell of a converted warehouse, Alex had created a warm, lavish atmosphere splashed with brightly colored wall fabrics and draperies. Velvet banquettes were arranged to give the appearance of a salon rather than a restaurant with forty tables. To my surprise the persistent hum and clanking of Gen-X diners in the usual variations on black nearly filled the place. At the far end of the room a quartet performed ambient chamber music on a platform carved into the wall above the bar. Alex stood underneath, near a winding metal staircase, conversing with the bartender. Wearing a tight wool mini-dress and Indian silk scarf, tied primly around her neck, she conveyed who was in charge.

"I'm amazed by the number of people with no place to go on Christmas Eve," I said, approaching her. Alex kissed me on the lips, briskly, yet we embraced long enough for the bartender to regard me curiously. "If you're busy," I added, "I could wait here."

She held my hands away from her body. "I guess I could buy you a drink." Alex seemed excited about our flirtation. "Did'ya eat?" she went on. "I'll send over some special appetizers for you to try. Okay? Kevin, bring us a dinner menu, please," she instructed the curly-haired young hulk, across the bar, as we stepped around the drink well and sat on the nearest upholstered stools.

"So, Ollie," Alex said. "What a pleasant surprise. I was wondering whether you'd come in."

"I'm truly impressed. All the details match so . . . effortlessly."

"Thanks very much. That's the idea, isn't it?"

"So it's true. Everybody comes here."

Alex rapped her knuckles on the lacquered bar without hesitation. "I'm kinda comfortable at the moment," she said. "Most of the time I see cockroaches floating in the bisque."

"Is that the holiday special?"

" . . . I hate Christmas," Alex replied, after smiling, rather weakly, I thought, at my remark. "Why aren't you with your family?"

"I dunno," I said, dodging her question. "Sometimes people you've known all your life become too much to face."

"It's a disgrace how I manage to avoid my parents. I'm so bad," Alex added, "My mother, who's always been afraid to get on a plane, is threatening to fly here for a visit."

"How nice that she misses her daughter."

"She can't wait to gloat over Lucien's situation. My mother has never thought much of my choices."

"That's exactly why I'd rather wallow in self-pity."

Alex laughed, but I remember her searching my face for signs of what loomed behind our link. This was my time to shine, too. She'd had ample opportunity to back away. Alex encouraged me instead with mussels soufflé, presented in an ornate parfait glass, seared foie gras to die for, and her body language opened a little wider, threatening to let me in.

"D'ya hear the good news?" she asked, perhaps noticing my personality change. "They're talking about dismissing Lucien's indictment. Judge Rotini agreed to plead guilty, but he's insisting Lucien didn't do anything improper in Mama's case. There's a chance this nightmare may end."

"That is terrific," I said, lying with every fiber in my being, unable to tell her that Lucien's hope for escaping prosecution was about to vanish. "There's a way to go before he's out of the woods," I added, trying to remain calm as we locked eyes, which, in my case, were cloudy windows to what passed for my soul. "The Justice department doesn't like tossing out cases," I said. "It's sure good news, though."

"You don't think very much of me," Alex replied, sounding like she knew what I was up to. "Do you?"

"Whaddiya mean?"

"I hope you respect me enough to let me make my own decisions about Lucien."

"Things aren't hard enough already?"

"Maybe I'm beginning to discover what I don't want . . ."

Alex's reply sounded reckless, her voice trailing off at the end. Certainly, here was the turning point. I hope I hadn't feigned indifference.

"I know why you're here," Alex went on, startling me. Then she took my hand in hers and held it while I looked back into her sweet, anxious face. "Don't be embarrassed," she said, getting to the bottom of things. "My intuition tells me you've come to set the record straight."

"I'm in way over my head," I admitted.

That's all she wrote. Far too many events conspired to overwhelm us at a vulnerable time. That worked for me. Anyway, I remained at the bar enjoying a snifter of Lucien's favorite brandy and jazzy Christmas songs performed by the quartet up in the bird's nest. Alex shifted stock in the backroom, wrote numbers in the company books, and fiddled with the cash receipts in the safe. At eleven-thirty the place was hopping. Without fanfare or discussion Alex led me out through the rear door and we happily surrendered to loneliness and betrayal.

In her car we were drawn together by the starry night and tranquil empty streets covered with fresh snow. While stopped at a traffic light, I took Alex's hand and held it between mine, bringing it up to the side of my mouth and nose. She turned, allowing me to kiss her fingertips, and our mouths found each other, softly at first, then greedily. We were twirling tongues when a lone car behind us began honking after the light had changed. We took ourselves the rest of the way with my hand tenderly massaging Alex's inner right thigh over panty hose. Holiday street parking was available a couple blocks away and we were soon tucked away on the couch in my living room.

"To a white Christmas," I said, toasting with my Snapple bottle.

"Hallelujah," Alex replied, clinking it against her water glass containing a concoction of fruit juices and cheap Agave I kept around. She took a gulp, sucked on a lemon peel, and smiled at me. "I guess you wouldn't have a tree? Would you?"

"No I don't," I said, a little upset.

"Too bad."

"Too bad?"

"Yeah, too bad," Alex repeated, her leg reflexively brushing against mine. "'Cause I got you a present and there's nowhere to put it."

"You did?"

"It's in the car . . . Don't look so surprised."

"How could you know I'd come to see you tonight?"

"Who says I know anything? If you don't like it, you can return it."

"I'm sure I'll love it," I offered, wondering what in the world she could have given me. "We can get it later."

"Whatever you want."

Whereas Alex seemed to accept our situation, she was more comfortable in her skin than I was in mine. Alex didn't believe that, of course, yet it was true.

"I have bouts of self-doubt followed by depression," she said, while we cuddled in each other's arms on the sofa. She was dissuading me from advancing further along the flip side of her confident social self. But her disclosure was tardy, following our rather intense kissing and fondling session, where I'd managed to unleash Alex's taut breasts while tangling up her scarf in the zipper of her tight dress. None of it mattered much by then. We'd gone over the cliff. The rest was negotiating our fall without a parachute. Naively, perhaps, our mental and physical show-and-tell kicked into high gear once we retreated to the bedroom.

"Are my ankles bloated?" Alex wondered when we were lying on my bed, side-by-side, half-naked and gauging how far we could go without confronting the important issues. "Don't hold me to my word when I'm drunk," she added, sneaking her tongue into my ear, after she'd nibbled on both of my lobes and sipped at her tequila mixture. "I don't drink for that reason," Alex went on, beginning to gently rub the outside of her hand across the inside of my thigh. "I'm surprised at myself to be here."

"You're allowed to be happy."

"A world of rationalizing won't change what I'm doing," Alex replied.

"How about happiness with a capital *Ollie*?"

"I don't know how permanent anything is," Alex acknowledged, smiling, as she continued massaging around and over my groin. "I'm talking about sharing a rare moment of well-being when we aren't absorbed in the issues of the day. There's a huge difference between recognizing what we're feeling and what we convince ourselves we could also be feeling if only this or that thing were happening too. . . . Hey, Ollie. Is something wrong?"

"No. What makes you say that?"

"I dunno. Maybe because your winky went soft."

"My winky? . . . That's what you call it?"

"It sounds better than cock. Don't ya think?"

"Yeah, I guess so."

"There he is," Alex encouraged me with her warm, gentle hand and then crawled along the quilt until she pulled down my briefs and took it into her mouth. Again I sprang to attention and began concentrating on Alex's breasts dangling in front of me, her hard pink nipples awaiting my eager touch. Here was the manifestation of my wildest dreams, the embodiment of my senses palpably conjoined with the universe in all its divine mystery. . . . Somehow, though, it was all wrong! The situation: Alex's motivation and vulnerability, my deception, the timing, our backstabbing betrayal, my fear of exposure and death, even the lighting was wrong. I'd reached the edge of an out of body experience. No doubt Alex and I were eternal soul mates. Only this time around we'd run into each other on a bad trip and I was required to surrender to some transcendental love that would carry us through.

My conundrum was greater than simple sexual dysfunction under extraordinary circumstances. I was raging inside against the terrible irony dooming me to celibacy rather than taking the easy way out. At that moment, I promise, I was alert to doing the honorable thing. We live in a time of such rudeness and inattention to each other that our basic human need of a little kindness goes more and more unrequited everyday. I'd like to assure you, I was doing my part to preserve civility, respect for traditional values, and the sanctity of one's word. But, try as I might, I couldn't stop picturing Lucien Echo shuffling down some lonely prison corridor, and I was unable to keep Mr. Winky aloft.

Dawn came while Alex and I continued to wrestle over our role in this theater-of-the-not-so-absurd unfolding around us. Put another way, it was Christmas morning and the Wise Men were nowhere in the vicinity. Alex and I seemed compatible. We shared the same rhythm, intellectually and sexually, although the latter remained subject to definitive penetration. If the bigger picture was at work, I didn't see it. We'd passed the night deposing each other on the subtleties of our aspirations and personal histories. More to the point, though, I sensed that our ephemeral cocoon was important to Alex. It was a lot better than worrying over the most likely fatal denouement at the time.

By seven-fifteen a.m., Alex was showered, dressed, and drinking a cup of my fresh-brewed coffee. I don't know why little more was said. The spell may have been broken, as we both faced disturbing decisions. After checking her messages for the third time, Alex explained that Lucien was scheduled to return from New York by noon. His melancholy presence hung around, and Alex soon left without offering to meet again at any specific time. Forgive me, here, for failing to properly translate the depth of my feelings. During the six months that Alex and I had come to know each other, in my opinion, ours was hardly some fluffy summer romance, and I still get emotional whenever I think about her walking out of my apartment that day.

The doorbell rang so soon afterwards I thought Alex had either returned to proclaim herself to me or to retrieve something she'd left behind. Imagine my surprise when I opened the door, wearing a shit-eating grin, and found Lucien standing there. It was bad enough that he'd secretly tracked the two of us together; it was more unnerving that Lucien had been cool enough to wait for Alex to leave before he bashed my brains in. It was downright eerie when he didn't say anything directly about her.

"We need to resolve some things," Lucien calmly said instead. "I know it's early. May I come in?"

Lucien's face was drawn, his eyes framed by dark circles of desperation. Still, he was defiant and proud like a wounded lion made more dangerous by the smell of his own death. After leaving his camel overcoat on the sofa, Lucien made his way through my tiny living room toward the round oak table near the bay window. I observed him meticulously dressed in black khaki pants and shirt, with a multi-pocketed vest and expensive all weather shoes—what any self-respecting stalker would wear on Christmas morning. Other than retribution over Alex, I didn't know what he was after. I didn't think Lucien knew what I was going to do to him. But I felt guilty enough to act the good host, keeping my eyes on his hands whenever he moved.

"You know my trial date's next month," Lucien said after we were seated, facing each other, sunlight streaming onto the tabletop. "Effram tells me the situation has changed, so I've decided against the publicity angle. I'm afraid your services are no longer required."

"I've been gathering material for months," I replied, fearful of disclosing anything I'd learned. "I was kinda' hoping to tie it together like we planned. It'll make a good book."

"I recall the only agreement we had was that you wouldn't print anything without my permission," Lucien said grimly. "On top of that, as my investigator, you'll have confidentiality problems if you get any funny ideas."

Lucien took a deep breath, gazed out the window, and slipped his right hand into one of the many pockets on his fancy vest. "Look, Ollie," he said. "I'm willing to compensate you for the time and effort you spent. I can't stop you from attending the proceedings, but I'm pulling the plug on this project. It's my final decision."

"I'm not sure that's possible anymore," I replied, realizing immediately that I'd decided to pull my own plug, so to speak.

"What's your point?"

"Y'see, Lucien, I know Arthur Hopkiss's ashes wound up in the Mississippi River," I said, standing up from the table, knees shaking, "because Tommy Goyle killed him. . . . Th . . . th . . . there's a witness who saw Goyle looking for Chillum two days before he was murdered. How long was that after you told Goyle where to find him?"

"Well, well," Lucien said, thin lips smiling at me through clenched teeth, withholding any reaction to my quivering accusation. "Now let's hear the rest," he added, as if he already knew, while he stroked his chin with his left hand and kept his right planted inside the same vest pocket.

"First you hustled Chillum out of town before the FBI came looking for him," I speculated, buoyed, I guess, by Lucien's apparent nonchalance. "Then you sent Goyle to make sure Chillum wouldn't expose you in Mama's case. Only it wasn't Rotini you paid off. It was Goyle. . . . I'm not the lawyer, Lucien, but I don't think your right to confidentiality will protect me from obstruction of justice charges in a murder case. I have to turn over this evidence and I hope you have one helluva good explanation."

"Let's be clear," Lucien's response was quick and decisive. He leaned across the table with his left elbow out in front of him like a blocker in football deflecting the bad news. "No explanation is necessary because you aren't going to turn over anything."

Lucien smiled at me again, his body relaxed, and he calmed down. For a time he gazed off into the living room, almost meditatively, and then he turned to me with resignation in his eyes. "I'm going to say this once, Ollie. I thought Goyle was going to keep Chillum *out* of harm's way until the investigation blew over. Goyle didn't want Chillum to tell the FBI that he was shaking Chillum down," he admitted, seemingly relieved to unburden himself.

"I only learned this after Mama became a witness," Lucien added, determined to set me straight. "The government tried to keep her away, but Mama contacted me, anyway, to ask if I thought she should tell them Hopkiss was dead. She also said Goyle had pressured Hopkiss to set her up in the first place. It was more profitable for Goyle if she stayed on the street, so he agreed to screw up the address on the search warrant. Now you understand why Tommy Goyle wasn't taking any chances that the FBI might get hold of Chillum?"

"Gimme a break, Lucien. You didn't know Goyle was going to kill him?"

"Keeping it quiet was difficult. They were prosecuting me for a trumped-up bribery charge. What was I supposed to do? Now that Auggie Rotini has decided to plea bargain in his other cases Effram tells me the government is dismissing mine. They're not going to trial because Auggie insists that I didn't give him any money. Do you see why your Lieutenant Colombo routine couldn't have come at a worse time?"

"You concealed Hopkiss's murder to avoid prosecution in a bribery. Why should I believe you didn't intend to kill him?"

"I could've reported it when Mama told me," Lucien replied softly, straightening in his chair; this time he looked directly at me. "For cryin' out loud, Ollie. How much did the government care about Hopkiss? Mama didn't tell them and they gave her immunity. . . . I'm paying dearly for my bad judgment considering the publicity, and I may still go to prison and lose my license."

Lucien stood up next to me and put his arm around my shoulder, drawing me towards him. I tried to pull free, but he continued to hug me for an awkward moment. Finally, he released his grip.

"Talk about poor judgment," Lucien sniped, as I backed away. "You were supposed to help restore my image, not snoop into the past and dredge up evidence against me.

Don't you think I've been carrying a huge weight around inside?"

He moved toward me again. "You know I agreed to help Mama because of our history. Whatever went on between Tommy Goyle and Chillum Hopkiss had nothing to do with me. When the government confronted me with the tapes, I made the mistake of letting Goyle know about the investigation. I never thought he was going to kill him."

"So you've kept quiet for a year to protect your ass?"

"I repeat," Lucien responded testily, as he followed me over to the Formica counter bar separating my tiny kitchen area from the living room, "I learned Hopkiss was dead *after* Mama was asked to cooperate in the bribery case. Then I was indicted and you entered the picture. You carried my message to Mama. Remember? You . . . the man with the proof that Goyle murdered Arthur Hopkiss."

"Am I supposed to make a citizen's arrest?"

"Where does the attorney-client privilege begin and end in a case like this?" Lucien replied, not being responsive, as he moved in closer and I noticed that his hand was back inside the same vest pocket.

"It *never* ends, Lucien. You have excuses for this and a shield of confidentiality for that. How many other dirty little secrets have you been piling up all these years? Bullshit in a clown suit is what you are, and you've wallowed in it for so long you can't recognize what a disgrace you've become!"

Echo slid backwards into the nearest captain's chair, alongside the bar-divider, as if the force of my remarks struck him. After sitting quietly for a moment, he pulled from his mysterious vest pocket a fancy Waterman pen and began to doodle on a Chinese takeout menu lying on the countertop.

"Of course, you don't know Tommy Goyle," Lucien said. "Don't worry, Ollie. Goyle will get his as soon as my case is dismissed. If you go to the US Attorney now, they won't believe I didn't have anything to do with Hopkiss's death. I'm the only one who can do that. You have to trust me a little longer."

"Stop it!" I exclaimed with all the fury I could muster. My face grew red and I flapped my arms like I was trying to shake off his words. "You have no right to ask for anyone's trust," I blathered on. "You're the keeper of society's rules and they don't apply to you." I shook from head to toe, although my mouth kept moving and words tumbled out as if disconnected from the rest of me. Lucien's eyes were fierce slits, filtering the force of my attack, and glaring right back through me. "You're out of control, Lucien, and I won't be conned anymore," I heard my own voice again, winding down. "How Alex finds any integrity in you is beyond me."

Following another uncomfortable silence, Lucien displayed his clenched jaw grin and quipped, "Thanks for your vote of confidence." He replaced the cap on his shiny black and gold fountain pen and rose impassively from the chair. "It's my fault for bringing you into this," he said. "How disappointing. I had high hopes for us. I'm afraid, though, you're the one who's out of control," he added, lowering his voice and giving me a hard look that was obviously his way of allowing me one last chance to back down.

"I wish you luck with your risky new philosophy," Lucien announced when I didn't reply. He walked over to the sofa, grabbed his cashmere overcoat and his soft Italian leather gloves, and started for the door. "How much integrity did Alex find in you?" he asked, turning around. Then Lucien added, for good measure, I'm sure, "What makes you think I wouldn't unleash Tommy Goyle on you?"

"You have twenty-four hours to turn yourself in," I replied with conviction, despite Lucien's dire warning, and without thinking. I was certainly out of control.

Yet, I felt satisfied, as though my life had value again. Our confrontation had seemed to confirm Lucien's timeless hubris. At least, he was stuck in his primitive musings and emotions threatening to take me down with him. I expected from him some wisdom and maturity, possibly a little compassion in deference to our long history. Lucien and I had come full circle since college, as I was the one who'd rather die than live this way another day. If Lucien believed me, then I needn't fear him any longer. If Lucien possessed any of this wisdom and compassion, it was his moment of truth not mine.

This theory kept me together for the next hour or so when fear crept back up through my stomach and lodged somewhere in my esophagus. In spite of the Christmas sermons and nativities inundating nearly every television and radio channel, it was impossible to sit at my desk and concentrate on what I'd outlined for the penultimate chapter of *Dr. Rob's Journey*. Real life events were more exciting and dangerous, and I hadn't grasped any relevant moral connection between ratting on Lucien and the resolution of Rob and Beverly's story. Don't get me wrong, I sensed that important parallels existed; lessons were there to be learned and applied. I hadn't figured them out yet, so I turned again to my dear sister, Annie, for illumination and escape.

Forty minutes later the snow was already melted under sparse traffic as I reached the Glenview exit off the Edens Expressway. Annie's rented cottage was situated above one of the wooded ravines running through the suburb's tiny downtown. Annie had promptly managed to transform this rather dismal, single story brick and stucco coach house into a warm and cozy country home for Jason, complete with Laura Ashley curtains, down comforters, working fireplace and a cobblestone walkway to their private entrance off the rear portion of the main residence lot. Bushes planted along the path and the vegetable garden out back were covered with sheets of winter weather protective plastic.

Unusual as it was for me to pop over without phoning, I was confident Annie would be home on Christmas morning. In my hands was a glow-in-the-dark Sammy Sosa key-chain flashlight for Jason, which I'd managed to score at a White Hen Pantry, the only place open on the way over. When Annie came to the door she hardly seemed surprised to see me. According to her, everyone had missed me at Dad's and she'd just tried calling to find out what was wrong.

"Nothing's wrong," I said, looking around her idyllic living room decorated with silver foil strung all over and four stockings hanging from the fireplace mantel. One was for Jason, one for Annie, one for Grandpa Katz, and one for Beaver, the six year old brown and silver tabby who'd been rescued from the pound as a kitten and managed to end up in Glenview, like the furniture, despite Annie's comings and goings. On the carpet, near the lighted tree, were the discarded wrappings, ribbon and empty boxes from Jason's haul, which had apparently included a skateboard and Gameboy, in addition to the practical but ever-boring three-packs of underwear and socks, and a plaid corduroy robe lying untouched. When Beaver stuck his face out of the skateboard box, his head and shoulders tangled in a bright red ribbon, I choked up with gratitude that I could rely on Annie at a time like this.

"C'mon, Ollie. What's going on? You're disheveled and distracted and you look like you're gonna cry any minute."

"Nothing's wrong," I repeated, unable to tell her what I'd found out about Lucien, or his threats, or what had happened between Alex and me. I'd lived in fear long enough to be paralyzed just processing the possibilities spread out before me. Despite my succession of sorely-missed opportunities—failing a better description of my life—things were so dire it dawned on me that I'd been committing suicide by increment all these years. That was far worse than the most violent or embarrassing fate awaiting me if I took on Lucien Echo.

I also couldn't bring myself to confide in Annie because I didn't want her to know I was full of rage and increasing desire to destroy Lucien. Self-defense, while not a strong suit of mine, seemed a plausible option depending upon how desperately Lucien wanted to stop me. And the more I thought about it, if Alex and I had a chance, our path together seemed smoother if Lucien was out of the way.

"Dad's here?" I asked, noticing his wool stadium coat with those old-fashioned wooden buttons, draped over the couch.

"He's in the den with Jason," Annie replied, circling around like a mother hen. "Last night, after dinner, Dad started giving Jason his Christmas presents. He's so excited to have Jason back that he decided to hold out some Hanukah gelt and come over this morning."

"It's a doubleheader for the mutant," I said, walking over to the sunken family room with blonde paneling and deep pile carpeting. In the far corner my father and my extremely slick, barely pubescent nephew were sitting in front of the video monitor connected to Annie's mega-gigabyte computer tower playing Texas Showdown poker. Dad's thinning silver hair was straight, unkempt and in need of a good cropping. I don't care how youthful a man appears, once he hits seventy-five he shouldn't keep his hair long. He starts to look like an old tribal chieftain or some other wild man of nature or, worse yet, Howard Hughes. My father resembled the Archie Bunker physical type. Except Dad was never blustery and, as far as I can remember, he seldom raised his voice at any of us.

"Hello, Son," Dad said after I came over and stood behind him. "What happened to you last night?"

"I just got home from a business trip to Mississippi and I . . . I had a date."

"So?" my father turned around to give me his full attention. Jason noticed something dynamic taking place and he perked up as well. "You couldn't bring your date over for dinner?"

"No Dad. I couldn't."

"Your brother brought *his* date. Sara, she was very sweet and quite attractive. Wasn't she, Jase? Michael didn't have a problem bringing her."

"Uncle Ollie was probably busy boning his date. . . . Right, Unc?"

"Jason!" my father interjected. "Did you learn that in Los Angeles? You'd better speak like a gentleman when you're in my house."

"This is *my* house, Grandpa. I'll talk any damn way I please!" Jason curled his lip into a smirk and jumped away from the mouse pad. "Just kidding," he added, waving his arms at both of us in surrender, when we didn't appear to get it right away; or at all, for that matter.

"Shut your hole you little shit!" I declared, grabbing Jason by the shoulders and holding him in front of me. "Not funny. If you disrespect my father or my sister again I'll rip your lungs out."

"Calm down, Ollie," my father interceded. "Jason's performing. He wants to be an actor. . . . Right, Jase?"

Jason silently pleaded with me to let him loose. I was shocked how handsome and vulnerable he looked. Pure Stanislavsky. This obnoxious know-it-all eighth grader had hoodwinked everybody including my sister. Still, no matter what you said about him, Jason possessed the fearless zest for life that I used to have when I was his age. Annie must've passed on our mother's quick wit and endless optimism, for Mom encouraged us to be and do our best. I remember thinking I was capable of anything. Lucky to have such a supportive parent, I wasn't certain when my adolescent joie de vivre turned into a cavalcade of "What ifs?" Nevertheless, determined not to expose my jealousy and resentment, I let the little smartass go.

It's a good thing I did because Annie walked in and looked at me as though she knew exactly what I was thinking. Before Jason squealed on me, I handed him the pitiful, glow-in-the-dark, Sammy Sosa trinket, straightened out the shirt of his flannel pajamas, and rubbed the top of his head while putting on my most innocent smile.

"C'mere, Ollie," Annie said. "I need your help in the kitchen."

"Thanks, Unc," Jason patronized me. "How'd you know I've been beggin' for a crappy key chain all year long?"

"Lemme see that," Dad said, grabbing it from Jason and flicking the flashlight switch. "Didn't you get any batteries with this thing?"

I followed Annie out of the room without further comment. She led me by the hand to the kitchen and deposited me into one of the cane chairs situated around the breakfast nook table. Annie sat across from me, patiently, staring me down until I began to crumble. In my last ditch effort to avoid talking directly about Lucien and Alex, I mentioned the possible ending to *Dr. Rob's Journey* that I couldn't focus on when I'd decided to drive out there in the first place. Please believe me, I wanted to tell Annie everything I was going through and ask for advice. I must say, though, upon reflection, I was beyond the point of reason, insisting on first talking about my novel. Annie seemed more concerned with my condition than I was; yet she encouraged me to go ahead. By then, I guess, she was willing to listen to anything I had to say.

"Well . . . y'see," I began hesitantly, "Dr. Rob's final quandary involves the imminent battle for his soul."

I was instantly uncertain where that was headed, as my real life moral dilemma was evidently intruding upon my fiction. "In one version," I went on, desperately trying to keep my stories separate, "Rob may be doomed for eternity to relive every experience that he's run away from, been in denial over, or lied about during his lifetime. When he finally succumbs, peacefully, in his own bed, with Beverly and the kids at his side, Rob faces neither heaven nor hell or judgment of any kind. Only his wrong choices will perpetually confront his spirit."

"That's the upbeat version?" Annie was fidgety already.

"Let's do this another time, okay?"

"I'm sorry, Ollie. I'll shut up. Please? I really want to hear this."

"In the other version," I continued, willing to suffer Annie's taunts, "Rob has accomplished much to correct his past mistakes and remained a good person till the end. He's compiled a list of sins he has managed to recapitulate since his time travel hallucinations began, including the name of each person to whom he feels he should atone. Rob is determined to contact every one of them, whether he survives or not, until he has wiped his slate clean. If our souls exist, why shouldn't his plan succeed? Why shouldn't Rob find the cure?"

"I don't know, Ollie. Why shouldn't Rob find the cure?"

"I thought you were going to help me decide what to do?"

"I don't know what you should do. For what it's worth, though, I'll tell you something Saint Augustine said: 'To have faith is to believe in something you can't see. And the reward for this faith is to see what you believe.'"

"What does that mean?"

"Unless Rob or you, Ollie—if that's who we're really talking about here—are willing to risk it all, spiritually and mortally, you won't resolve whatever is driving you crazy. Capiche? . . . But I have to warn you," Annie went on before I could respond, "There won't be a happy ending just because you have absolute faith in the course of action you've chosen. The truth is, Ollie, some of history's most noble commitments have ended in the bloodiest disasters. I know you hate it when I toss that word into the mix. But to the extent that we must follow through on our doomed promises, aren't we all prisoners of the truth?"

"Prisoners of truth?" I wondered aloud. "That's pretty good," I went on, turning the phrase over in my head.

For the first time I began to understand the significance of Annie's statement in the context of what to do about Lucien Echo. Once I carried out my threat there would be no recapitulating this event whether I was proved right or not. I was dizzy from traveling back and forth in time since the odyssey had begun on the rainy pier in Madison. Yet, the first thing Lucien had said to me was ringing in my ears:

> Heroes are only lucky fools. There's an instant of decision when the outcome is spontaneous and anybody who follows that plan for life is certainly a fool.

Nearly two months passed before I saw Lucien Echo again. Not for lack of trying on my part. Although crap started raining down right after I delivered my raging ultimatum, I'd given Lucien one extra day. Just when I'd decided to call Sandy Turbot, the assistant US Attorney prosecuting Lucien's case, eerily, the doorbell rang. Upstairs came two dark-suited FBI agents requesting that I accompany *them* to Mr. Turbot's office on Dearborn Street. Being wholly unconcerned with my anxiety, they refused along the way to discuss anything other than the fact that Mr. Turbot wanted to confirm my relationship with Lucien Echo.

"Is it true, Mr. Katz?" Turbot asked as soon as we were facing each other across the desk in his cluttered office. "Myrtle Batts told you she could identify Detective Goyle?"

I watched Sandy Turbot straighten the Windsor knot on his green and gold club tie, not exactly matching the pointed collar oxford shirt and off-the-rack navy blue pin-striped suit. He fixed his beady eyes on me and officiously declared that Lucien had instructed Abrahamson to report the death of Arthur Hopkiss thirty-six hours before.

I remember looking around the tiny room for the first time. Tall metal file cabinets framed the curtainless window, every available space stacked with legal papers and poster-board diagrams, and I felt my perpetual stomach knot begin to loosen and, blessedly, unfold. The government had gotten it right and Turbot wasn't bothering to squeeze me for more information. He went on to say that Lucien had agreed to plead guilty to obstructing the Rotini investigation and cooperate in Tommy Goyle's prosecution for murder.

"Is he in custody?"

"He was here yesterday," Turbot smirked. "I'd stay as far away from Lucien Echo as possible. You're lucky he came forward, Mr. Katz. We'll be in touch if we need you."

Ten days later, I read in the papers that Lucien had appeared before Judge Plunkem who accepted his guilty plea, dismissed the bribery charges, and ordered him to return for sentencing in six weeks. I was too uncomfortable to attend that first session, mostly in dread of seeing Alex, so I tried phoning Lucien several times. I wanted to acknowledge what he'd decided to do in spite of everything, but I didn't leave a message. I sensed that it was better to stay away from Alex in light of what she probably thought of me. While I didn't stalk her, I often waited outside their apartment contemplating whether to ring the bell or approach Alex when she came home alone.

When the morning of Lucien's sentencing arrived, I couldn't avoid the spectacle, slipping into the back row of Plunkem's courtroom just in time to hear Sandy Turbot recommend an eighteen-month prison sentence. As it turned out, Abrahamson's assessment was closer. Judge Plunkem stared Lucien right between the eyes and coolly ordered him to spend the next nine months inside a government country club in Florida contemplating the greater moral implications of his illegal deeds.

During what must've been Lucien's lowest moment on earth, Alex's stoic support from the second pew in the gallery probably made it worse for him. Alex was flanked by the scabrous media and her inappropriately done up and over-tucked mother. Braving her lifelong fear of flying in the hope of witnessing her daughter's idyllic life—and to load up on the silverware in first class—Mother Carlton ended up touching down into this shameful ordeal. From where I sat, anyway, Alex's mother could have been attending the theatre instead of watching her future son-in-law get fitted for a pair of trap-door pajamas. Considering that she made a loud whelping noise when Judge Plunkem announced Lucien's fate, for a moment, I thought that she might charge the Bench.

By the time I made my way out to the corridor, Alex and her mother were standing near the bank of elevators across the hall. After Alex fended off the last two metro reporters, I walked over and she introduced me as her "dear" friend. Eva Carlton calmed down long enough to smile at me in an odd, almost sexual way. Alex appeared pleased that I was there, under the circumstances, especially since this was our first contact since Christmas morning. On the other hand, she seemed dismissive, as though she'd decided I had taken advantage of Lucien.

Lucien had remained with Abrahamson at the defense table, having promised to surrender himself in two weeks directly to the converted air force base near Okaloosa, Florida. But as soon as they exited the courtroom together, Mother Carlton nearly knocked me down trying to get to Lucien. Using Abrahamson as a shield he briskly stepped past her while he shot Alex an exasperated glance, and they kept on going toward the men's room at the end of the long hallway. Out the corner of my eye, I watched Alex look after him, her heart surely breaking, and I decided to make myself scarce rather than become the consolation guy. That's where things stood until Lucien sent me the following e-mail on St. Patrick's Day:

Dear Ollie:

The worst reminder of my current whereabouts is the persistent sound of keys rattling followed by the clanking of steel doors opening and closing. All night long I hear the comings and goings of other inmates on my floor inside our modernized mini-mum-security quarters. For the first six nights I lay awake in the dark fearing that any light might attract one of the wandering wolves or a guard; both types have been known to enter your locked room and demand grotesque favors or services from you. But I soon learned to distinguish hype from reality here in the boot camp atmosphere. Having never served in the military, I heard this comparison from some of the other "corn dodgers" who I've come to know during the fourteen days I've been confined to my tiny single cell.

In the daytime a television set blares incessantly in the common room, the wait is tedious to use this computer, and our exercise is limited to an hour of voluntary participation in any sport. The men are mostly drug dealers and other white-collar criminals

like me. We have several bankers, a judge, a state leg-
islator, and there are two guys with six figure book
deals who promised to put me in touch with their
agents. . . . I'll talk to you about that when I see you.
That is, if you want anything to do with me. . . . I
must admit, for a while, I didn't want to see you.
That's why I'm writing to you now. It's taken me
this long to say that you saved my life. I've denied
this to myself and to Alex too long. Luckily, though,
you exhorted me to reexamine things and understand how I ended up in this place. I wanted to say
thank you and I hope you'll consider coming to
visit while the weather remains chilly up in Chicago.

Friday is visiting day in our zoo. We're allowed
ninety minutes, under the hot sun, on opposite
sides of an old wooden picnic table in the grass exercise yard. Nevertheless, visitation is the height of
culture here, so I'd like to fly you down and put you
up at a fancy beach resort for the weekend. I apologize for sounding glib, I haven't completely figured
out how to accept this. And despite the lack of privacy, the perpetual boredom and solitude, it has
become a game. Even the food can be mastered with
a little imagination and patience. In five months, I'll
be eligible for early release and then I'll find out
whether it's possible to start over. But I don't know
if I'll ever be able to forget the fear that grips me
whenever I hear keys rattle and doors clank.

I know that a man is dead because of me. Being in
here doesn't compensate for that. Moreover, the lesson is appropriately ironic. If I'd come forward as
soon as Mama told me, I might never have been
indicted. Instead I thought of the scandal and my
disgrace, and the permanent stain on my all-impor-

tant reputation. Well, whenever I return to my cell, after eating a starch-laden pile of glop, or taking a walk inside the barbed-wire fence surrounding the compound, I can no longer pretend to be a disinterested observer of my own life. Not when Tommy Goyle is in the Bolivar County jail awaiting trial for capital murder and I may have to testify against him.

For what it's worth, apologizing to you and Alex means much more to me. . . . No, I am not in a twelve-step program. Ever since I arrived here I've taken to long periods of silence. Maybe I'm not ready to get on with my life yet, and that's why I don't contribute much to the conversations. The cons try to draw me in, provoking me at times. These days, however, I much prefer to listen. I've spent too many years working on my own agenda, telling other people what to do with their lives. For now, anyway, I'm learning to listen to Alex and other people who care for me about the things that matter. Which brings me to the other reason I'm writing to you, Ollie. If you decide to take me up on the free vacation and visit offer, would you bring Alex with you?

I suppose this sounds strange, considering what I know about you two. Alex didn't tell me, as I'm sure you're wondering. I've never accused her or discussed it with her. And I'm only bringing this up now because I don't want you to be uncomfortable if we do see each other again. As far as I'm concerned the matter is over. Alex maintains that she and I have a work in progress, despite her missing the first visiting day. While she has been blowing hot and cold lately, Alex said she'd probably still go through with marrying me after all that's happened. We've decided to wait and see how things develop. I don't know whether I'll ever deserve a second chance. As I write this the flower I selfishly damaged stands strong, her scent lingers on my hands and in my hair. Like a house pet left in the kennel, with an article of its master's clothing, I'll survive off Alex's perfume until she returns to claim me.

I believe Alex would come down here with you, Ollie, if you ask her. I have no idea whether you two have been in touch since I've been inside, so I don't know how hard this might be for you. I think I know how Alex feels about you and I trust that you will do the right thing as far as everyone is concerned. Well, that's all I have to say for now and I hope to see you soon.

Your grateful friend,
Lucien Echo

Do you believe that guy? He confessed to major crimes and asked me in the same sentence to do his laundry. I won't tell you my initial reaction, but after I read the bloody thing a few more times I realized that Lucien was keeping alive in me whatever remaining hope I had to wrest Alex away from him. . . . "The flower I selfishly damaged stands strong?" Are you kidding?

It also burned me up that Lucien was right about most things. I *had* nearly called Alex following our unsatisfying exchange in the hallway outside the courtroom. But I held to the notion that she should initiate the contact, and I didn't follow through. This fresh opportunity to see Alex, at Lucien's behest, was clearly meant to finish this thing among the three of us. So I reached Alex at the penthouse the next afternoon and she suggested I come over straightaway.

When Alex opened the door wearing a silk dressing gown, tied at the waist, I wasn't sure whether she was trying to send a signal. I reached out to hug her and we ended up kissing on the mouth longer than I think she may have wanted. Alex led me into her dressing room with a story about changing her clothes for a meeting with some wine supplier. I don't know, maybe it was my fault; maybe *I'd* been the one who insisted that we get together immediately.

"Ollie, I don't think I've seen you look so stressed out." Alex leaned across the comforter covering her four-poster bed, reached for the clicker, and turned off the Sony resting atop the dresser on the opposite side of her boudoir. She walked me over to the brocade loveseat and held my hand while we sat down. The fresh strawberry scent that I'd first inhaled around her returned and we stared at each other for what seemed like an erotic moment to me. When our lives were first thrown together, who could've thought that Alex and I were destined to share that connubial ride along the road through Crate & Barrel, not to mention Home Depot, and one day, possibly, Gymboree?

"When I didn't hear from you, I knew you understood," Alex said, getting up from the sofa. She had turned it off like a switch and I didn't get it. "Isn't this unbelievable?" she wondered out loud, walking over toward the closet.

"Wanna go for truly absurd?" I replied, retrieving the e-mail from my coat and handing it to her. "Lucien wants me to bring you there."

Alex sat down on the bed and commenced reading. I watched her expression go from sadness to anger until, finally, she was smiling a little nervously as she set the paper down beside her. "You gotta hand it to him," Alex said. "Lucien knows what he wants."

She grabbed her apricot-colored blouse, lying nearby, opened a mirrored closet next to the bed and took off her robe behind it. "I've already decided not to visit him. So you're off the hook."

"Whaddiya mean?"

"Lucien needs positive support during his ordeal. I couldn't see him now without telling him we're not a work in progress anymore."

Alex selected a charcoal pantsuit, put on the pin-striped trousers, and came out from behind the mirrored door carrying the jacket. "The truth is," she went on, tucking in her blouse and putting on the double-breasted suit coat, "I'll be moved out before Lucien comes home and I don't think he needs to know that right now, on top of everything else he's going through."

I hadn't expected this. Not by a long shot. Yet, it made perfect sense at the time in light of my single-minded determination that we belonged together. It sealed the deal for me and it became difficult to keep a straight face over Alex's gut-wrenching decision to dump Lucien. I told myself to be sensitive, supportive, and not gloat. Instead I slowly turned the screw for our future.

"Where are you going to live?" I innocently asked.

"I'm not sure. Not too far, I suppose. By the end of the year the restaurant could be in the black and somebody might want it. I'm thinking about going back to New

England for a while, doing something quietly. Maybe a small bed and breakfast. Something practical. I dunno, have a normal life, whatever that is."

"And when Lucien comes home?"

"Maybe I've learned what not to settle for in a relationship again. Lucien is manipulating both of us from his prison cell."

"I have to tell ya'," I chimed in, getting up from the sofa and coming over to where Alex sat at her lighted vanity, applying unnecessary finishing touches to her big round eyes and tight cheeks. "I'm here on my own account."

I couldn't help but rub my hand up along the arm of her suit coat. It was done more from my own sense of feeling comfortable with her rather than out of lust. She looked up at me, put her hand over mine, and leaned her head against my chest. During the ensuing silence I felt our heartbeats communicating, a sign that she loved me. For that shining moment we were connected to one another in a way that made me realize what was best for me, after all. The great Titan, Prometheus, whose name is synonymous with knowledge and forethought, was condemned by the gods for stealing fire from heaven to benefit mankind. While I hardly expected to be chained to a rock, where the vultures would come each day to eat my liver—talk about nobody being perfect—I guess that I must have decided to go out with testosterone blazing.

"Did I hear you say normal life?" I asked her, "As in us together?"

"This is *so* not the right time."

Alex got up from the dressing table and walked over toward the bed. Before I could follow her, she stopped, came back and put her arms around me. I hugged her tightly feeling as much of her lithe body and smooth face as I could touch. I could hang on for as long as she would allow.

"I am late already," Alex went on, way too soon, it seemed, as she broke free and headed toward her purse resting on a chair near the doorway. "I'll call you, I swear," she said, turning around one more time to look me in the eyes. "The moment I feel comfortable to consider such a serious thing. Ollie, please walk me to the elevator and ride down to the garage with me."

And I believed her. Time was on my side according to the big picture philosophy I had been espousing lately. Our deepest moments together were yet to come and I'd be ready. In the end, though, I was glad to get out of there. I must have clenched my jaw too tightly while I was hugging Alex all over, as I heard my faulty bridge finally snap off the upper bi-cuspid, and it was just luck and glue on the back crown keeping the whole thing from falling out of my mouth right next to her in the elevator.

Three months later, Alex hadn't called. Lucien, on the other hand, had become my prime pen pal. He sent weekly updates on his existence in stir interspersed with interesting accounts of some of his most memorable cases and other experiences. Lucien seemed to have accepted that Alex wasn't coming to visit since he'd stopped mentioning her except as a thinly-veiled character in his e-mail memoirs.

In fact, Lucien took seriously the idea of publishing his autobiography, having convinced me to collaborate with him after all. The draft of *Dr. Rob's Journey* had been finished for a couple months. I had nothing new going on. Besides, if Lucien did contact Alex when he got home, what better way to keep track of her? So I agreed to punch up the three best Lucien Echo anecdotes and sent them to New York, through Annie, with a proposal for *Prisoners of Truth: The Life and Times of Lucien Echo*, as told to Ollie Katz. What I'm trying to say is . . . as luck would have it—I swear, that's all it was—within a few weeks, from out of the blue, Annie called.

"You're taking me to Positano next month," she declared mysteriously into the receiver.

"What're you talking about?"

"Jason has a summer job in Michael's stock room. He can stay with Dad when we go to Italy."

"C'mon, Annie. What's the deal already?"

"I hate being cryptic but we've got a good news-bad news situation here."

"Gimme the bad news first."

"Moira Benson, over at Rosydent, rejected *Dr. Rob's Journey*. Apparently," Annie went on, and I sensed she was choosing her words carefully, "she liked the book very much. She didn't like the ending. Anyway, Moira thinks it just isn't right for their list."

"Whaddiya mean? What didn't she like about the ending?"

"I don't know, Ollie. I didn't ask her. I already told you what I thought about it. Rob isn't saved or his soul released. He dies. Boom! The end. Where's the payoff? Doesn't Rob atone for every sin he's committed? Why didn't Rob's plan succeed?"

"The fate of humanity seems bleak for a reason," I replied, sorry to say that my experiment had failed. "I've found no evidence of a universal truth that transcends time."

"Too bad, Ollie. We all need something to believe in."

"It sounds sappy, but I think love is as close as I'll ever come to believing the truth about anything. If we spend our time in the past we are absent from the present, and that's how things got screwed up in the first place. Love is an end unto itself. The only one worth thinking about."

"All the more reason to hear the good news," Annie replied impatiently. "They want to publish your book about Lucien Echo. Moira thinks it'll be a hit. They're getting behind it and they're willing to pay for a tell-all. We're talking six figures, Selection of the Month and, dare I say it? . . . 'Oprah.' For my commission, you're taking me to Italy."

"Moira really said that she didn't like the ending?"

We have finally reached the end of this tale as well. If Annie's friend has the clout, and Lucien and I produce a few more stories, you might be able to read *Prisoners of Truth* one day. As I write this we are well on the way to finishing the first draft, and the darn thing is pretty good, if I do say so myself. I won't tell you what's happened between Alex and me. I'll leave that to your imagination. The doubters among you will say that I remain in serious denial, that we'll never end up together and I'm too afraid to face it. With apologies to future historians, that's my story and I'm sticking to it.